Praise for *Life Flight*

"This book is an edge-of-your-seat suspense thriller from start to finish. With great character development and enough excitement to keep readers hooked, this novel is sure to keep patrons talking for months to come."

Library Journal

"*Life Flight* by Lynette Eason is a heart-stopping, breath-stealing masterpiece of romantic suspense! I read it in one gulp and could not put it down. It's the best novel I've read this year. Highly recommended!"

Colleen Coble, *USA Today* bestselling author
of *A Stranger's Game* and the Pelican Harbor series

"I highly recommend this for those who love romantic suspense with enough twists to keep the most astute reader guessing."

Cara Putman, award-winning author
of *Flight Risk* and *Lethal Intent*

"A life-threatening medical emergency, a helicopter crash, and an escaped serial killer . . . Lynette Eason packs in all the ingredients for a thrilling edge-of-your-seat read! *Life Flight* will grip readers by the throat on the very first page all the way to the shocking ending, leaving them gasping for breath."

Elizabeth Goddard, bestselling author
of *Present Danger* and the Uncommon Justice series

"Lynette Eason's latest book, *Life Flight*, grabs you from the opening words and doesn't let go until the final chapter. I'm green-eyed with envy over her ability to craft such a heart-pounding, nail-biting story."

Carrie Stuart-Parks, award-winning,
bestselling author of *Relative Silence*

T0036245

"Once again, Lynette Eason delivers a suspense-filled romance in *Life Flight*. Prepare to stay up all night as this book grips you from page one and won't release you until the satisfying conclusion. The twists and turns had me holding my breath. Highly recommend!"

Robin Caroll, bestselling author of the Darkwater Inn series

"When you pick up Lynette Eason's *Life Flight*, buckle up and brace for a wild ride! The story dips, twists, and spins with danger and deception on every page, all leading to the breath-stealing conclusion."

Lynn H. Blackburn, award-winning author
of the Defend and Protect series

Praise for *Crossfire*

"Expertly plotted and relentlessly paced, the narrative drives home its message that 'God is there to get us through whatever we have to face.'"

Publishers Weekly

"*Crossfire* is another great addition to this series by Lynette Eason— one of my favorite Christian Suspense authors. . . . A truly exceptional story."

Interviews & Reviews

"Lynette Eason has blown me out of the water. She took my heart through a roller coaster of emotions with *Crossfire*."

Life Is Story

CRITICAL
THREAT

Books by Lynette Eason

WOMEN OF JUSTICE

Too Close to Home
Don't Look Back
A Killer Among Us

DEADLY REUNIONS

When the Smoke Clears
When a Heart Stops
When a Secret Kills

HIDDEN IDENTITY

No One to Trust
Nowhere to Turn
No Place to Hide

ELITE GUARDIANS

Always Watching
Without Warning
Moving Target
Chasing Secrets

BLUE JUSTICE

Oath of Honor
Called to Protect
Code of Valor
Vow of Justice
Protecting Tanner Hollow

DANGER NEVER SLEEPS

Collateral Damage
Acceptable Risk
Active Defense

EXTREME MEASURES

Life Flight
Crossfire
Critical Threat

EXTREME MEASURES #3

CRITICAL THREAT

LYNETTE EASON

R

Revell

a division of Baker Publishing Group
Grand Rapids, Michigan

© 2023 by Lynette Eason

Published by Revell
a division of Baker Publishing Group
PO Box 6287, Grand Rapids, MI 49516-6287
www.revellbooks.com

Printed in the United States of America

Library of Congress Cataloging-in-Publication Data
Names: Eason, Lynette, author.
Title: Critical threat / Lynette Eason.
Description: Grand Rapids, MI : Revell, a division of Baker Publishing Group,
    [2023] | Series: Extreme measures ; 3
Identifiers: LCCN 2022020824 | ISBN 9780800737344 (paperback) | ISBN
    9780800742607 (casebound) | ISBN 9781493439652 (ebook)
Subjects: LCGFT: Novels.
Classification: LCC PS3605.A79 C74 2023 | DDC 813/.6--dc23/eng/20220428
LC record available at https://lccn.loc.gov/2022020824

Some Scripture used in this book, whether quoted or paraphrased by the characters, is taken from the (NASB®) New American Standard Bible®, Copyright © 1960, 1971, 1977, 1995, 2020 by The Lockman Foundation. Used by permission. All rights reserved. www.lockman.org

Some Scripture used in this book, whether quoted or paraphrased by the characters, is from the New King James Version®. Copyright © 1982 by Thomas Nelson. Used by permission. All rights reserved.

Baker Publishing Group publications use paper produced from sustainable forestry practices and post-consumer waste whenever possible.

23 24 25 26 27 28 29   7 6 5 4 3 2 1

Dedicated to the men and women
who put their lives on the lines for the rest of us.

For God so loved the world, that He gave His only Son, so that everyone who believes in Him will not perish, but have eternal life For God did not send the Son into the world to judge the world, but so that the world might be saved through Him.

John 3:16–17 NASB

CHAPTER
ONE

"A third victim has been found and a serial killer is once again thought to be terrorizing the Northeast—just east of the territory Peter Romanos paralyzed with his string of murders," Rachel Goodwin reported from her position outside the prison. "Peter Romanos, who is incarcerated in the new high-security DC federal penitentiary, is serving twelve life sentences. Only this time, instead of teenage girls, this particular killer is targeting older women. That's all the information I have at the moment. I hope to know more soon."

The camera panned away from the woman, and clips of Romanos's arrest thirteen years ago took over the screen.

The man in the recliner stood and frowned. Peter Romanos had gotten what he deserved—caught.

Because he'd been stupid.

The killer walked down the hallway, grabbed his keys off the table near the door, stepped outside, then crossed the yard to the barn. He unlocked the padlock, lifted the wooden beam, and stepped inside, surveying his office. It wasn't what most people considered an office, but it was definitely where all the important work took place.

He stepped into the stall on the left of the area where he'd dug the hole. It had taken him a month to get it just the way he wanted. Once he had it deep enough, he smoothed concrete on the floor and then concreted the walls most of the way up. High enough that no one could climb out. The remaining sides, up to the barn's floor, had fencing with chicken wire to hold back the dirt and a heavy chain-link fence on top that would allow air in. He didn't need anyone suffocating in there. *He* was the one who chose the time of death. *He* was the one who decided *how* they died. And, because he paid attention to details, everything had gone according to the plan so far. No one would ever trace anything back to him. Ever. Because he was smart.

Not like Romanos.

Who leaves evidence in their house for their kid to find?

So dumb. And it was infuriating that Romanos had treated killing like it was a game, a sport. Killing was *not* a game *nor* a sport. Romanos's victims hadn't deserved to die like that. They were young. Innocent. They'd had so much to live for.

Not like some.

The ones who weren't innocent. The ones who deserved what they had coming.

Like Sonya Griffith. What a mean old bat. He'd taken care of her and made sure she never had a chance to spread her poison ever again.

His phone buzzed and he glanced at the text.

See you at noon for lunch, sweetheart.

He stopped and tapped back his response.

So sorry, hon. I need to cancel. Looks like a long day. I'll let you know when I'm on the way home.

So much for plans for lunch. He tucked the phone back in his pocket and headed into the workroom, where he wiggled the mouse on the laptop. It was thrilling to see all his hard work finally paying off.

Because killing wasn't a game. It was very serious business.

CHAPTER
TWO

FIRING RANGE, QUANTICO

Supervisory Special Agent Grace Billingsley adjusted the ear protectors, aimed her weapon at the target fifteen yards in front of her, and pulled the trigger three times. Agent Mark Davis, in the space next to her, let out a low whistle. "That's pretty deadly aim there. I don't think you're going to have any trouble requalifying." Quarterly firearms qualification was required, and Grace was always ready to prove her skills on the range while praying she never had to use them in any other scenario.

She eyed the holes in the paper with satisfaction. "Don't worry, Mark, you keep practicing and maybe one day you'll be just as good."

He snorted and holstered his weapon. "Better watch out or you won't be able to get that head through the door."

She laughed and reloaded her weapon. The lighthearted bantering was good for her soul. Healing. Dealing with what she had to see on a regular basis, she'd come to appreciate the moments when she could laugh.

Early this morning, she'd been sitting at her desk located in the CIRG—Critical Incidence Response Group—building just outside of Quantico, scrolling through ViCAP, reading the latest information on new crimes. The Violent Criminal Apprehension Program was a database containing the details of certain violent crimes—solved and unsolved—as well as unidentified recovered bodies and missing persons believed to be victims of violent crime. It was created as an attempt to link crimes with similar methods of operating, signatures, et cetera.

She made it a point to keep up with the new entries. Unfortunately, not all departments entered their crimes into the system, but most did.

Six months ago, against some stiff competition, she'd applied for and been offered the position as behavioral analyst, formerly known as a profiler, with the Behavioral Analysis Unit 4—crimes against adults. Finally. She'd set her sights on this job when she'd been a teenager in juvie and had befriended the psychiatrist who'd worked with her and the others who'd been incarcerated there. It had taken hard work, a lot of sleepless nights, and some unappealing assignments, but she'd made it.

The range door opened and Jerry Stevens stepped inside. "Hey, how about an early lunch? I'm starving. The food court good with y'all?"

The Academy had a food court with an assortment of choices. Mark grinned and Grace shook her head. Jerry was always starving. At six foot three and two hundred twenty pounds, the man could put away some food.

"I'm in," Grace said. "Just got to clean my weapon and change out my ammo."

"Same here," Mark said. "We'll meet you there."

"Text me your order so I don't have to wait on you." He left, and she and Mark did as requested before turning their attention to their weapons.

Fifteen minutes later, they walked into the cafeteria and Grace drew in a deep breath. Fried eggs and crispy bacon were on the menu today. She waved to two of the workers she often chatted with, then spotted Jerry at the table, food already in front of him and two empty seats.

She slid into the chair, said a quick blessing, then dug in. Three bites later, Jerry's phone went off. He answered, listened, then nodded. "Grace is with us. Ask Frank if she can come along."

Grace raised a brow but continued eating. She'd know the details soon enough. Frank Boggs, her unit chief, would say yes, but they still had to ask. Mark shoved the last of his food in his mouth and waited.

Finally, Jerry nodded. "Great." He hung up and snagged his tray. "Got a body."

Mark sighed. "Right."

And just like that, her good mood darkened.

Jerry's gaze switched to her. "Looks like we might have a serial, so this is going to land in your lap at some point. Frank okayed you to go."

Grace nodded. "Just need to make a quick stop back at CIRG so I can grab my laptop and vehicle. You can give the details on the way."

They hurried toward the exit and Jerry's vehicle.

The men had been partners for almost fifteen years. They'd caught more than one serial killer and were ready to stop the next one—should this one turn out to be what was suspected.

Grace found she liked and admired both men. Thankfully, they respected her, too, and they made a good team when they had the opportunity to work together.

She climbed into the back seat of Jerry's Bureau-issued sedan, better known as a Bucar, and buckled her seat belt. Mark could ride shotgun.

Jerry slid into the driver's seat and glanced in the rearview mirror. "Local detective is at the scene and thinks he's got something we need to see," he said. "Says the killing is very similar to Gina Baker's death from last week and Carol Upton's from two weeks ago. He also said the media is already on the scene."

"The media?" Mark nearly shouted the question. "How are they already there?"

"Someone tipped them off, obviously."

Jerry cranked the engine and aimed the car toward the scene.

"The detective put that together about the three killings? That they're similar?" Grace asked. They'd deal with the media when they got there.

Jerry shrugged. "Apparently, he has his sights set on the Bureau and keeps up with cases. He read about the one in the paper last week, so it was fresh in his head when he was called to this one. Since this is number three, he decided to give us a heads-up." Three was the magic number that labeled the cases as a probable serial killer, bringing in the FBI.

"Huh. I just reviewed Gina Baker's case this morning and told myself her killer was going to kill again." She rubbed her forehead. "Didn't expect it to be this soon."

As much as she hated the necessity for her job, she loved what she did—and excelled at it. And now, she was going to crime scenes, using her skills to track killers.

"Where's this one?" Grace asked.

"Prince William Forest Park. Two hikers found a dead body and called it in," Jerry said. "When park security responded, they called the local police. Thankfully, Detective Morgan caught the call and noticed the similarities to Gina's murder."

Mark ran a hand over his blond head. "Any ID on the victim yet?"

Jerry nodded. "Her purse was tucked up under her right shoulder. Sonya Griffith. She was a fifty-one-year-old history teacher at the local high school."

"Any history of violence?" Grace asked. "Affiliations with the unsavory types? Relationships gone bad?"

"They're in the process of finding that out."

"What was the similarity to the other two killings?"

"Caucasian middle-aged woman with her purse tucked next to her. Fingernails gone. White forget-me-nots in her right hand. Bullet hole at the base of her skull and her tongue was cut out and placed on her chest with a Bible verse pinned to it. You know, the one from Proverbs."

Grace grimaced. "'The mouth of the righteous flows with wisdom, but the perverted tongue will be cut out.'"

Jerry shot her a look. "Yeah. That one. Someone is really not liking what these women are saying."

Grace mentally ran through what she'd read just a few hours ago in her scan of new cases. Fortunately, Gina's murder had been entered into ViCAP. "Gina Baker, fifty-eight years old, wife, grandmother of three, churchgoer, movie lover—and part-time X-ray tech at the hospital. She was found in a neighborhood park—put there in the wee hours of the morning according to detectives, three days after her disappearance—with her tongue cut out and placed on her chest with the same verse pinned to it. And he took her fingernails so there was no DNA." The pictures had disturbed Grace on a deep level. Deeper than just about anything else she'd worked on. "Her car was found parked in the Howlson Soccer Complex and the crime scene unit has it at the warehouse lab. No camera footage of it being parked or left there."

"When we talked to her husband, Adam Baker, he had no idea why her car would have been at the sports complex. She had no reason to be there."

"Killer dumped it there, of course," Grace said. She looked at the iPad in her lap. "And Carol Upton, the first one killed, is the same setup. Neighborhood park, posed against a tree, tongue pinned to her chest, no fingernails, purse next to her. Disappeared and found three days later like these last two. And no phone to be found. What else?"

"That's it for the moment. CSU is on the way, as is the ME."

She nodded. "Has an analyst been assigned?"

"Daria Nevsky."

A flash of relief slid through her. She loved Daria and admired the heck out of her. "Good. We'll have something soon then."

Jerry pulled into the parking lot of CIRG, and she ran in to grab her laptop. She'd take her own Bucar to the scene because she'd probably head home from there.

The drive to the park was short. She followed the guys to Mohave Road, and they all pulled to a stop behind the line of other emergency vehicles parallel to the South Fork of Quantico Creek. Grace found the scene as she expected—taped off and buzzing in an organized manner. The act of processing a crime scene was nothing short of amazing professionals doing what they did in the hopes of catching a killer sooner rather than later. She let Jerry and Mark bypass her, parting the crowd made up of media and other rubberneckers. Ignoring the shouts of the reporters, she ducked under the crime scene tape. The path to the creek was dense, but manageable. While she walked, she let her gaze scan the area. Trees and a gurgling creek were about all she could discern from her current location, but it was quiet. Peaceful. Serene. If one could mute the noise from the activity just a little farther ahead.

She made her way down the incline and came to a stop at the bottom where she turned her attention to the body covered by a black tarp.

Jerry was kneeling next to it, using a pen to lift the edge to see under.

"Don't touch that body 'til the ME gets here," Mark said. He stood at the edge of the minuscule beachy area where the victim lay propped up against a tree. "He'll have your head."

Jerry scowled at his partner and Grace bit her lip. The two had been partners for years, but Mark still liked to get his digs in, treating Jerry like a rookie.

"Not touching a thing," Jerry said, "as you well know. Just looking."

"I don't suppose there are any cameras out here, huh?" Grace asked, walking over to join Mark.

He looked at her, with brow raised. "Please tell me you're using that dry humor of yours."

She shrugged. "Not exactly my environment. I'm a city girl."

He just shook his head. "No cameras, city girl."

"Not even one of those wildlife live-cam things? Seems like this creek would be a good spot to aim one. You know, you catch the animals coming in for a drink or something."

He frowned. "Good point. I doubt it, but guess it can't hurt to ask."

She glanced at the road. "Where's the ME?"

"On his way."

Jerry stood and walked over to them. "She fought hard. Hands are messed up bad."

"Good," Mark said, "maybe we'll get some DNA this time."

"I doubt it. Just like Gina Baker and Carol Upton. Nails and tongue." Grace shuddered and prayed the woman had been dead at that point.

Footsteps to her left dragged her attention from the body to a pair of feet clad in brown loafers. She let her gaze travel upward to meet familiar hazel eyes. "Sam?"

"Hi, Grace."

She smiled at the man she'd met eight months ago at a psychiatric conference—and hadn't been able to get him out of her head. "Good to see you. What are you doing here?" Sam Monroe was a prison psychiatrist but also an FBI agent with Health Services at HQ. She could have looked him up, but he'd made it clear he wasn't interested.

"I had an interest in the case."

"As in . . . ?"

"I called him," Jerry said. "The first person who was killed—"

"Carol," Grace said, her voice low, "her name was Carol."

Jerry paused, then nodded. "Right. Carol. She was missing her phone. Same with Gina." He pointed to Sonya. "And I can't find hers either."

Grace frowned. "What's that got to do with you?"

Sam raised a brow. "Because of who my father is." He cleared his throat. "It's not like I advertise it—in fact, only a few people know—but my father is . . . unfortunately . . . Peter Romanos."

Grace stilled. Her eyes went from him to Jerry to Mark. Mark gave a slow nod and Grace pursed her lips. "Peter Romanos. The Cell Phone Killer?"

"That's the one."

■ ■ ■ ■

Saying his father's name always left a bad taste in his mouth, but telling Grace Billingsley that his father was the infamous killer left him a little nauseous. At the conference, he hadn't introduced himself as Sam Romanos, but instead as Sam Monroe—the name he'd taken in order to acquire some anonymity from his being related to an infamous killer.

His and Grace's time together at the conference blipped at warp speed through his mind. They'd hit it off on the first day, hung out and talked late into the night. He'd gotten her number and then done nothing with it. Divorced for eight years, he'd written romance off, deciding it wasn't for him—especially since he'd have to tell a potential love interest who his father was. And he hadn't been tempted to change that decision. Until her. Then he'd wimped out. Thankfully, she didn't look mad, just surprised.

"I thought you looked familiar at the conference," she said, "but I didn't place you until after I got home."

"Oh. How?"

"I followed the case as it unfolded. Your picture was on the screen a lot." She studied him. "You'd shaved the mustache and the five o'clock shadow, but I thought I knew you from some-where."

With her trained eye, that didn't really surprise him. "You never said anything."

"When you didn't seem to recognize me, I figured I was just imagining things, but later, after I was home and going over a case, pictures from Peter's trial came up and there you were."

He rubbed a hand over his smooth-shaven chin. "Even as the trial unfolded, I was already planning how I could change my appearance—and my family's last name." He dropped his hand and curled his fingers into a fist at his side. "We took my ex-wife's maiden name. I figured it would make life . . . easier." He shrugged. "Or at least less stressful if every time we said our full names, we didn't get asked if we were related to the serial killer."

"I can see that. Peter Romanos *was* a household name for a while. And Romanos isn't exactly common," she said.

"I couldn't let my kids go through life knowing . . ." He shook his head. "All of our friends disappeared during that time, so I figured it would be a good way to start over. With the move to a different neighborhood, different schools, and a different last name . . . it's been good for all of us. Anyway . . ."

"Yeah. Well," she said, "I can understand why Mark and Jerry would have you here." She turned back to the body. "You think we have a copycat?"

Thankful for the redirection, he shook his head. "I don't know, but no one knows my father's cases better than I do, so . . ." Because he'd studied them ad nauseam trying to find out what he'd missed, how he hadn't known.

"Right." She glanced up at him. "You're still at the prison when you're not working with other agents' trauma?"

"I am."

The same one where his father was now incarcerated. It had been thirteen years since the man had been arrested and imprisoned—and thirteen years of dodging any contact with his dad.

The fact that Sam continued to work at the prison even after his father had managed to get himself relocated there last year probably said a lot about him. Something he hadn't been willing to explore just yet.

She nodded. "You have someone in mind who could be responsible for this?"

He shook his head. "I've been mentally going over every person my father has been in contact with to see if I can find any kind of connection, but I've got nothing. And besides . . ." Could his father have managed to bypass the security and monitoring to influence someone to continue his twisted killings?

"Besides what?" Mark asked.

"The age of the victims doesn't match up. My father stayed in the under-twenty-five range. The three you've got are quite a bit older."

"So, you don't think the missing cell phones are somehow connected to your father's MO?" Mark asked, his gaze hard.

Sam ignored the man's chill and fell silent, studying the scene, thinking back to the reports he'd memorized. Not because he wanted to, but because he'd read them so often, they'd become engrained in his brain. "I . . . don't know. My gut says no, but I don't want to say that and be wrong. Then again, I don't want to say yes and have you chase an angle that's not what you need to be chasing."

"We'll chase them all," Jerry said. "We can't afford not to."

Sam's phone buzzed and he glanced at the screen. A number he didn't recognize, but the text identified the sender.

> It's me. Your daughter. Mom won't let me have a phone for my birthday. Will you PLEASE get me one?

> Working right now, sweetie. I'll call you when I can.

> Call me? On what? Because this is my friend's phone. Not mine. The one that I could text you from if I had my own and you could call me on. But I can't do that because I don't.

> I love you. Will talk later.

He sighed and tucked the device back into his pocket. Raising a preteen was harder than he'd ever imagined it would be. Then again, he'd never thought he'd be doing it as a divorced father.

"You okay?" Grace asked.

"Yeah. Just . . . family stuff. Nothing that can't wait." Eleni would be thirteen in a week, and while her nagging for a phone was driving him straight up the proverbial wall, he had to admit he grudgingly admired her dogged persistence in going after something she wanted. If he could channel that in the right direction, it would serve her well in the future. He just prayed he managed to hold on to his patience that long.

The medical examiner arrived, pulling Sam's attention back to the present situation. One that had him thinking this killer and his father really had nothing in common. Mark and Jerry were still waiting for him to give them a definitive answer. He shook his head. "I can't say one way or the other. I'm sorry. My father didn't take their fingernails or cut his victims' tongues out." But he did leave them in public parks, posed against a tree, one red rose placed in their right hand. Like an apology. *I'm sorry I killed you, so I got you a flower. Am I forgiven now?* He cleared his throat. "And he didn't leave any kind of note or verse with his victims. Did you find a rose with her?"

Jerry shook his head. "No, but she had a bouquet of forget-me-nots in her right hand. All three victims did."

"Forget-me-nots," Grace murmured. "Interesting choice. Wonder why he chose those."

A chill skated up Sam's spine. "I'm sure there's a reason. Just like my father had his reasons. All of these similarities are well-known. His killings were described in detail by the media. It could be someone who is sick enough to admire him and want to honor"—he used air quotes around the word—"him by using some of those details in his own killings. But, if you're wanting a yes or no answer, I would lean more toward no."

Mark crossed his arms. "Come on. How can you say that? We've got a victim in the park, with a flower, propped against a tree. And a missing cell phone. All shades of a Peter Romanos killing."

He wasn't wrong. But . . . "There are too many significant differences. Killers don't change some of the differences. Like age. The kind of flower. Everything has meaning in what he does." He shook his head and glanced at his watch. "Like I said, I'm leaning toward no, simply because I just don't have enough information to connect the killings to a copycat." He hesitated. "Although, I suppose you could talk to my father. He's in prison not too far from here."

"I know exactly where he is," Mark said, the chill in his tone obvious.

Sam raised a brow. "Okay, then. Well, since it doesn't look like you need me anymore, I've got a client to see in about an hour, so I'm going to head back to Headquarters." It would take him about that long to make the drive depending on traffic. Which was usually horrible.

"I've basically gotten what I need here too," Grace said. "I'll walk to your car with you, then come back and wrap up."

He nodded and they fell into step together as they navigated the scene to arrive back at his vehicle. He placed a hand on the door handle and paused. Turned back to her and cleared his throat. "I . . . um . . . owe you an apology."

She raised a brow. "What for?"

"For leading you to believe I'd call you."

"Oh, that." She shrugged. "It's okay. I just figured you weren't interested."

"But I was," he blurted. She tilted her head and studied him, waiting. He sighed. He'd started this, now he had to explain himself. "You know that phrase, it's not you, it's me?"

She gave a quiet laugh. "I'm familiar."

"Well, there's truth in that. It wasn't you, it was me."

"Okay."

He sighed. "And I'm sorry I didn't say anything the night we were at dinner and talking," he said in reference to the meal they'd shared at the conference.

"Our conversation wasn't that deep, Sam. If I remember correctly, we talked mostly about our jobs."

"True."

"And I guess it's difficult to find the right time to bring that topic up," she said.

"That's putting it mildly." He struggled to find the words. "I haven't dated anyone in a very long time. Not seriously. If . . . when . . . I ask someone out, I will have to be honest with that person and tell her about my father up front. At least I feel like that's what I should do. I guess I just wasn't ready to do that with you. To see the look come into your eye . . ." He shrugged.

"I understand."

When she said nothing more, he blinked. "That's it?"

"Of course. I can see how that would be terribly . . . terrifying. I can't imagine having that hanging over my head." She paused. "And I'll be honest too. I was a little disappointed you didn't call, but I wasn't waiting by the phone either."

"I didn't mean to imply you were. I just . . ." He groaned. "Now I've gone and made things awkward—more awkward. I'm sorry."

She patted his bicep. "It's okay, Sam. Let it go. I told you, we're good. I understand."

"But I don't want to let it go, because now that we've run into each other again, I'd like to actually take you to dinner."

"Why? Because it's what you feel like you're supposed to do?"

He hesitated. Was it? For a brief moment, he rolled the question around in his head. "No," he finally said, "because I'd really *like* to. And the fact that I don't have to explain about my father is no longer an issue, so . . ."

"Oh. Okay then. When and where?"

"Uh . . . how about tonight?"

"Fine."

He blinked. "Are you this easygoing all the time?"

She tilted her head. "Easygoing? Hmm. Yes, most of the time. I've had to learn to let most things roll off and not take offense. And besides, I've never been one to turn down free food."

He nodded. "All right, then. Good enough. I have your number in my phone." He tapped the screen. "There. Text me your address and I'll pick you up?"

"I live in Springfield. That's a little out of your way from Headquarters."

"I'm in Alexandria. You're worth the drive."

She raised a brow at him. "All right, then. Sure." She texted him her address and then tucked her phone back into her pocket. "But we'll go to a nearby restaurant so you're not doing even more driving."

"You pick the place."

"Even better." She glanced back over her shoulder at the scene, then turned her gaze to his once more. "He's not done, Sam."

"I know."

She shot him a tight smile. "And I know you have an appointment to get to. See you tonight."

"I'll be there."

She walked away and he couldn't help but watch—and wonder. Her dark hair held a slight wave, like she'd gathered it into a loose ponytail earlier, fastened at the nape of her neck. Her flawless light-brown skin glowed with health and her brown eyes hinted at mystery, tinged with humor and fun beneath the serious exterior. In other words, she was attractive, with a smile that got under his skin. Again.

The first time, he'd managed to chalk it up to a fluke. This time? Had to be more than that.

CHAPTER
THREE

Once Sam drove away, Grace stood there until his taillights disappeared. He still had her number programmed in his phone. Interesting. All her instincts shouted that he was a good man. A kind man. And his father was a serial killer, so he was most likely a *troubled* man.

Then again, everyone was troubled in their own way, weren't they? About something? She sure was, which was why she was the last person to judge another by their past baggage. And she'd readily admit, she was looking forward to seeing him later this evening. But for now . . .

More media had arrived, and a reporter caught her eye. When the woman beelined for her, Grace turned and ducked back under the tape and walked toward the scene once more. While she'd told Sam she was basically done, she still needed to listen to the ME's assessment and take another look around the scene.

When she was far enough away from the media and not quite back in the thick of the scene, she stopped and drew in a deep breath, tuned out the activity behind her, and closed her eyes. The wind whispered through the fall leaves, a gentle breeze that should have sounded like peace.

Only it didn't.

It sounded like secrets.

Like if she listened hard enough, she could hear the thoughts of the disturbed individual who could do such a thing to another human being. In his mind, the killings were justified, and to him, he'd done a good thing. The right thing.

But why?

The women were gossips? They talked too much? Said things they shouldn't say? Spread lies? Their words hurt someone else?

All were possibilities, of course, and the verse left behind seemed to convey that message.

Or there could be some other motive behind the killings. Whatever the case, he wasn't going to stop until someone stopped him.

It wasn't so much the chill in the air as it was the pictures in her mind that generated the icy feeling in her. What this poor woman—and the other two—had suffered. Tears welled and she had to shut off the empathy. As CSU continued to gather what evidence they could find, she stayed still, her mind struggling to focus on her surroundings, on the killer, not the victims.

He'd be thrilled at all the excitement he'd generated. He hadn't tried too hard to hide the body. He'd done just enough to make sure he could get away. What had these women said that was offensive enough to make someone want to cut out their tongues?

And where was he hearing the conversations? Or was he? The odds seemed like he would be.

She walked over to join Mark and Jerry once more. "I want to work up a geographic profile on the three victims," she said. "I need to know every place they went on a regular basis." If their phones had been available, that might have made things a bit easier.

Mark nodded. "I figured."

"Thanks. Just send it my way when you have it." She paused. "I'll know more after I talk to some of the relatives. Husbands, boyfriends, children." Behavioral analysts didn't necessarily investigate crimes, but Grace did everything possible to build her profile of the killer, and sometimes that meant going the extra mile or thinking outside the box. "I'd really like to know the time she was brought in and left here. The security cameras at the park entrance should give us information on every car that drove through the gates."

Jerry smiled. "I'm already ahead of you. Got someone pulling the footage from the last two days to start with. We'll go back more if needed."

"Of course."

His smile slid sideways. "We need your profile as fast as possible, Grace."

"I know, but you also know it can take up to two weeks to get it." He scowled but nodded and walked back toward the body. She eyed Mark. "I sense a coldness toward Sam. Everything okay?"

"Fine." He slipped away to join his partner.

Not so fine, but he wasn't talking to her about it. She let it go. For now.

Again, she let her gaze roam the area while Mark and Jerry turned to the park security officer to discuss blocking access to the area until CSU was ready to release it. The ME had finished his examination of the body and motioned for his assistant to bring the black bag. Agents talked with the park officers and local police. They'd all work together to gather as much information as possible about the victim.

Grace walked over to the ME. "Any idea how long she's been dead?"

"I'd say no longer than twelve hours. Maybe less. Once I do the autopsy, I'll have a closer estimate."

"Of course, thanks." But according to the missing persons report she'd pulled up on her phone, Sonya Griffith had disappeared three days ago. So, where was she before she was killed?

Grace was basically done here, and yet she lingered, letting her eyes scan higher this time. The birds in the trees chattered, not happy to have their sanctuary disturbed. A glint of light from the leaves of a tree just across the creek bounced at her, and she paused, lifted a hand to shade her eyes. "Mark? Jerry?"

"Yeah?" Mark returned to her side. "What is it?"

She pointed. "There. Do you see something up there? About halfway up that oak?"

He squinted and frowned. "No."

"Come stand where I'm standing."

"What do you—" He shifted more toward her and stopped. "Oh, wait. Yeah. Looks like sun shining off glass."

"If it was a rifle, I think someone would have fired it by now."

"Hey, Jer, bring me some binoculars, will you?"

"Yeah, hang on a sec." Jerry scrambled back up the incline. When he returned, he passed the binoculars to Mark, who peered through them. "What is it?"

"Not sure." Mark was quiet while he adjusted the focus. "Well, Grace, congratulations."

"What?"

"I think you found her phone."

"Her phone! What's it doing in the tree?" But a hard knot formed in her gut.

"Getting ready to find out." Mark handed the binoculars to Jerry. "Just need to find a place to cross to the other side."

"Look at the rocks in the creek. You can cross it." She hesitated. "I'm guessing that's probably the place he crossed as well—unless he just waded through the water." But the water was cold, and it was more likely he would have used the rocks.

"There's probably nothing there, with the water washing over them, but I'll get CSU to check it out."

Three minutes later, one of the techs waved to Mark. "Nothing here."

"I figured."

She and two crime scene techs she'd worked with before, Jennifer Henson and Blake Manning, followed him across the water. Grace found the rocks smooth and slippery. She was surprised when she made it across without falling in.

Hands planted on her hips, Grace waited at the edge of the creek while the others approached the base of the tree.

"I got this," Jennifer said. "My whole childhood was training for this moment." She climbed up the lower branches and reached for the phone from behind. Only, she paused. Withdrew her hand and climbed back down. Grace frowned. When the woman was back on the ground, she held a finger to her lips and motioned them to back away from the tree.

Confused, Grace followed.

"Okay," Jennifer said, "this is far enough."

"What is it?" Mark asked.

Grace curled her fingers into a fist as it hit her. "The phone's connected, isn't it?" she asked. "He's watching." She glared at the device.

"Yep. He's got it on FaceTime." She held up a hand. "And before you get your hopes up, no, you can't see him. His little box is blacked out."

"How'd he have the phone secured to the tree branch?"

"Looks like a homemade contraption. Brown, yellow, and orange painted piece of wood with wires holding the phone in place. Very well done and hardly visible. How did you see it?" she asked Grace.

"The sun reflected off something. Probably the camera lens."

"We need someone to trace the number ASAP," Mark said.

Jerry grabbed his phone. "I'll get Daria working on that."

"I suppose it's worth a try," Grace said, "but he's not going to be using his personal phone to watch."

"Might be using a laptop or something. Let's see if we can track the IMEI number to find out for sure," Jerry said.

Grace shook her head. "He's too smart for that—he'll have changed it. And while that's illegal, I'm guessing he's not too worried about that aspect." She never took her gaze from the device. "You're watching, aren't you?" she whispered. She walked forward, circled the tree, and looked up. "Why are you doing this?"

"Grace?"

"I'm going to find you," she said, ignoring Jerry's questioning tone, her voice still soft, her gaze unwavering, "and when I do, you're going to spend the rest of your life behind bars. You might think you're going to get away with this, but you're not. And that's a promise." What was he seeing? What was he thinking, watching the chaos he'd caused? Did it give him pleasure? Or was it just a way to stay informed of what was happening in the investigation? "I'm going to find you. One way or another."

Mark shifted to a different angle and lifted the binoculars again. "It's been disconnected."

"Because he knows we found it," Grace said. "I don't think he expected that—or wanted it. It's too well hidden." She finally looked away and turned to Mark. "Did you find phones hidden at the first two crime scenes?"

Mark and Jerry exchanged a look.

"I'll take that as a no," she said. She nodded to the device still in the tree. "What you want to bet the killer's not too happy right now?" She blew out a breath. "Who wants to take a little trip back to the last crime scene and see if we find a phone?"

"Was one found at the first one?"

"No, but this one is more recent. I think we should at least try."

"I'm right behind you."

■ ■ ■ ■

They'd found the phone. *She'd* found the phone. And after all the work he'd put into hiding it so well. Camouflaged it and everything. The pretty one had spoiled the fun. He slammed a fist against his palm and let out a low growl. *That* hadn't been in the plan. He pictured her holding a hand to her brow, shading her eyes—and then pointing to the phone. The only thing he could figure out was that the sun had betrayed him, and she'd spotted it. Now they would be looking for a phone with every body they found.

Because there were more bodies to come. He wasn't sure how many more. As many as it took to make sure the innocent were protected.

He circled back to the phone issue and his ire rose once more.

The phones were his lifeline, his way to watch the fallout and enjoy seeing the guilty one get her due. Only when the crime scene died down did he plan to remove it. And now he wouldn't get the chance.

He had to watch! He replayed the footage all the way up to when she stopped and looked up at the phone. Zooming in on her, he watched her face. She had smooth, tan-colored skin, and her brown eyes held . . . what? What was that expression? Rage? Yes, there was anger in them.

But determination. A hard, steely look that said she had a goal and wasn't going to stop until she achieved it. Her lips moved, her eyes were locked on the screen like she was looking straight at him. Like she could see right through the phone and into his home. The breath left his lungs. She was speaking *to him*. She'd crossed the creek to do so, but her voice was too low for the mic to pick it up. *What* was she saying? He played it over and over, trying to read her lips, and still couldn't figure it out.

He had to know!

He raked a hand over his head and rose from the chair to pace. Now what?

How was he going to be able to see and hear those who came to clean up the scene?

This was all *her* fault. What was she doing there anyway? She hadn't been at the first two scenes. Neither had the other man. Who were they?

He blew out a low breath. That was a problem he'd have to address.

After he got back.

He took a moment to review his escape routes. He had a number of them all over the city although he didn't expect to need them. But . . .

"Always be prepared, kid, always be prepared. You never know what's around the corner, but be ready for it." He grabbed his coat, gloves, and ski mask. It was cold outside, so no one would think twice about his outer garments. But where he was going, there were also cameras and he couldn't afford to get caught. He glanced at his watch and groaned. He was going to be late to work, but nothing could be done about it. There were too many innocents who still needed his protection.

And too many others who had to pay for their crimes. If only there'd been someone like himself to take care of the guilty ones years ago. His life would have been so different. But the task had fallen to him, and he'd make sure he fulfilled it.

■ ■ ■ ■

Sam pulled to a stop at the red light, his mind still on Grace Billingsley. She drew him like the clichéd moth to the flame. He shouldn't think about her. Or take her to dinner. But he was going to. His phone pinged and he glanced at it and saw it was a text from Grace.

> Might be a little later than planned. Will text you
> an update soon. Headed to the last crime scene
> to take a look around.

With another glance at the still red light, Sam voice dialed her number and waited for Bluetooth to connect the call.

She answered mid-ring. "Hey."

"You're going back to the last crime scene? What did you find at this one that makes you want to see the last one?"

A short laugh, light as a breeze on a summer day, filled his ear. "You're a smart one, aren't you?"

"Just makes sense."

"We found her phone, Sam. The killer was watching us the whole time. He shut it down only when he realized we'd spotted it."

Sam sucked in a breath. "Whoa."

"Yeah."

"Let me guess. No one found a phone at the other scenes, so you're going back to find them."

"Like I said, you're smart."

He hesitated. "Can you get permission for me to meet you there?"

"What about your patient?"

"I can postpone. He's one I can do that with."

"I'll ask."

"What's the address? I'll head over, and if for some reason I get a negative, I can always turn around."

"What's the reason for you being there?"

He hesitated. "While I know for a fact my father didn't kill those ladies simply because he's sitting in a prison cell, I'm circling back to the idea that he might be involved on an advisory level somehow."

"So, not just a copycat wanting to pay homage, your father is somehow *mentoring*—and I used that word very loosely—someone in his ways?"

"Yes. Only, making sure it doesn't *look* like he's mentoring. The more I think about it, it could be he's found someone who's as disturbed as he is, and is simply using that to develop a different MO. The fact that phones are involved and that the bodies are placed where they are—and the flower . . . well, as much as I hate to admit it, Mark might be right. There are enough similarities to have me reluctant to dismiss the possibility of his involvement outright."

"All right, I'll text you a thumbs-up and the address if you get the all clear."

He'd get it. They'd want his input if there was even a microscopic chance that his father was involved. "Thanks."

Within a minute, her text came up and he pulled over to put the address in his GPS. He didn't recognize the area, but it looked isolated. Like a neighborhood park?

He put the sedan in gear and aimed it toward the location.

Twenty minutes later, he pulled into a parking lot and cut the engine. He could see Grace in the distance, hands on her hips and talking to Mark and Jerry. He walked toward her and she turned to wave him over.

"Another open area," he said. "Not a state or national park, but a park all the same."

Grace pointed. "She was tucked under those trees. Not exactly in plain sight, but not exactly hidden either."

"Any phone?"

"Not yet. They're looking."

The park was mostly wide-open grassy space. Brown right now, but a vibrant green in the spring and summer. A small man-made waterfall sounded to his right, and the walking trail wrapped around the large pond straight ahead.

Sam sighed. "Peaceful out here."

"And it was peaceful at Prince William. Why kill someone in a horrible manner, then bring them to a place that's quiet and serene?"

Mark raised a brow at her. "You think there's something to that? Some reason he picked the parks?"

"I feel sure of it. No idea what, but yes." She closed her eyes and breathed deep.

Sam allowed himself a lingering stare. Only to finally look away and catch Jerry watching him. Jerry's lips tilted in a smile and Sam refused to acknowledge the "caught you" smirk. He and Jerry had been friends since high school.

Instead, he pursed his lips and waited a few seconds longer. "Okay, what are you doing?"

"Listening. Trying to hear what he heard." She paused. "I hear people talking, but their voices are muted. The wind is rustling the leaves and the water is cascading over the rocks of the waterfall."

"Geese are on the water of the pond," he said, his voice quiet, "honking, calling to one another."

"And their wings are flapping."

"Children are laughing."

"But . . . no traffic," she said. "Do you hear any?"

"No."

She finally blinked her eyes open and looked around. The other two agents had moved to the area she'd indicated the body had been found.

"Anything that reminds you of your father?" she asked.

"No, not really. But dead bodies, parks, flowers, and missing phones still bother me."

"We found one phone and I have a feeling we'll find another one before we're done. And maybe the third."

Mark returned to Grace's side. "Nothing so far. There's no place to put a phone and have it aimed at the tree. I had hopes but have to admit I'm starting to think this is a dead end."

Grace drew in a breath and Sam found himself doing the same. "No, it's not," she said. "It's here. Somewhere."

"Okay, then where?"

Her gaze scanned the area, stopping at various points before she started walking. "Grace?"

"Okay, you're right. There's really no place for a camera. In the park. But her body was found under the tree kind of toward the edge of the waterfall, right?"

"Right."

"He'd want a good view of the area, so maybe the phone's not in the park."

Mark nodded. "The garage?" He pointed to the back of a parking garage across the street."

"That's what I was thinking. He would've mounted a telephoto lens on the phone for the shot. The lens could make it harder to hide."

"I'll let Jerry know I'm going to check it out."

"Do you mind if we come along?" Grace asked.

He narrowed his gaze at Sam, then cut his eyes to her. "Sure. I'll meet you up there." He spun and stalked away.

"He doesn't like me," Sam said.

"I noticed."

"So, it's not my imagination. I was hoping it was."

"No, sorry. It's pretty obvious, even to me."

"You have any idea why?"

"I can make a guess. He puts serial killers away and you found a way to let one go."

"That's not what happened." The desire to defend himself rose swift and hot, but he bit his tongue. "I found evidence that proved Josiah Cartwright was innocent and he was released because of that. What was I supposed to do? Keep my mouth shut?"

"Absolutely not." She placed a hand on his arm. "I'm just telling you what might be going through Mark's head. To know for sure, though, you'll have to ask him."

She and Sam walked across the street to the garage. "I'll do that if it becomes a thing," he said. "For now, let's focus on what we came here to do."

"Works for me."

They stopped on the sidewalk before rounding the corner to the entrance, and Sam noticed Grace looking at the building, then back at the park. "What floor?" he asked.

"Third would probably give him the best view."

"I'm following you."

She found the stairs and they headed up. At the third floor, she pushed through the door and stopped. Sam stepped up behind her. The garage was quiet, no one around. "There." She headed for the wall that faced the park.

The squeal of tires echoed through the level and a black car roared around the corner of the ramp.

Straight toward Grace.

CHAPTER
FOUR

Grace registered the squealing tires and revving engine about the time Sam slammed into her, taking her down to the hard concrete. Air whooshed from her lungs and pain arced through her left shoulder and hip. She ignored it and rolled, eyes searching for the car. It disappeared around the concrete post, heading for the exit. Too fast for her to get a plate.

She turned back to Sam, who groaned and scrambled to his knees. "Are you okay?" she asked him.

"Yeah." He pulled in a deep breath and rubbed his knee. "You?"

"Better than I'd be if I'd gotten hit."

He gave her a grim smile. "No kidding."

"Seriously. Thank you for sparing me that."

He rose to his feet, then held out a hand. "Absolutely."

She grabbed his fingers and let him pull her to her feet. Her body protested but nothing she could do about that now. "Don't suppose you got a plate."

"Nope." He nodded to the post next to her. "But maybe the camera did."

The door to the stairwell opened and Jerry stepped into view.

Sweat beaded his forehead and he swiped it with the back of his sleeve. When he caught sight of them, he frowned. "You guys okay?"

"Just great," Grace said. "Did you see the car that almost ran us over?"

Jerry lifted a brow. "Sorry, what?"

"You must have been in the stairwell." She explained and pointed to the camera. "Whoever it was needs a lesson on safe driving in a parking garage." Tracking down the driver and calling him might not make any difference, but it would make her feel better. "We can worry about reckless drivers later. I want to find that phone."

"Right."

She walked to the wall that lined the perimeter of the level and looked out over the park. "This angle's not quite right." Sam joined her. Then moved to the right. "This is better." She scanned the area and frowned. "Nothing." She didn't understand. There was a camera here somewhere.

But . . . there wasn't.

She planted her hands on her hips and took another look around. "It's not here." She studied the concrete and pointed. "Look."

Jerry walked to her side. "What?"

"That. What do you see?"

"Grease?"

"Three little dots in the grease."

"A tripod," Sam said. "He had the phone on a tripod."

Jerry pinched the bridge of his nose. "And he came back and got it."

"The car." Grace stomped a foot. "That was him. He knew we found the other phone and came to get the one from here."

"I'll get the footage and we'll get the plate and hopefully a picture of the guy."

Sam shook his head. "You won't get a picture of him, and the plate will be stolen—maybe even the car too."

Grace raised a brow at him but didn't disagree. In fact, she nodded, then sighed. "Well, I guess this was a bust." She glanced at Jerry. "Will you let me know when you get the results back on identifying the car?"

"Sure."

She nodded to Sam. "Walk with me back to the scene?"

"Of course."

They headed to the stairs. "Are you still interested in an early dinner?" he asked and opened the door for her.

"I am." They fell silent until they reached the lower level. She stepped through the door back into the chill of the outside and turned to him. "Are you?"

"Definitely."

"Why don't I follow you?"

He shook his head. "If you're okay with it, I'd rather drive you, so we have time to talk in the car."

"Like I said before, that's a lot of driving time for you."

"I know."

She studied him and smiled. "Your pants are torn at the knee."

He glanced down, shrugged, then looked pointedly at her shoulder. "You've got dirt streaking your sleeve."

"Well, thankfully, my pants are black. We may look a little bedraggled, but I'm fine with it if you are."

"Sure. Or . . ."

"Or?"

He hesitated. Took a deep breath. "Okay, this is going to be way out there, but . . . I have steaks in my fridge, a salad, baking potatoes, and a chocolate cake. Would you want to come to my place and just hang out for the evening? We can drop your car at your house, and I'll bring you home when we're done."

Okay, that was unexpected. "What about your family?"

"The kids are with their mother and my mother-in-law—who lives with us—but that's a story for later. I've got the evening free."

Grace mentally scrambled for a moment and Sam shoved his hands into his pockets.

"Or we can hit a restaurant somewhere near your house like we originally planned," he said.

"Sure. I'd love to. Go to your place, I mean. You're right. It's been a long day already and just hanging out sounds nice."

He blinked. "Okay then. You ready?"

"Sure."

His phone rang and he glanced at the screen before giving a grimace and letting the call go to voice mail.

She was curious about the caller but rolled her shoulder and bit her lip at the ache. "I don't suppose you have a hot tub."

"No. Sorry. I do have a big bottle of ibuprofen."

"That'll work."

He frowned at her. "I tackled you pretty hard. You sure you're okay?"

She wrinkled her nose at him. "The shoulder is just going to be bruised and sore. I'll be fine." She took one last look around and sighed. "Let's get this attempted assault reported, then I'm ready when you are."

Twenty-five minutes later, she pulled into her garage and cut the engine while Sam waited at the end of her drive. She thought he was crazy to want to cart her over to his place, then back home, but it also touched—and intrigued—her that he thought she was worth the trouble.

She held up a finger indicating he should wait while she ran inside and changed. Her shoulder and hip protested the hurried movements, but soft yoga pants, tennis shoes, and a long sweatshirt were all she wanted at the moment. The most comfortable outfit she could find. When she stepped out her front door, she caught Sam's eye and noted the small approving smile that curved his lips before he climbed out to round the front of the car and open her door.

"You look great."

"I look comfortable, and you don't have to open my door," she said. Some might call it old-fashioned. She called it thoughtful and definitely nice.

"I know, but I want to."

"Well, thank you. I'm one of those women who enjoys it." Grace buckled up and looked over at him after he did the same in the driver's seat. "This is crazy, you know. I can drive to your place and back home."

"I don't mind being a little crazy sometimes." He smirked. "Just know that this is about as crazy as I get, though."

She laughed. "Noted."

They rode in silence for the next few minutes and Grace found herself studying the man beside her.

"I can feel you looking at me," he said without taking his eyes from the road. "What?"

"Sorry. I was just thinking."

His jaw hardened. "Thinking about what the son of a serial killer looks like?"

Grace winced. "Uh . . . no. That actually hadn't crossed my mind. I was just wondering how you came to be a psychiatrist."

"Oh. Sorry." He shot her a sheepish look. "I might be a tad defensive sometimes."

"Nah, really?"

He chuckled and rolled his eyes. "But, in answer to your question, it's because I found out I was the son of a serial killer."

"How old were you when it all came out?"

"I was twenty-six years old and the father of a four-year-old and a newborn."

"Oh my. I can't even imagine how shattering that was. For all of you."

"Shattering." He nodded. "That's a pretty good way to describe it. Eleni is the fortunate one. She doesn't remember anything about that time. Xander has a few vague memories, but thankfully, not many."

"How old are your children now?"

"Alexander—who goes by Xander now—is seventeen and Eleni is twelve, almost thirteen. Xander remembers the chaos, but not really what it was all about. He thinks his grandfather's dead."

Grace raised a brow at him. "What did he think when you changed his name? Doesn't he remember the last name Romanos?"

Sam's fingers clenched the wheel tighter before relaxing. "At first, he was a little confused, but still young enough that it didn't take long for him to accept Monroe as his last name. Especially since it was his grandmother's last name as well."

"And now?"

He shook his head. "I don't think he thinks about it. If he does, he's never said anything to me or his mother. Or grandmother."

They fell silent a moment. "That sounds terribly hard."

He nodded. "Although, to be honest, I'm not sure raising a teenage daughter won't rival that level of difficulty. In a different way, of course, but we're already at difficult and heading toward making me insane. I'm still wondering where my sweet girl went."

Grace couldn't help the smile that pulled at her lips. "She was texting you earlier."

"From a friend's phone. She wants her own."

"Oh. And you don't want her to have one?"

He shook his head. "I don't know that she *should*." He sighed. "Then again, I don't know that she *shouldn't*. Her mother is adamant that she not have one—which kind of surprises me in a way, but . . ." He shrugged. "If I go against that, then . . . well, let's just say that might be more rocking of the boat than I can handle."

"Do you and your ex get along?"

He shrugged. "Depends on how you define 'get along.'" He pursed his lips. "Is it too soon to tell you personal things like why we divorced?"

■ ■ ■ ■

Sam's phone rang before Grace had a chance to answer his stupid question. What was it about her that made him trip all over his words, say things without calculating how they might be perceived? "Pretend like I didn't ask that, okay?" He activated the car's Bluetooth when he saw it was Nathan Kingston, the warden at the prison. "Nate?"

"Sam! Sam, thank you for answering. We need you here ASAP.

We have a hostage situation and Pacman said he'd only talk to you."

Pacman. Hal Brown's nickname. "What happened?"

"About thirty minutes ago, he was watching a football game on television. Then all of a sudden, he started banging on the bars and yelling about his sister being in danger. Guards told him to settle down. He grabbed his chest and fell to the floor shaking like he was having a seizure. Mitch Zimmerman called for help, then went in to try and help him. Only—"

"Only it was a trick," Sam said. Hal was one of his most violent patients—but only when provoked. He didn't just spontaneously erupt like Nate described.

"Exactly. He grabbed Mitch, held a shiv to his throat, and demanded he get him out of the prison. He was ranting that his sister was in danger and he had to warn her."

"His sister's in danger? From what?" Sam braked and pulled the car off to the side of the road.

"He didn't say. Just said he had to talk to you and only you would understand."

Well, he didn't. Maybe Hal would reveal his reasons when Sam got to the prison. "He's never done anything like this before. Well, not in prison anyway. He's been a model prisoner up to this point." Sam spun the situation through his brain and managed to come up with . . . nothing. What had he missed? What would lead Hal to believe his sister was in danger? "It'll take me twenty more minutes to get there."

"SWAT is on the way."

"I have someone with me. I may need her to help with Hal."

"What do you mean?"

"Just bear with me. There was something he said in therapy a few sessions ago. Depending on his mindset, having a woman with me may be a plus. And she's an agent. Special Agent Grace Billingsley."

"I know her. She's been here before. We'll have an escort waiting for you. We need you here *now*."

He glanced at Grace and she pointed to the road, indicating he should go. He frowned, torn. He had no idea what he'd be walking into and didn't want to force her to be there indefinitely. "Nate, hang on a sec." He muted the phone. "This has never happened before, believe it or not. I have to go, but you don't—in spite of what I said to Nate."

"Of course you have to go. Get back on the highway. I can always take an Uber home later if I need to."

He groaned and went back to Nate. "I'm on the way." He hung up. "I'm so sorry. This was not what I envisioned for the evening. On all accounts."

"Stop apologizing," Grace said. "Everything that's happened today has been out of your control. And mine."

"True."

"Tell me about this patient of yours."

"He's different than any other serial killer I've worked with. I almost don't even know how to explain it. But . . . while he's a killer, I don't believe he's a sociopath. I *do* believe he's mentally ill."

"Does he belong in prison?"

"Yes. Absolutely. He was in a psychiatric ward and it was a failure. He killed an orderly."

"Oh, gah. Why?"

"Said the guy made a pass at his sister when she was visiting."

She grimaced. "Okay, he's obviously super protective of his sister."

"That's an understatement. The first guy she was with was abusive in a brainwashing kind of way. He was into reincarnation and influenced Hal in his beliefs. Only Hal came to believe the boyfriend was an uncle reincarnated. An uncle who'd abused his sister. So, he killed him. Same with the others."

"Reincarnation." She rubbed her eyes. "I've come across that a few times. How do you handle that during Hal's therapy?"

He shrugged. "I counter it with truth and just pray that some of it sticks." He glanced at her from the corner of his eye. "That in some corner of his heart, there's a crack for the truth to sink in and God to work."

"You're a believer."

"I am." He paused. "Are you?"

"Since the age of seventeen."

"Good to know." He shot her a quick smile, then frowned. "Does it make a difference for you when you work with those you come into contact with? Offenders or victims?" He grimaced. "Sorry, dumb question."

"Not a dumb question. Depends on what you mean by making a difference. If you're asking if my faith influences how I interact with the people I investigate, find, and put away—people who seem to have no remorse or conscience? Yes. It does. Does it have an influence on the spiritual lives of those people? I don't know. I leave that part to God. But mostly, it has an influence on me. I know the truth, and I pray for wisdom to see through the lies of those I come into contact with, such as those who'd protect a killer. Being able to discern a lie from the truth can mean saving an innocent person's life."

"Have you ever been wrong?"

She hesitated and a dark cloud flashed across her features for a brief moment. "Yes."

"I'm sorry."

"I am, too, but we can talk about that later. Tell me more about what I'm walking in to."

"Of course. Hal's weakness is women. He adores all women, but he's elevated his sister, Brenna, to goddess status. She comes to see him on a regular basis, and he just worships her. She can do no wrong in his eyes." He pursed his lips. "Honestly, when she's around is when he seems the most . . . normal. He keeps it together for her."

"You think he'll listen to me? Because I'm a woman?"

"I don't know, but if he won't listen to me, I need a backup plan." His fingers flexed on the wheel. "I really don't want them to kill him."

"I don't mind being plan B. Give me more to work with. You've listened to their conversations?"

"I have." He shrugged. "They're recorded and Hal knows it. But I think he probably forgets about it. I listen to the latest visits before his sessions, trying to pick up on anything that could help me reach into his mind. Brenna's very encouraging and upbeat. She talks to him about God and how the enemy has Hal deceived and he needs to take off the blinders so he can finally heal and be free of his torment."

"What does he say?"

"He counters with a lot of New Age mumbo jumbo, and she patiently refutes his claims with truth. From what I can tell, she's legit, but so far, I can't tell that it's made a difference in his beliefs."

She fell silent for a few moments. "All right, tell me some of his favorites. Favorite movie, book, quote. Anything like that."

"Even though he's young, he talks a lot about old shows from the fifties and sixties. His favorite movie? That's easy. *Going in Style*. He says he likes the humor in it, but has great admiration for the characters doing what needed to be done to protect their families and get what was owed to them."

She frowned. "I've seen that. That's the one where the old men are getting cheated out of their pension and plan to rob the bank holding the money?"

"Yeah, the company froze their pension and they figured they'd take only what they're owed. It's a comedy of errors, of course, but in the end, they get away with it. You couldn't help but be glad about it in spite of the whole illegal aspect of it."

"So," she said, drawing out the word, "you said 'the first guy' in reference to her boyfriend. Tell me about the others."

"He killed three of them over a ten-year period. With this last one, she finally put it together and turned him in."

"Oh. My. What was it about them that he didn't like?"

"Some background on that. When Brenna was twenty, their parents were killed in a car accident. Hal was sixteen. She worked two jobs to take care of her little brother. Then she started dating someone—the someone with the reincarnation beliefs. Six months later, he was dead. Killed with a blow to the back of the head late one night when he was finished with his shift at a local restaurant. He took the trash out and never came back in. Owner found him the next morning."

"How terrible."

"Hal was three days shy of his seventeenth birthday when he killed him."

A light shudder ran through her.

"And the others?"

"Same story. She started dating another guy a couple of years later. She was twenty-three and Pacman was nineteen. Guy came out of work and was bashed in the head. No cameras, no witnesses."

"How old is Hal now?"

"Twenty-seven."

"So that would make his sister thirty-one. And the third one?"

"From the police report, it seems like she'd finally met a good one. Nice guy, took Hal to ballgames and was trying to be a father figure to him—or at least an older brother kind of guy. He confided in Hal that he planned to ask Brenna to marry him. The next day the guy was dead from a blow to the back of the head. He'd been hit so hard it broke his skull, sending fragments into his brain. When Hal finally confessed after Brenna confronted him—and recorded the conversation she shared with the police—he told her he was protecting her. That none of them were good enough for her and that it was the uncle reincarnated come back to hurt her again."

"I'm guessing that, in his head, he truly believed that he was doing the right thing in his belief that he was protecting her. It was definitely the wrong thing, but in protection of his sister, to him, it was the right thing." She paused. "Is that confusing?"

"Not at all."

"Okay. So, if you follow the reasoning of the movie, it sounds like he's saying it's okay to do something wrong as long as you have a good reason for it? The end justifies the means—especially when protecting someone you love?"

"That's my takeaway. If he has another explanation for why the movie is his favorite, I haven't heard it—or been able to discern it."

She frowned. "Did someone steal something from him before he started killing?"

He shook his head. "If so, he's never mentioned it."

She nodded while chewing on her lower lip. "So, he's being proactive, working off the fear that she's going to be hurt again? And it's possible that while he's concerned about her, he's still looking out for himself. She's his only visitor?"

"Yes. I honestly can't think of anyone else. We could check the prison records, of course, but I think Hal would have told me."

"Then it stands to reason that he's afraid if she meets someone else, she'll forget about him. If that was his fear originally—that he'd lose her to another man—he'd be so compelled to get rid of them."

He blew out a low breath. "Yeah. That's pretty much the conclusion I've come to, although Hal hasn't come out and said anything about fear of losing her. He always plays the saint and insists it was for her protection." Sam pulled to a stop at a checkpoint and showed his ID. After two more stops, he finally parked and hurried toward the entrance, with Grace on his heels.

CHAPTER
FIVE

Passing through security with Sam went smooth, and Grace soon found herself traversing a maze of corridors to a part of the prison she'd never seen. The most violent inmates were kept in isolation, away from the general population.

A gentleman in his early sixties with graying hair, ruddy cheeks, and hard blue eyes met them in the area of the prison that had been locked down.

"Nate," Sam said.

Nate hurried forward. "Thank God you're here. SWAT is in place and one of the negotiators has been talking to him, doing a good job of keeping things somewhat under control, but Hal's still demanding to see you—and that someone go to his sister's home and get her."

"Have you dispatched anyone to locate her?"

"No." He raked a hand over his head as he frowned at Sam and narrowed his gaze. "I'm only giving that lunatic so much."

Grace could almost see Sam biting his tongue on his initial response. "I suggest we get her here," Sam finally said, his voice low and calm. "On the off chance her presence might help diffuse the situation. Because that's our priority, right?"

For a moment the warden hardened his jaw and clenched his fist. "Fine. Yes, of course." He bit out the words and turned to one of his guards. "Get the sister here, will you?"

The man left to do as ordered, and Sam stepped toward the window that looked out into the area under lockdown. The cellblock was arranged in a U-shaped formation, with each cell measuring eight by ten. Inside the individual rooms were a bed, a sink, a toilet, and a shower. Most of the men housed in those cells were released for one hour of solitary exercise per day.

Grace stayed next to Sam. She took in the scene, processing it, and was already working on a dialogue if Sam should decide he needed her. She could see into the area where his patient held the guard in the hallway, the shiv resting against his neck. The other prisoners shouted their encouragement for Hal to kill the guard, and she could only pray he continued to ignore them.

Sam pressed the button that would allow him to communicate with Hal, and Grace made sure she stayed out of sight but still had a good view of the man and his hostage.

"Pacman," Sam said. "Hal. I'm here."

"Sam!" Hal's gaze focused on the glass and Sam. "You came!"

"Of course I did. I told you I'd be here for you whenever you needed someone to talk to."

Grace scanned the guard with the shiv to his throat. His eyes were narrowed, a determined glint in them. This man had decided he wasn't going to die today.

"Sam," Hal said, "you got to get Brenna safe. He's going to kill her."

"I understand you're worried about Brenna. I'll make sure she's safe. She's on her way here."

"Without an escort?" His pained scream echoed through the speaker. "He'll catch her!"

"Who, Sam?"

"Open the door! You have to let me out! I'm the only one who can save her!"

The man's agitation was escalating with each passing second.

"Hal!" Sam raised his voice. "Breathe! And look at me. You know I can't just open the door and let you out. So, let's talk about this and figure out a solution that works for everyone."

Hal drew in a ragged breath. "No, you don't understand. You'll just talk and talk, wasting time, and drag this out while he's with her and is going to kill her."

"Who, Hal? I need to know who, so I can stop him."

"I don't know his name! And *you* can't stop him! Only *I* can. Don't you get it? I only needed you here to get me out. I thought you would help me get out when I told you Brenna was in danger, but you're as worthless as the rest of them." He let out a string of curses that Grace let bounce off her ears. But it was obvious, Hal was right on the edge and about to slip over.

Grace glanced at Sam, who wasn't responding. His focus had shifted away from Hal, so she followed his line of sight. One of the prisoners in the cell behind Hal had turned and was looking straight at Sam.

"You hear me? Sam?" Hal's agitation continued to rise, and Sam seemed frozen solid.

Grace placed a hand on his arm. "Sam?"

He flinched. Glanced at her, then back at Hal. "I hear you, Hal. Let me see what I can do." He muted the audio to the room and turned to her. "This isn't working. Try talking to him. I'm only aggravating the situation."

"Sure." Something more was going on than Sam wanted her—or anyone else—to know.

Sam glanced at his phone. "Sniper is in place. He doesn't have a shot yet but is working on getting one. Hal doesn't have much longer if this doesn't go well."

"I understand. Introduce me."

Whatever had rattled Sam seemed to have passed. He pressed the button and cleared his throat. "Hal, I have a friend here who wants to talk with you while I get Brenna on the phone. I want you to hear that she's safe."

Hal stilled. "You're getting Brenna on the phone?"

"Yes. If you'll talk to my friend. She's really nice. I think you'll like her."

"Her?" The idea seemed to intrigue him, and his tension lessened a fraction. The guard's eyes widened slightly, and his fingers curled into a fist at his side. But he was ready to act as soon as Hal gave him the opportunity.

"Yes," Sam said, "her name is Grace. Will you talk to her while I take care of Brenna?"

While Sam talked to Hal, she locked eyes with the guard. *Hang on, don't do anything yet,* she silently pleaded with him. His eyes narrowed and his jaw tightened.

"Yes," Hal said. "Yes. Whatever it takes." He cleared his throat. "I know you have a sniper, but I'm not moving from this spot. Then again, if I have to die to get your attention on Brenna, that's what I'll do."

Sam blinked and a flash of uncertainty darkened his eyes.

Grace frowned at him, muting their voices. "Could there be something to what he's saying?"

"I would have said no right up until this moment." Sam raked a hand over his head. "His whole world is wrapped up in protecting his sister, and he's convinced he's the only one who can. So, that last comment has me thinking there might be a grain of truth in there somewhere."

Grace nodded and hit the button once more. "Hi, Hal. Or should I call you Pacman?"

At her voice, the man drew in another deep breath, and the guard met her gaze for a flicker of a second before she focused back on Hal.

"Hal is fine. Who are you?"

"I'm a friend of Sam's. We were getting ready to have dinner when he got the call that you needed him."

"Dinner?"

"Yes, he dropped everything, and we came straight here."

"He did? Dropped everything? I . . . see." He paused. "You're pretty."

"Thank you, Hal. Hey, listen, Sam's on the phone right now, making sure the police have Brenna in sight and that she has an escort like you wanted." Sam waved at her and pointed to the phone, then gave her a thumbs-up. "And you know what? He just signaled that she's fine. She's with the police officer who's going to bring her here."

"Really? She's okay?" A tear slid down his cheek and dripped off his chin.

"Yeah, Hal, she's really okay. Can you let the guard go now?"

"Not until I see her."

"Of course. Can we just talk until she gets here?"

The hostage shifted and Hal scraped the shiv along the man's throat. "Be still," Hal ordered.

The guard obeyed even as a fine line of red appeared on his skin and a blaze of fury ignited his eyes.

"Hal," Grace said, "I understand you have no reason to believe anything I say, but I promise, Brenna is safe."

"You can't let him get to her. You can't. He hates women. He'll hurt her. He'll cut her tongue out and—"

Grace jerked. "What? What do you mean he'll cut her tongue out? Who will?" Her gaze shot to Sam's, and he leaned in.

"He will!" Hal insisted. "I'm not kidding!"

"What's his name, Hal?"

"I don't know, but—"

The shiv lowered and the guard slammed an elbow back into his captor's belly. Hal cried out, bent double, then dove for his weapon. Only the guard beat him to it and jammed it into Hal's neck.

■ ■ ■ ■

"No!" Sam raced to the door. "Open it up!" The door buzzed and he pushed through. "Get the doctor here now!" He dropped to the floor next to the bleeding inmate while Mitch backed away, breathing hard, his eyes fixed on the man he'd just stabbed.

"Can you help him?" the guard asked, his voice low and tight.

Sam ignored the question. Someone passed him a towel, and he pressed it around the shiv still sticking out of the side of Hal's neck. He kept his attention focused solely on the wounded man in front of him.

Hal coughed. Scared brown eyes met his. "I don't want to die," he whispered. "Don't let me die. Have to save her."

"Just hang on, Hal, you're going to be okay. What's the guy's name? Who am I looking for?" He had no idea how the man was able to talk but took it as a good sign that there might not be permanent damage. If he survived. Blood pumped around the blade, soaking the towel. If his carotid artery had been hit . . .

"You're not a good liar, Doc. Take care of Brenna. Don't let him . . . hurt her."

"What did you mean about cutting out her tongue? What's his name, Hal? Give me a name."

Hal's lips moved. "Don't . . . know." Then stilled. But he was breathing. Barely. He'd slipped into unconsciousness.

Sam looked up at Mitch. "You okay?"

"Yeah." The man swiped a hand across his lips, and Sam noticed the subtle tremor. "Fine."

"Hello, Sam. Fancy meeting you here. It's been a while." The voice came from the cell behind him.

Sam froze for a brief second but ignored the inmate's statement and monitored Hal's pulse while he waited for the prison doctor to arrive. Paramedics had been called and now all he could do was pray Hal made it.

Finally, the prison doctor rushed in, bag in hand. Sam looked up. "Pulse is weak. I don't know how close the shiv is to the carotid. I didn't dare pull it out until he's had an X-ray."

"Got it." She worked fast and efficiently, getting an IV into his arm. Just as she finished, paramedics arrived.

Sam glanced at Mitch. The man watched the proceedings with hooded eyes and Sam stepped over to lay a hand on his shoulder. "It's okay if you're not okay."

"He gonna make it?"

"I don't know. I'm going to the hospital to be there if he wakes up."

"You'll let me know when you know something?"

"Of course."

"Thanks."

The warden pushed through and strode up to Mitch and Sam. "Mitch? That was impressive how you handled yourself there. I'm glad you're okay. Take the rest of the week off." He paused. "I'd tell you to report to the prison psychiatrist, but . . ." He waved at Sam. "What do I do in this situation?"

"I can make a referral if he doesn't want to talk to me."

Nate turned to Mitch. "What's your preference?"

Mitch shook his head. "I don't know. I don't care. I don't need to talk to anyone."

"Yeah, you do." The warden nailed the guard with a laser-sharp scowl.

"Fine," Mitch said. "I'll talk with the doc here."

Sam nodded. "Let's talk in the next couple of days."

Mitch nodded.

"Coming through." Sam turned to see paramedics with Hal on a gurney hurrying toward them. "Who's going with us?"

Nate assigned two guards to the transport detail, and they headed for the ambulance.

"Sam," the inmate behind him spoke again. "Can we talk a moment?"

Sam ignored the man, placed a hand on Mitch's arm, and nodded to the door. "Why don't we go in there? I have a few questions for you."

"Of course." They walked away, and the man behind the bars didn't say anything else. Once they were through the door, Sam breathed a little easier. He led the way to a small conference room where he, Mitch, the warden, and two other guards entered.

Sam looked at Mitch. "Any idea what set him off?"

"No. He was in his cell watching television. Then he started pacing and muttering to himself. I asked him what was wrong, and he said nothing. Then all of a sudden, he started shaking the bars, hollering about his sister. When I told him to calm down, he really cranked up. His face was red and he was sweating like a pig. Then he grabbed his arm and went down. Started convulsing like he was having a seizure. I ran in and he grabbed me." He raked a hand over his blond hair and shook his head, disgust written on his features. "Been doing this job for almost twenty years and never have I been played like I was today." He glared in the direction of the exit where Hal had been rolled out. "Won't happen again, I can promise you that." A knock on the door interrupted him, and an officer waved at him through the window. "Guess they want me to put that statement in writing. You know where to find me if you have any more questions."

"Thanks." Sam turned to Nate as Mitch left. "The last time I talked to Hal, he seemed fine." As fine as Hal ever was. "Has he had any visitors lately? Ones that I wasn't made aware of?"

"No. I can check the log, but I'm pretty sure the only person he's seen is his sister. She was here yesterday."

The sister who was on the way. "Where is she? She getting close?"

"We rerouted her to the hospital. Figured if he regained consciousness, her presence would keep him calm and make things easier for the doctors."

"Good thinking. I'm going to head over there and see if she has any insight into this." And he still had to take Grace home. And check in with his mother-in-law, who was bringing his kids home.

Sam stepped out of the room and found Grace talking with two members of SWAT. He approached and she turned to him. "I'm heading to the hospital," he said, "but I have time to take you home first. Hal will probably be in surgery for a while. But his sister is on her way there and I want to talk to her."

"I'd like to go to the hospital with you if you don't mind. Hal's reference to someone cutting out his sister's tongue is . . . interesting. The Bureau hasn't released that particular detail in any of the killings. Could be just a coincidence, but I'm thinking there's more behind the comment."

"Of course, I don't mind. And I agree. He's got some kind of connection with the killer."

"Let's hope he lives to tell us what."

CHAPTER
SIX

Grace was no stranger to long days and longer nights, but sitting in the hospital waiting room, fatigue pulled at her. She closed her eyes and pressed her fingers to her temples. Hal's sister had arrived two minutes before them and had been ushered to her brother's side before he'd been rolled into surgery.

"You okay?"

She looked up at Sam's question and found him holding a cup of steaming coffee and a wrap in front of her face. She took both. "Thanks."

"It's the least I could do since we aren't getting dinner."

"I have to say, I was really looking forward to that steak."

He smiled and settled in the chair next to her. "You and me both." He unwrapped his food and took a bite. "Did they say how long it would be until we could talk to Brenna?"

"Just a few minutes, I think. She wouldn't calm down until she'd seen him. We'll have to wait on Mark and Jerry. They're on the way."

He blew out a low breath. "You think they'll let me listen in?"

"Yes, of course. You know the sister and you know Hal. You may have information related to the case you may not realize you have."

"True." He tipped his cup to drain it. "We're going to need more coffee, aren't we?"

"Definitely." She paused. "What happened back at the prison? With that inmate? I couldn't get a good look at him, but he seemed to know you."

He winced. "He does."

She raised a brow. "So . . . who is he?"

"My father."

Grace snapped her lips shut. Okay, she hadn't expected that.

"I haven't seen him in almost ten years, but I recognized his voice immediately. Apparently, he recognized me too."

"It threw you."

"Oh yeah."

She fell silent a moment, thinking. "You said he was the reason you went into psychiatry? What was it you were hoping to figure out? How he thought? Why he did what he did?"

He chuckled without humor. "Yes. Partly. Mostly."

"You're going to have to elaborate on that answer."

"There are so many reasons that I chose psychiatry, you'd have a field day analyzing them, but yes, to the reasons you stated. And more."

"I was just curious. I don't want to analyze you."

"Hmm. Then you're the only one who doesn't." He sighed. "The simple answer is, yes, I got into psychiatry and working with sociopaths because of who my father is."

"That would have been my first guess."

He shrugged. "But there were other reasons too."

"Like?"

He opened his mouth and shut it. Opened it again and said, "Okay, all the reasons probably circle back to him. I had to figure out how he thought. What was it about his mind that made him capable of doing what he did to other humans? What does he lack in his brain? Was it a chemical thing? A spiritual thing? Or was it something else?"

"What's your conclusion?"

"It's not a popular one."

"I'm intrigued."

"He made a choice."

Grace pondered that. "Yes, he did. But what made him make that choice?"

"He's a classic narcissist. Selfish, wrapped up in himself. I'm not even sure he feels real emotion, although he knows how to mimic it."

She shot him a sideways glance. "Most do."

"But I believe he knows right from wrong. He's not insane or mentally ill, he just doesn't have the ability to care." Sam rubbed a hand over his chin. "He's never once expressed regret or remorse for his actions. At least, not that I've ever been made aware of. So, he can still be held accountable."

"What was his childhood like?"

His tight smile pressed lines into his cheeks. "It was a good one. He wasn't abandoned by his mother and he wasn't abused. He just wanted what he wanted and went after it. Which led him to be successful. A loaded bank account—and . . . bored."

"Bored?"

"I talked to him shortly after he was arrested. I was hoping for some answers. Instead, I just got more questions. Because when I asked him why, he said he was bored and needed to find something to make life interesting."

Grace shuddered. "Bored."

"He's a sociopath, Grace. As skilled as we are, as much knowledge as we have, we'll never be able to wrap our minds around it." He swallowed. "And frankly, I look at that as a good thing."

"It definitely is," Grace said, "but he also wanted his family. And he knew if he got caught, he could lose it."

"Exactly. Because he knew what he was doing was wrong."

"I don't know that I agree with that." He scowled at her and she held up a hand. "Hear me out. It's possible that he thought what he was doing wasn't *wrong*. He probably thinks the whole justice system is stupid and kept him from freely having what he deserved, doing what he wanted. So, in order to get that, he had to circumvent it. But he didn't necessarily think what he was doing was wrong."

Sam studied her a moment. Then sighed. "Yes. And that's something I think about. Often."

Of course he had. He had the same training she did. Had studied the same cases she'd studied. His knowledge just hit closer to home than hers did. "You said there were other reasons you chose your career path."

His eyes darkened. "Yes." The door opened and a woman with dark hair and red-rimmed blue eyes stepped through. "And I guess we'll save that reason for another time."

An officer walked at Brenna's side. Grace stood, as did Sam.

"Brenna," he said.

She approached. "Sam. Thank you for coming. I can't believe he did this. I mean, I can, but . . . I can't."

"I know." Sam introduced Grace, then asked, "How is he?"

Brenna ran a shaky hand over her eyes. "Stable. And in surgery. He was unconscious when I got back there, but I was able to talk to the doctor a bit. She thinks she can remove the shiv, but that there was a lot of damage, and she won't know more until she gets in there." Brenna pressed a tissue to her nose and shook her head. "I don't understand, Sam. You said he was doing better."

"He was. I have no idea what triggered this. The guard said he was watching television right before the incident. It could be something he saw that reminded him of you or the uncle he believes was reincarnated. A commercial or something one of the announcers said. Really, it could have been anything, and the only one who knows for sure can't tell us yet."

From the corner of her eye, Grace spotted Mark and Jerry hurrying their way. "Let's hold up on the conversation so they can join us."

Once the introductions were made, Jerry led them to a conference room across the hall. "I don't want to be overheard."

Grace grabbed a seat and let Jerry take the lead. "All right,

Grace filled us in on the incident at the prison. You were there visiting with him yesterday. Did anything happen?"

Brenna swallowed and looked away. "I . . . maybe."

"Gonna need a little more than that," Mark said.

Her gaze swept to Sam's, and Grace admired the fact that his expression never changed. "Go on," Sam told her.

"We were talking and he was fine. Until I told him I was seeing someone."

Sam sucked in a breath. "Why would you tell him that?"

"Because I have a right to live my life without being afraid." She leaned forward. "He's in prison with no chance of getting out—especially after this stunt—and I'm not letting him influence my decisions. It took me years to even be able to agree to go out with someone else. Grant knows all about Hal and he doesn't care. He knew about him before he asked me out and he's not scared. He refuses to live in fear." She pressed fingers to her eyes and swiped the tears from her cheeks before she dropped her hands to rest them on the table. "I admire that. I want that." She paused. "No. I *need* that. God didn't create us to live each moment waiting for the other shoe to drop. And Hal would find out eventually, so I wanted him to hear it from me." She twisted her fingers, then pressed her hands flat to the table as though making an effort not to fidget. "I want to get married, have a family, children, a normal life—whatever normal looks like for me." She lifted one shoulder in a small shrug. "Sorry. That was a really long explanation, but that's why I told him."

Sam nodded. "I understand that. I even agree with it. I just wish you'd given me a heads-up."

The woman sighed. "I didn't plan to tell him yesterday. It just slipped out." She linked her fingers and studied them. "Honestly, I'd had a rough day at work and shouldn't have come yesterday, but I knew it would upset him if I didn't."

"Rough day?" Grace asked.

"I'm an oncology nurse. One of my patients who I'd grown close to passed away yesterday morning."

"Oh no. I'm so sorry."

More tears welled, then hovered on her lashes. She sniffed. "Look, I told Hal this yesterday. Told him all about Grant and made sure I was clear that he was nothing like our uncle." She flicked a glance at Grace, Mark, and Jerry. "I was abused by my father's brother. One day, Hal came home early from a friend's house and saw what was happening. He grabbed a knife from the kitchen and stabbed our uncle in the back." She swiped the tears from her cheeks. "Hal changed that day. He never wanted to leave my side. He kept apologizing for not knowing, for not protecting me. I tried to assure him that it wasn't his fault, but he shouldered the blame anyway. He was only twelve years old," she whispered. "He shouldn't have seen that." She paused and let out a low breath. "Some days I wish I'd lied to the police instead of spilling the whole ugly truth, but Hal wasn't having any of it. He told the cops and the medical personnel, everyone. There's no way I could lie about it without making Hal look like the liar. And I wasn't going to do that to him."

"That's a horrible situation," Grace said, "but telling the authorities was the right thing to do."

"I know that. In my head. My heart wants to argue."

"Where's your uncle now?"

"Dead. He hung himself the night he was escorted from the hospital to the prison."

Grace blinked. Her heart broke for the brother and sister who'd suffered so much. For the mental illness that had ruled Hal's life. For all of it. Grace raised a brow at Sam, silently asking permission to give her input. He nodded.

"I think telling him about your new boyfriend triggered all of his old issues. Before, while it's possible he was afraid you'd be hurt again, I think it's highly likely that he was more afraid of the other man in your life taking you away from him."

"I've thought about that," Brenna said, "of course I have. But what am I supposed to do? Live like a nun the rest of my life? If God called me to that, I'd do it gladly. But he hasn't and I *need* to move on."

"Absolutely, but I think now that Hal's behind bars, he's simply afraid he'll lose the only person he has any contact with. You give him something to look forward to each week. In other words, he's afraid he'll be forgotten."

"Again, I've thought about that too. I've also assured him he won't be. I've gone there week after week, trying to show him how much I love him and want him to be a part of my life, but it's like all of my efforts bounce off of him. It's like he simply can't seem to process it. Or allow himself to believe me." A shuddering sigh slipped from her and the desolation in her gaze pulled at Grace's sympathy.

"I understand," Sam said. "But we have a question for you that goes beyond your situation."

She frowned. "What?"

Mark leaned in. "He said something about your new boyfriend being a danger to you. That he'd cut out your tongue."

The woman flinched and sat back twisting her hands in her lap. "I have no idea why he would say something like that. He's never met Grant, never even seen him. Didn't know about him until yesterday. It's just too bizarre." She sniffed and shook her head. "I'm finally living a normal life. I have someone who cares about me. I'm going to dinner, openly dating a guy I'm falling in love with and who seems to feel the same about me. I went to a football game for the first time in years the other night. Grant's cousin is the star quarterback, and I sat there in awe and so grateful that I was finally *living*. And now this? I love Hal, but I'll be honest. I don't know how much longer I can continue to include him in my life," she whispered. "I really don't."

■ ■ ■ ■

Sam sympathized with the young woman. He knew exactly how she felt. He'd turned his father in for being a serial killer, and she'd done the same with her brother. But she'd taken things a step further. She was doing something he'd never been able to bring himself to do. She'd recognized her loved one's mental illness, accepted it, and then forgiven him for the pain and tragedy he'd caused in this world. She offered him grace and love.

Granted, there were differences in the crimes—and the motivation behind them—but Brenna's choice was to try to save her brother. Sam's choice was to ignore the whole "my father is a serial killer" thing. As much as he could anyway. And while he and Brenna shared another similar aspect of having a loved one behind bars—they were both responsible for putting them there—she could be letting the guilt from her role in putting Hal away influence some of her actions.

Sam had no guilt. Not related to putting his father behind bars anyway.

"What did you tell him about the guy you're seeing?" Jerry's question jerked Sam back to the conversation.

"Just that he was nice, treated me well, and that I thought he'd like him. And that if he loved me, he'd understand that I needed someone in my life. Someone to be with."

"And Hal's reaction?"

"Not really what I expected."

Sam frowned. "What do you mean?"

"He just said he needed to think about that." Her gaze flicked up to meet Sam's. "He said y'all had talked a lot about me and what it meant to really love someone. That love was putting the other person's needs above your own."

Sam nodded, glad to hear some of what they'd talked about in sessions had sunk in. "So, that brings us back to what set him off today?"

She shrugged. "I don't know. I guess the more he thought about it, the more delusional he became, and it was too much for him to deal with." She dropped her head, dark hair falling around her face. "I shouldn't have said anything." She peered up through the strands. "Or I should have at least talked to you about the idea of telling him. I'm sorry. This is all my fault."

"Brenna, that's the last thing this is. This is Hal's fault. Mostly.

I'm not saying just because he's mentally ill, he gets a pass, but it does factor into the situation. Whatever the case, you're not to blame for any of this."

"But if I'd just not said anything, this wouldn't have happened."

"Maybe. Assuming that's what set him off. But," Sam said, "you're right in that you had to tell him at some point. If you didn't, someone else would. Somehow." Without visitors, he wasn't sure how word would have gotten back to the man, but he had no doubt it would have. Eventually. Possibly through the man's lawyer. "I mean, if you wind up marrying this guy, you'll have the engagement announcement, the wedding announcement, and more. Right?"

She nodded. "I guess."

Sam shook his head. "It's best to be honest with him, because finding out from someone else would not go over well at all."

"Well, that's kind of how I looked at it, but now . . ." She spread her hands, then linked them back together and fell silent.

"We watched the footage of Hal's episode or whatever it was," Mark said. "He was in his cell when the guard made his rounds like usual. He had his television playing. He spoke to the guard— Mitch, the one he attacked—then went back to the television. Sat there for three minutes and thirty-seven seconds, then started screaming. The guard returned, Hal faked his seizure, and as the guard entered the cell, Hal attacked him."

"With no idea of what set him off," Sam said.

"None."

"Okay, here's the plan," Jerry said. "We're going to wait for Hal to wake up and see what he has to say for himself. We're simply going to ask him why he did what he did and what he meant by the whole 'cutting out her tongue' thing."

"Assuming he wakes up," Mark muttered.

Brenna flinched and Grace shot him a frown. Mark shrugged. "Sorry. I know this is hard for you," he said to Brenna, "but I don't think we can count on him to give us the answers we need."

"You have a better plan?" his partner asked.

"Not at the moment, but if Hal's our plan A, we need to be thinking of a plan B."

"Yeah."

Brenna stood. "If you're done, I need to go see where my boyfriend is." She checked her phone. "The last I heard from him, he was on his way to the hospital."

"Of course." The men stood while she left, then settled back into their seats. Mark and Jerry eyed Sam.

"What's your take on this?" Jerry asked him. "You're the one who's been working with Hal. Could he possibly have any connection to the guy we're after?"

"Hal and the serial killer? I honestly can't make that call since I don't know who we're after."

"Good point," Jerry muttered.

"What about your father? Any more thoughts there?" Mark asked.

"I have to admit the similarities have been nagging at me, but who would he talk to without someone knowing? Everything he does is monitored. On camera and on paper."

"We'll get a visitor's log. See if your father and Hal had some of the same visitors."

Sam shook his head. "That's just it. The only visitors Hal had are his sister and his lawyer—and a woman in the church he used to attend. She feels like it's her duty to visit him once a year."

Mark frowned. "No other family?"

"None. And no friends. No church. Nothing."

"What about you?" Mark eyed him and a familiar chill crept into Sam's soul. "You see him on a regular basis. You're the link between Hal and Peter Romanos."

"Mark!"

Grace's shocked response reached Sam, but he kept his gaze steady on the other agent. "I meet with Hal on a professional basis. I have never once had any contact with my father since he's been incarcerated."

Mark's expression didn't change. Neither did the judgment there.

"Well, that's just sad," Jerry muttered, slicing into the awkward moment, his gaze bouncing between Sam and his partner. "About Hal, I mean. No wonder the guy is so fixated on his sister. If she ditches him, he really would be all alone."

Grace cleared her throat. "So, you two have a place to start, right? You can talk to the lawyer and find out who's been in contact with Hal? It's possible there's someone that Sam isn't aware of. Will you keep us updated?"

Mark looked away, and Jerry frowned at the man but nodded in answer to Grace's question. "Of course. I know you'll be studying everything we gather, trying to put together a profile for us."

"As soon as possible."

"Perfect."

The agents rose and left the room and Sam stood. "I'm going to do one last check-in with the doctors, then I'll take you home."

"Sure. Sam—"

"We can finish talking in the car." He couldn't meet her eyes and had no idea what he'd say to her in the car. But he'd just had a harsh reminder that romance and relationships weren't for him.

Twenty minutes later, on the highway headed toward her home, he still hadn't said a word to her.

"No one thinks you had anything to do with what happened today," she finally said.

"Someone does."

She sighed. "Mark's a good agent, but he can be a jerk sometimes."

"Yeah."

Grace fell quiet once more and Sam pressed the gas. The sooner he dropped Grace off at her house, the better. He'd made the mistake of trying to have a normal life, but each time he'd let his heart open up, it had been trampled by the truth that he was the son of a serial killer. He liked Grace and was attracted to her, but he'd have no more contact with her if he could help it.

It stunk, but it was just the way things had to be.

CHAPTER
SEVEN

Grace walked into her home and got a whiff of spoiled chicken. Great. She'd forgotten to take the trash out last night after she'd cleaned out her refrigerator. She shut the door and flipped the overhead light on to chase away the shadows, wishing there was a switch she could hit that would allow her to see into the darkness that had invaded Sam's spirit tonight. She worked quickly to tie off the bag and lift it from the can. As she opened the door that led into the garage, she felt her phone buzz.

She set the bag next to her car, backed into the house, and shut the door, snagging her phone to see a message from Jerry.

Sorry about Mark

Grace tapped her response while she walked into the den.

Not your fault. That's on Mark.

She went to the fireplace and turned on the gas logs. Something about the dancing flames was soothing for her tattered nerves—or for trying to work out something in her mind.

Such as Mark's attitude toward Sam today.

It hadn't been hard to figure out the agent had scraped a raw wound for Sam. She just had no idea why the agent would imply that Sam had anything to do with the situation. In fact, while she'd been truthful with Sam that Mark could be less than tactful in some situations, he wasn't usually flat-out rude. But apparently he was angry about a case Sam had solved.

Sam had been convinced one of his patients was innocent and had set out to prove it. He'd investigated and found the real killer. So, could it be Mark didn't believe the innocent man had deserved to go free in spite of the evidence Sam had turned up?

She couldn't say for certain, of course, but it seemed Mark's animosity was something more than that.

While the flames flickered, Grace made her way to the kitchen, hung her keys on the hook just inside the door, then aimed herself toward the refrigerator. The wrap from the hospital had helped take the edge off, but she was still hungry. She pulled a frozen dinner from the freezer and popped it in the microwave. While the timer ticked down, she checked her messages and found two voice mails from Julianna Jameson—soon to be Julianna Fox. Julianna currently worked as a crisis negotiator with the Bureau and was assigned to the Charlotte, North Carolina, office.

She dialed Julianna's number, got her voice mail, and left one of her own. "Got your message to call you. Feel free to do the same. It's been a long day. If it can wait until tomorrow, great. If you need to talk, call me when you get this."

Just as she was about to hang up, Julianna's name flashed across the screen as an incoming call. She answered with a tap. "Hey. What's up?"

"I'm just calling to check on you. How's your day been?"

Grace filled her in, thankful for close friends with whom she could speak freely about her work—and just about everything else in her life. The microwave dinged.

"Are you eating one of those nasty, frozen fake things again?" Julianna asked.

"No."

"Liar."

Grace laughed. "Fine. Yes, I am. I don't feel like cooking."

"That's why they have takeout. Or food delivery services."

"They take too long. I'll be asleep by the time it gets here."

She dumped the steaming food on a plate and set it on the table. Her stomach rumbled, and she dropped into the chair and took a bite. "Ugh."

Julianna laughed. "One day you'll listen to me. If you don't buy them, you won't eat them. Now, finish telling me about the case."

Grace did so in between bites, and Julianna let out a low whistle when Grace finished. "So, you have a serial killer on your hands and no idea for motive."

"That about sums it up."

"And Sam Romanos—aka, Sam Monroe—is involved?"

"Indirectly, but yeah."

"We studied his father's case in class right after the man was arrested. Sam found the evidence the Bureau needed and turned him in."

"I know." Grace shook her head. "I can't imagine how hard that was."

"Oh, it was hard, all right. One of the case agents said he'd never seen a man so broken. Thought he'd crash and burn for sure."

"But he didn't," Grace said, her voice low. "He channeled whatever his emotions were and did something good with them."

"Well, he had a family to think about when all of that went down. I'd heard he divorced, though."

"Yeah, he did."

"Too much for the wife?"

"Apparently. He hasn't come right out and said." And she wasn't going to ask anytime soon. She sighed. "What do you think, Jules? How could the attack at the prison be related to these killings?"

"You've got to look for the connection between the guy from the prison and the victims. But you already know that. Because, that's like . . . your job."

Grace smiled. "I also know that running things around in my head without taking notes and using my system is worthless."

"And yet, you persist in doing it," her friend teased.

Grace stuck her tongue out.

"Stop it," Julianna said. "Sticking your tongue out is so childish."

A snort of laughter escaped Grace. "I never could get anything over on you."

"Well, I am older . . ."

". . . and wiser, smarter, and cuter," they finished together.

"It's always good to talk to you, Julianna. You're great for my self-esteem. But enough about work. How's Clay?"

"As ready for this wedding as I am."

"And y'all are still planning on eloping?"

"Well, sort of. Reese and Dottie were furious when they found out, so they'll be eloping with us." The sisters of each of her friends.

"That sounds . . . um . . ."

"Weird? Tell me about it. Add in Clay's parents and friends, you, Penny, and Raina, and I might as well just plan a big to-do."

"A big to-do is not your thing. But family is good."

"Yeah," Julianna said, a smile in her voice, "family is definitely good. We're going to let y'all be there for the ceremony, then throw you on the next plane home while Clay and I soak up some sun and alone time."

"That sounds like a lovely plan." And it did. Julianna and Clay had opted for a small ceremony on the northern coast of the Dominican Republic in lieu of a traditional wedding. Grace squelched the shaft of envy with a grimace. She didn't have time to date—and when she made the time, she usually wished she hadn't bothered.

Of course, thinking about dating sent her thoughts scurrying straight to Sam. But that was different. Sort of. Even though their date had turned into chaos, she'd still been glad to be with him. To watch him work and get a peek inside the mind of the man she was attracted to. And not because his father was a serial killer.

"Helloooo? Grace? You there?"

Grace blinked. "Oh, yeah. Sorry. Just thinking."

"Glad to know I don't bore you or anything."

"Ha. It's not you." To share or not to share? Always a question for her. "I've met someone."

She could almost see Julianna's brow raising. "What kind of someone?"

"A guy someone."

"I'm listening."

"Well, that was an underwhelming reaction."

"I was afraid if I screamed, you'd hang up. Now spill it, my friend."

Once again, Grace couldn't stop the smile that curved her lips. "I've known him a while. Or rather, known *of* him. Well, we've spoken a few times and attended a conference several months ago where we had dinner and talked a lot there."

Silence.

"I'm not expressing this very well, am I?"

"Which I find exceedingly interesting, but keep going. I'll filter."

Grace closed her eyes. "I don't know, Jules. He asked me out and I said yes. Then everything fell apart and we wound up working a case."

"So, you work with him."

"Yes. And no. Sort of. It's complicated." Grace picked at a loose thread on the padded seat, then curled her fingers into fists when she realized what she was doing.

"And not confusing at all. So you don't work together, but you sort of do. Got it. Isn't that a conflict of interest?" Jules asked.

"No. He works on a contract basis for the Bureau. The rest of the time he's at the prison working with inmates." Julianna fell silent once again and Grace wished she could see her friend's face. "What are you thinking?"

"Just wondering if I know this guy."

"If you don't know him personally, you've definitely heard of him. It's . . . Sam."

"The Sam we were just talking ab—"

"Yes."

"Wow."

"I know. The problem is I don't have time to pursue a relationship. Not really." She rubbed her eyes. "I haven't had time to process everything."

"So, you're going to hang up with me and overanalyze?"

"Pretty much."

"Okay. Well, you know where to find me if you want to verbally process some more."

"Thanks, Jules." She paused. "Hey, wait, how's Raina?" Raina Price, another friend she'd met in juvie, who worked with Penny at Life Flight in Asheville. "Have you talked to her lately?"

"Just the last time we were together—which has been much too long, by the way. Why?"

"I've texted her a couple of times and gotten vague one- or two-word replies, a thumbs-up, or a like. She's usually a little more wordy. These responses aren't really like her."

"Maybe we all need another get-together to just hang out and catch up. Calls and FaceTime are nice, but . . ."

"That would be amazing."

"I'll arrange it. Sounds like you've got enough on your plate right now."

"And you don't?"

"Eh, you know how it is."

Grace did. "Text me the details when you know them. I'll get away if I can. If not, then you and Penny take care of Raina."

"Absolutely." A pause. "And Grace?"

"Yes?"

"You take care of yourself. I'm all for you having a personal life, but if you get involved with Sam, and the media gets wind of it . . . well, it may have been thirteen years ago, but they'd still chase that story."

"I've thought about that." Briefly. She should probably think about that some more. "And, the truth is, the way we left things tonight, it might not be an issue anyway." She gave Julianna a brief description of Mark's attitude toward Sam and the basically silent car ride home. "I can't say I'm not curious what that was all about." She sighed. "Okay, I really am hanging up now. Talk to you soon."

"Bye, Grace."

Grace disconnected the call. She cleaned up her tiny mess in the kitchen, then wandered back into the den to stand in front of the fireplace. Warmth bathed over her, and she let it soothe the chill in her soul while she looked at her phone.

Should she call him or not?

She tapped the screen until she found the number she'd memorized the first time it came across her phone. Sam Monroe—Sam Romanos. Son of a serial killer. She liked him and wanted to see him again outside of work, to get to know him better. But Julianna was right. The media would be like a shark in a feeding frenzy if they got wind of it. Did she really want to open herself up to that? Assuming she had the opportunity to do so and Sam's coolness wasn't anything to take personally. She bit her lip and dropped onto the couch with a low sigh. If she was smart, she'd let it go. Let *him* go. Then again, she'd never been one to play it safe in life.

Why start now?

■ ■ ■ ■

Sam had been home for thirty minutes when the front door slammed open and Eleni burst into the den, tears on her cheeks. She glared when she saw him. "It's not fair and you need to do something about it!" Before he could ask her what was wrong or take her to task about her rudeness, she'd bolted past him and up the stairs. The bedroom door slammed and he grimaced.

His mother-in-law, Vanessa Monroe, and his son, Xander, entered at a slower, infinitely more peaceful pace. Sam met Vanessa's gaze with a raised brow, and she blew out a low breath and gave a roll of her eyes before she disappeared into the kitchen. His buzzing phone distracted him for a split second before he ignored it and turned to Xander. "What was that about?"

Xander's eye roll was an exact imitation of his grandmother's. He dropped onto the couch. "What do you think?"

"Eleni wants a phone."

"Give the man a gold star." Sam let the sarcasm roll off while he waited for the rest of the story. "She and Mom argued about it the entire weekend. I'm surprised my ears aren't bleeding." He narrowed his eyes at Sam. "I'm not going over there anymore until this issue is resolved one way or another, so you and Mom need to talk."

Sam bit the inside of his lip and refused to smile. "I'll talk to her."

"Good." Xander pulled his phone out of his pocket, and Sam dropped onto the couch and placed a hand over Xander's.

"Three things," he said. Every time his kids came home from the weekend at their mother's, he had them tell him three good things that happened or that they did. He'd catch up with Eleni shortly.

Xander sighed. "One, we had pizza twice. I'm not sure if that's a good thing or not, but since it wasn't Mom's cooking, I'm counting it as good. Two, I finished my essay early, so I don't have to worry about it anymore. Three, I also finished two college applications and am working on a third."

Emotion hit Sam from out of the blue and he cleared his throat. "Hey, man, that's awesome. I'm proud of you."

"Hmm. Thanks. Although I remember when teacher workdays were student fun days. I might as well have been in school today for all the work I did." He held up his AirPods. "May I?"

"Go for it. You've earned it."

His son hesitated and Sam frowned.

"What is it?"

"It's just . . . Mom and Brett leave El alone a lot."

"What do you mean?"

"It's a recent thing. Mom said El was old enough to stay by herself, but I can tell she doesn't like it."

"Stay by herself for what?"

Xander shrugged. "For them to go out to eat or whatever."

"And what are you doing?"

"Football practice, hanging out with friends I have over there, whatever. I usually don't realize they've left her alone until I get back from wherever I've been. I think that might be why she wants a phone so bad. Brett and Mom don't have a landline."

Sam worked hard to keep his anger at bay. "I see. Have you talked to your mom about this?"

"I kind of tried to, but she blew me off, told me to mind my own business. Said I wasn't El's parent and to leave that to her."

Sam's fingers curled into a fist, and he drew in a deep breath while he held back the words he wanted to say. He cleared his throat. "Okay. I'll figure out what's going on."

"Thanks, Dad. She might get on my nerves with all of her preteen drama, but I love her and don't like to see her afraid or whatever."

"You're a good brother, Xander."

"Hmm. Sometimes, I guess." He put his AirPods in.

Sam walked into the kitchen, drawn by the smell of coffee and the sound of dishes being loaded into the dishwasher. "I was going to get those," he told Vanessa.

She shot him a quick look before dropping a soap pod into the dishwasher. "You won't let me pay any rent. How else am I going to earn my keep around here?"

"You watch my kids. I should be paying *you*."

"Today, I would agree with that. I'm reminded why Monday has earned a bad rap."

Sam laughed and leaned against the counter. "Thank you for all you do. I feel like I don't say it enough, but I really don't know how I'd make it without you."

"You'd manage."

He studied her. In her early sixties, she could pass for ten years younger. She worked out at the gym three times a week, ate healthy, and enjoyed socializing with her circle of friends—when she wasn't watching her grandchildren. The cross tattoo on her right forearm rippled when she moved, sending the verse dancing. "I can do all things through Christ who strengthens me." Every time he saw it, he appreciated the reminder.

"I want to ask you a question," he said. "Two questions, I guess."

She paused and turned to face him. "Sounds serious."

"First, what do you know about Claire leaving Eleni alone so she and Brett can go to eat or whatnot?"

She sighed. "El said something about it, but honestly, I was leaving Claire alone at that age. Not long, just an hour or two at a time. Some kids are babysitting at that age."

"Yeah, I know. I guess it's just hard to wrap my head around the fact that she's old enough for that."

"She's almost thirteen, Sam."

"Stop. Don't remind me. I don't like that she's alone with no way to call for help, though. At least when you were leaving Claire alone, you had a landline in your house."

"Well, that's true enough. I'll mention that to Claire when I see her tomorrow."

"Thanks."

"And your other question?"

He pressed his thumb and forefinger to his eyes and tried to figure out how to phrase what he wanted to say. Finally, he dropped his hand and shrugged. "Am I doing my job as a father?"

She blinked. "Okay, didn't see that one coming. What triggered that?"

Sam studied her, holding her gaze. "I want to be a good dad, and most days, I think I pull it off, but then there are days where I . . . I just don't know."

She stilled and narrowed her eyes. "Again, what happened to bring this on?"

"Just something someone . . . inferred." Sam glanced away, not sure he could hide the torment raging through him.

"That you're like your father."

He flinched and looked at her. "I'm that easy to read?"

"Not really, but I'm not stupid either. I pick up on things."

No, the woman definitely wasn't stupid. "You think it's possible

I could—" He broke off. "Never mind. I know in my heart that I'm not like him. I just hate that people still think I could be."

"The media was brutal after your father was arrested, I get that. But just like I told you back then, I'm telling you now, you can't let them get under your skin."

"I know, but . . ."

"But?"

"I saw him today."

She froze. "Saw who?"

"*Him.*" Talking about him felt strange. He'd managed to avoid allowing the man even a fraction of head space for a very long time. Of course, he'd loved his father once upon a time—and, if he were honest, probably still did in some little-boy part of himself. Sam had considered Peter Romanos a role model for fatherhood. A good man who'd been knocked down by Sam's mother but had managed to pick himself up and do what he'd had to do to raise his kids. To discover it had all been an illusion had nearly killed Sam.

"You saw your father," she repeated. "At the prison. Why? How?"

Her confusion was understandable. She knew how much he went out of his way to avoid anything related to the man, much less *seeing* him in person. "There was an incident with a patient near Dad's cell. And when I say near, I mean right behind the whole thing. I was called to help and . . . there he was."

"I thought he was in isolation."

"No, just in a cell by himself, but not in general population. His movements are more restricted."

"I can't believe they let him move to your prison. How could they even consider moving him out of Colorado?" His father had been in the supermax facility there since his sentencing. "I was hoping he'd be there forever and away from everyone." She sighed and shook her head.

"You know as well as I do that money can buy a lot of things. Sometimes even the prison cell you want. His sister is still dispersing his funds as he orders."

"She's as bad as he is," Vanessa murmured. "She just hasn't been caught yet."

He paused. "You don't think she could be behind the latest killings, do you?"

Vanessa raised a brow and laughed. "No, not her. She wouldn't sully her hands in that respect. I'm just saying she's always done Peter's bidding."

"Which is why he's in a cell near us." Sam sighed. Before his arrest, his father had been friends with a lot of influential people. People who didn't mind taking money from a killer. And now Sam's aunt controlled the accounts and his father controlled her. He pressed his palms to his temples. "But he's held up his end of the deal. He's caused no one any trouble since he's been here, so I guess there's that." He dropped his hands to link his fingers. "And the supervision is impressive, so I suppose it's a win-win for everyone. He gets what he wants and so do the prison officials—no trouble from him."

"That they're aware of."

"Yeah."

Vanessa patted him on the shoulder. "You're a good man, Sam. You're not a perfect one, but you have a conscience and you listen to it. You love the Lord, and you make sure you're active in your kids' lives and they know you love them. And you don't bash their mother. It still shocks me that the kids don't even know the real reason for your divorce."

"I don't want them to know."

She grabbed a bottle of water out of the refrigerator and twisted the cap off. "I, on the other hand, can bash all I want. And believe me when I say you're a better father than my daughter is a mother. So don't ever doubt that. Don't listen to the voices that would tell you otherwise."

His eyes burned, but he refused to acknowledge the sensation. "Thank you for that, but . . ."

"But?"

"I don't want you to feel like you have to take sides or defend me over Claire."

She laughed and reached out to squeeze his hand. "Son, I live with you and my grandkids. I chose sides when she left you for another man at what was most likely the lowest point in your life. You may have forgiven her for that, but I'm still working on it." Before he could respond, she said, "Eleni's asking questions, though. I overheard her tonight. She asked Xander why you two aren't together."

Sam stilled. "What did he say?"

"'Irreconcilable differences. They couldn't get along anymore.'" She eyed him. "Exactly what you told him when you had to explain the situation to him eight years ago—although, I think 'irreconcilable differences' might have been a tad over his head."

"Good. That he explained it to her."

"Not really. He then went on to say, 'There's probably more to it, but no one's ever come out and said. I expect Brett had something to do with the divorce.'" Sam groaned and she held up a hand. "I intervened at that point, but don't be surprised if he asks you for the details."

Sam sighed and raked a hand through his hair. "I never wanted them to know the truth."

"I've got something I want to tell you," Vanessa said. He stilled at the abrupt change of subject, and she laughed. "Come on, it's not a bad thing."

Relief wilted his shoulders a fraction. "All right. What is it?"

"I've . . . met someone."

"Met someone? As in a male someone?"

She shot him an amused look. "Exactly. We're going out Friday night after the game. Eleni didn't want to go to the game, so Xander said he'd pick her up from school and meet Claire halfway to drop her off. Then he's heading for the football game." She raised a brow at him. "The one you're supposed to be at."

"I've no intention of missing it." Xander played wide receiver and had colleges looking at him. Sam had been doing something right for the kid to turn out like he had.

"Good." She waved a hand. "Now, I'm tired and think I'll go to bed a little early tonight."

"I guess I need to go have a chat with El." He bit off a groan before it could escape.

"Yes, I'd say you do."

"Any tips?"

"Pray for patience?"

"Yeah."

"Night, Sam."

"Wait a minute. Aren't you going to tell me about this *someone*?"

"Nope. Not yet. Night."

Sam shook his head, then aimed his footsteps toward Eleni's room, dreading the confrontation, but knowing he had no choice. He climbed the stairs and took a right. Her door was the first one on the left and he gave it a light rap. She didn't answer and he tried the knob. It turned under his touch, and when he peered inside, he found his daughter sound asleep, tears dried on her face, her stuffed zebra clasped to her chest. She'd hate knowing he saw her holding it. He rubbed his forehead, debated about waking her, then let out a low breath and shut the door. He'd drive her to school in the morning, and hopefully, during the twenty-minute commute, she'd talk to him.

His phone rang and he glanced at it. Grace. Again.

He hesitated. It could be work related. His finger hovered over the screen. Then he dropped his hand and let the call go to voice mail.

■ ■ ■ ■

She was home. Finally. She lived in a small but nice middle-class neighborhood with three cul-de-sacs. Her home backed up to the wooded area with a fence he'd already made sure he could easily scale should he need to.

Grace Billingsley. *Special Agent* Grace Billingsley.

He'd been watching and waiting for hours. And once she entered her home, he waited some more. Letting her go through her evening routine, not realizing she was in any kind of danger. For a moment, uncertainty tugged at him. Could he take on someone with her kind of training? He smiled and banished the thought. Of course he could. He had some training himself, and it had served him well up to this point. True, he'd never taken on a federal agent before, so it would be interesting to see how it played out. He'd have to kill her, of course, but first he had to know what she said.

He lifted the binoculars and scanned the area once more. It was dark, but the streetlamp cast a good amount of light on the front of her home. She had one of those doorbells with a camera and motion sensor, but that was easily avoided. The alarm would go off when he broke the window to get in, so he'd have to act quickly and get her out of the house before the police arrived.

A shot of excitement bolted through him. This was going to be a challenge. Something new.

He couldn't wait.

CHAPTER
EIGHT

Grace stared at the screen of her phone after hanging up without leaving a message. He'd see she called twice, and if he wanted to talk, he'd call her back. If not . . . then she could take a hint. Although she'd really like the chance to explore his reaction to Mark's rudeness today.

A low sound at the back of the house caught her attention and she frowned.

When several moments passed with no other noises, she told herself it was just the house settling. It had to be, right?

Her phone rang, and she snatched it to swipe the screen even as she rose and walked into the kitchen to snag her weapon from the counter. "Hello?"

"Hi."

"Sam. Hi."

"I saw you called."

He left off "twice." "And you didn't answer."

"Because I . . . yeah. I didn't."

Another soft scuff, this one a little closer to the den, sent her nerves humming. "Thank you for calling me back." Her fingers tightened around the grip of her gun. "I was concerned about you." A quick glance at her alarm keypad confirmed that she hadn't armed it when she'd come home. Ugh. She'd set the chicken outside the door when her phone had gone off. And she'd never set the alarm. Which didn't mean there was someone in her house.

Didn't mean there wasn't either.

"No need to be," he said. "I'm fine."

"Mark was rude."

"I'm used to it."

She walked toward the foyer. If she stood near the front door, she could see down the hallway. "Not something you should get used to." The open floor plan allowed her to see into the kitchen but not down the hall. "Sam?"

"Yeah?"

"I think someone's in my house," she whispered.

A slight pause. "In your house?"

"I'm going to have to hang up and call 9—"

The figure stepped out of the master bedroom at the end of the hallway and Grace sucked in a sharp breath. For a flash of a nanosecond, she wondered if she could be hallucinating, but the young man stood there, dressed in black yet unmasked, his eyes locked on hers. She lifted her weapon. "Don't move!"

He stopped.

"Grace!"

Sam's yell echoed in her ear, but her eyes were locked on the large shears in her intruder's left hand. He saw her on the phone and hesitated. Edged toward her and the kitchen.

"What do you want?" she asked.

Ignoring Sam's demands to answer, she set the phone down. She was going to need both hands.

The intruder shifted and she tracked him with her gun. "You get one more warning. Get out of my house."

"Or what?"

"I'll shoot you."

He laughed and the sound chilled her to her soul. This was no ordinary intruder.

"Who are you?" she asked.

"Before you decide to shoot me, just know that I have a woman who will die in less than two hours if I don't return."

"What?" She had no clue what he was talking about but understood exactly what he was saying. Everything in her wanted to squeeze the trigger. "Okay, let's see if I have this right. You have a hostage as leverage to keep me from killing you. That means you came prepared for a confrontation. What do you want?"

"I want to know what you said."

Grace narrowed her eyes, ignoring the pounding in her heart, the fear that wanted to overcome her training. "What I said? When?" She ran her gaze over him. Five ten or eleven, broad shoulders, trim build. Eyes were an odd color of blue. Probably contacts. And most likely left-handed. She registered all of this in less than a second, then returned to his chest. He had on a vest. She'd have to aim for his head.

"At the scene in Prince William," he said, backing into the kitchen. She followed. "You looked right at the phone and said something too low to hear. I want to know what it was."

The chills turned to ice. The serial killer—the one who'd killed three people and cut their tongues out—was in her home. She could pull the trigger now and it would be a clean shoot. But if he really had another victim . . . "Why does it matter?" she asked. The woman was already dead—whether she'd stopped breathing yet or not didn't factor into it.

If he was telling the truth.

"It matters. Tell me."

"No. Put the shears down. Now."

Those weird blue eyes hardened, and he blinked, taking a couple steps back. "Why won't you tell me?"

"Because I don't think you need to know that."

His right hand fumbled behind him.

"Be still!" Her shout echoed in the spacious kitchen, but he pulled the door open and stepped back. Did he think he was leaving? "Prove it," she said.

Her words stopped him. "Prove what?"

"That you have another victim."

He frowned. At least she thought he did. There was something about his face—

"Why would I do that? I don't lie." He seemed genuinely confused. "Now, if you come with me, I'll let the other woman go."

Would he? She doubted it. "Sorry, I'm not falling for that."

He huffed a short laugh. "You're making this harder than it has to be."

"How's that?"

"I thought I would have to break a window and set off the alarm to get in," he said, his tone mild, "but this is easier."

"What's easier?"

"No alarm to navigate."

Finally, she could hear the sirens screaming toward her home. So could he. "I really need you to come with me."

"Not likely."

"Then I will have to take you, and by the time I'm done with you, you'll tell me everything I want to know—and the other woman will have to die too." He lifted the shears, lunged toward her . . .

. . . and Grace squeezed the trigger.

She'd aimed for his head, but he'd spun at the last second, and the bullet slammed into the side of his shoulder. He twisted again and her second bullet gouged a hole into her doorjamb. He staggered back with a harsh cry, hitting the flimsy kitchen storm door. It gave way and he fell out, down the four steps to the concrete floor. The shears clattered from his grasp. Before she could unload the other bullets, he rolled, spun, and raced out the garage door that led to her backyard. She bolted after him, absently noting the sirens growing closer.

She couldn't let him get away. He had another terrified victim somewhere. Someone praying for rescue. Grace didn't bother yelling at him to stop, just pounded after him only to see him hit the fence with his right foot, follow with his left, and then he was over with a pained grunt. Like it was no higher than a fallen tree log.

There was no way she could do that. She bolted for the gate, unlatched it, and swept her weapon right, then left.

Nothing.

Breathing hard, she stood there, listening, trying to hear over the rushing blood and pounding heart beating in her ears. She'd lost him. "Ugh!" She spun and ran back inside the house to grab her phone. She pressed it to her ear. "Sam?"

"Grace! Are you okay? I heard gunshots."

"Yes. That was me. I hit him." She pulled in a deep breath. "Officers are on the way."

"I know. I called them from my son's phone."

"The serial killer. He was here."

"I heard."

"I'm hanging up now. We've got to get a chopper and dogs out here ASAP."

"They're on the way. When I realized who was in your house, I called them too."

"Thank you. I've got to go."

"Keep me updated?"

"Of course." She hung up and pressed a hand to her forehead, then went to meet the officers pulling up to her house.

A helicopter roared overhead, and a spotlight swept the area. They'd mobilized at warp speed to get here so fast. One of the perks of living practically in the FBI's backyard.

She braced herself for the coming inquiry and for the investigation into the shooting. With Sam's testimony as someone who heard the entire exchange, hopefully it wouldn't take long for everything to be cleared up. Tremors set in at that moment, and she clenched her hands into fists while she drew in and blew out slow, even breaths. She'd been terrified, but she'd handled it. And when she looked at the blood on the floor of her kitchen near the door, she smiled. Having a serial killer show up in her home wouldn't be her first choice in how to track him down, but at least they now had his weapon and DNA.

■ ■ ■ ■

Sam hadn't been able to stay away in spite of his vow to do so. After listening to the confrontation with the serial killer, he'd had to see for himself she was okay. And give the statement he'd be asked for.

It was closing in on midnight when he pulled back in front of Grace's house for the third time that day—would the day *ever* end?—and spotted her on the front porch huddled in a heavy coat. She'd already turned her weapon in, no doubt, and would be on re-stricted duty until the investigation into the shooting was wrapped up—which shouldn't take long. Not with his testimony.

He got out of his truck and walked toward the porch. When she spotted him, she offered him a tight smile. "Sam, you didn't have to come."

"I wanted to."

She raised a brow at him as though she wasn't quite sure whether to believe him or not. He didn't blame her after the way he'd given her the silent treatment on the way home, or the way he'd dropped her at her house and run like a scared—

"I appreciate it."

A car pulled to a stop at the curb, and Sam had to turn his head to hide his grimace when he recognized Mark Davis. Great.

The man headed straight for them and hurried up the steps, his gaze on Grace. "You okay?"

Had the agent purposely snubbed him? Or was he just that wor-ried about his friend and fellow agent? Sam wasn't sure and hated that the thought even crossed his mind.

"Yes, I'm fine," Grace said. "Wiped out with the adrenaline crash, but I'll be all right. Any idea who the woman could be he mentioned?"

She'd no doubt filled Mark in when she'd called him. The agent shook his head. "No, but we're scouring the missing persons data-base with matching filters from the other three, looking for who it could possibly be. So, we're on it, but it's going to take time."

Time the woman probably didn't have. Sam pressed his lips together to keep from stating the obvious.

"How'd this guy find you?" Mark asked.

Grace gave a light shrug and her frown deepened. "That was my first question, but there's no way to know."

Refusing to let the man make him feel invisible, Sam stepped forward. "Could he have gotten your plate from when he was watching at the scene?"

Grace's gaze met his. "I don't think so. My car was parked up on the hill. There's no way he could have seen it with the phone in the tree."

"Well, this is a disturbing thought," Sam said, "but what if he wasn't watching from a remote location?"

"You mean he was there? At the scene?"

"Wouldn't be the first time a killer stayed to watch the action. Depending on where he was watching from, he could have followed you home."

She stilled and locked her eyes on his. "He could have. I wasn't looking for a tail, so . . ." She shrugged. "There were no cameras out there—other than his—so there's really no way to know." She stilled. "Except maybe there is."

"What do you mean?"

She tapped a number into her phone and held up a hand. "Hey, yeah, I need a geofence warrant. I'll send the coordinates for the net. Thank you." She ended the call and looked over at them.

Sam nodded his approval. The warrant was a long shot but could be worth it if the killer had used his phone from the location. He shifted and ran a hand over his head. He desperately needed sleep but wasn't sure that would happen anytime soon. For a variety of reasons. "There'll be another scene." The others looked at him, and he suppressed a sigh. "I don't know what it is about these women that makes them targets, but he's not finished."

"Thank you, Captain Obvious," Mark said. "I think we've figured that out all by ourselves."

Sam bit his tongue on his first response to the snarky comment.

He'd get the guy alone and ask him what his problem was at some point, but not right now, not here in front of the others. He'd be professional if it killed him. Grace was frowning at the agent as well, so Sam figured it wasn't just a bad mood making the man ill-tempered. Sam really wasn't imagining the slights—or the chill in the air that was more than the weather. Grace had said he wasn't imagining it, but he'd kind of hoped he was.

"All I meant," he said, keeping his tone cordial, "was that, assuming you don't catch him beforehand—which is obviously the goal—you could be prepared to record the people at the next scene. There were crowds at all three, and he'll make sure there's a crowd at the fourth."

"I thought the whole reason for stealing the phones was to watch," Mark said. "Why steal the phones if he's going to stick around?"

"He records them," Grace and Sam spoke simultaneously and Mark raised a brow.

Grace sighed. "He probably watches them over and over. It's a thrill for him."

Mark nodded. "Yeah, I can see that. We'll be prepared for the next one—assuming we don't find a way to stop it. Which, as you said, is the goal."

"Of course," Sam said. He turned to Grace. "As for you, I don't think you should be alone."

"He's right," Mark said. Sam was surprised the man didn't choke on the words. "We're going to put you up at a safe house."

"Absolutely not." Grace shook her head. "I'm not letting this guy upend my life. I have an alarm system. A good one. Windows, doors, motion detectors, the whole deal. I'll be diligent about turning it on."

Mark scowled. "You're going to be cozying up to a desk any-way while you work on this profile. Might as well do it from a safe house."

"No. I need to talk to the victims' families, friends, coworkers. I can't do that in a safe house—or tied behind a desk."

He sighed. "All right. I'll check in with Jerry. He was with his kids while his wife was with her parents for the night. Her mom wanted her to come to an early morning doctor's appointment. Promised him I'd update him."

"Thanks, Mark."

"Yeah."

"I'll be working on the profile. You know how long it takes to compile."

"I know." The scowl on his face said he wasn't happy with that.

"Don't worry, I'll be sending you what I've got as I get it. Just like always."

"We'll be waiting to hear. Now, I'm going to get this guy's statement"—he gestured to Sam—"then grab a couple hours of sleep. I recommend you do the same."

She shot him a weary smile. "I'll just go inside and write my own statement while you two talk."

"This won't take long," Sam said.

She went inside, and Sam rattled off every detail he could remember. Mark was finally satisfied, but with the other officers around, Sam couldn't find a good moment to talk to the man in private.

The agent finally left and Grace stepped outside next to Sam. They watched the taillights disappear. "I really don't know what his deal is with you," she said, "but you should talk to him."

"I'd already planned to do so but didn't have a chance without an audience. And honestly, his issues with me are kinda low on the priority list at the moment."

"Yeah."

"You're really going to stay here alone tonight?"

She shrugged. "Like I said, I have an alarm system. It'll work just fine as long as it's on." She led him into the house and gestured for him to take a seat. It was now going on one o'clock in the morning.

Her phone buzzed and she pulled it from her back pocket.

Sam frowned. Who in the world would be texting her at this

time of night? Or morning? "Please tell me he hasn't killed someone else."

"No. It's . . . my brother."

"He doesn't own a watch?"

She sighed. "Bobby's an artist. Time doesn't have a whole lot of meaning for him." She walked to the desk in the corner, opened a drawer, and pulled out a gun. She checked it, then slid it into her shoulder holster. "Any word on Hal?"

"Nate texted me. Hold on while I read it." He scanned the text that had come in while he'd been giving his statement. "Looks like he made it through surgery but is being kept in a medical coma for the time being. As suspected, the shiv came very close to his carotid artery, and they want him to do some healing before he wakes up. A wrong move could tear the wound and do more damage."

"He knows something about this killer," she said. "There's no way his reference to the tongue was an off-the-wall thing."

"I agree." He tucked his phone back into his pocket.

"So . . . let's figure out what."

Sam nodded. "I've already thought about that and requested every scrap of information on him from the prison, from his sister, and his former employers."

"Like I told Mark, we'll need to talk to former friends and coworkers as well," she said, her voice soft, almost as though she were thinking out loud. She finally met his gaze. "He wanted me to tell him what I said at the crime scene."

"Did you?"

"No."

"Why not?"

"Because it bothered him enough to risk breaking into my house. As long as he wanted to know what I said, he'd keep me alive."

"And as soon as you tell him . . ."

". . . it's highly likely that he'd have no more use for me."

"And will kill you."

"That's my take on it."

Sam palmed his gritty eyes. "Then, it's also highly possible that he'll be back."

Grace nodded. "Again, we're on the same page. He'll be back, but this time I'll be ready."

"You'll be *ready*?" Sam narrowed his eyes, then groaned. "That's the whole reason you didn't want to go to a safe house. You're setting yourself up as bait."

"Not the whole reason. The reasons I gave Mark were valid and very real. But if me being bait is what it takes to catch him, then that's what I'm going to do."

CHAPTER
NINE

The absolute horror on his face echoed her own thoughts, but she knew—they *all* knew—that this guy was going to kill again unless he was stopped. "Look, I know setting myself up as bait probably seems a bit drastic—"

"You think?"

"But," she continued as though he hadn't spoken, "I've already attracted his attention, right? He may or may not return. Who knows? But if I don't go on the offensive, I'm simply going to be doing my best to deflect his attempts to . . ." She spread her hands. "What? I don't know. Kill me? Probably. I mean, it's not like he wants to have me over for dinner and a nice chat, right?"

"He wants to know what you said."

"Yeah, well, too bad. I'm not telling him."

Sam raked a hand over his head. "I honestly don't know whether to admire your stubbornness or be terrified of it. For your sake."

"Well, let's face it, it's easy to say that at the moment. If he was holding a pair of shears and threatening to use them on my tongue, I'd probably cave and tell him." Maybe. He was right. She was terribly stubborn. Sometimes to her own detriment.

He grunted, and she wasn't sure if it was meant in agreement with her statement or not. Her phone buzzed once more and she glanced at the screen. "I'd better answer this."

"Go ahead."

She tapped the screen and lifted the phone to her ear. Music blasted and she could hear the din of voices in the background. "Hi, Bobby."

"Grace? Finally. Thank you for answering."

"I don't guess you're keeping track of time?"

"Um . . . no. Why?"

"Bobby . . ."

"Oh. Sorry. It's really late, isn't it?"

"Yes. But what is it?"

"I . . . uh . . . need you to come get me."

Grace closed her eyes and counted to ten.

"Grace?" A frantic edge broke through in his voice.

She couldn't leave him on his own. As much as she probably should practice some tough love with him, she couldn't. For more reasons than one. The main one being he'd call their parents, and she wanted to avoid that if at all possible. "Share your location with me."

His sigh of relief sent shards of pain crashing through her heart. "Thank you," he said. "I'm sorry. I just . . . time got away from me and my friends left and I . . . I don't have the money for an Uber or—"

"Bobby, I'll be there. I'll be waiting for the location."

He hung up and five seconds later, her phone pinged. He was thirty minutes away. Fatigue hovered, just waiting to crash down on her. She shoved it off and walked into the kitchen to grab her keys.

"What's going on, Grace?" Sam asked.

"I have to go pick up Bobby. He's at some bar thirty minutes away. Then I'll have to drop him off at his place and come home."

"He doesn't have a car?"

"No. It was repossessed for nonpayment. He has friends—and trust me, I use that term lightly—who transport him to wherever they're going. If he's not ready to leave when they are, they ditch him."

"And he calls you."

"Pretty much."

He stood. "But, Grace, you have a serial killer after you."

"Well, we don't know that for sure. Maybe we scared him off." He raised a brow at her, and she sighed. "What else am I supposed to do?"

"I'll go get him."

Grace blinked. "Uh. What?"

"I'll go get him."

"No." She reached for the doorknob and Sam stepped up beside her, putting his hand on the door.

"Then call someone else to pick him up. You have plenty of friends in the Bureau. Surely one of them could do this for you."

"They could. And they would. But I can't ask. Not this."

"You could send him money for an Uber."

"Money he wouldn't spend on an Uber, Sam. He's an addict."

He studied her for a quiet second, then nodded. "All right. Then I'm coming with you."

She didn't bother protesting. He would just follow her. She slipped out the door and hit the garage door opener. "Lock it, will you?"

"What about the alarm?"

"I'll set it from my phone." She climbed into her Bucar.

Sam slipped into the passenger seat, and soon the alarm was set and they were on their way to one of the seediest areas of town.

Grace drove, her jaw set, her blood humming. She hated that her brother had so many issues. She hated that he wouldn't get help. She hated a lot of things, but she didn't hate *him*.

"What's Bobby's story?"

"Like I said, he's a drug addict. He has ups and downs. I guess he's in one of the downs at the moment."

Sam winced. "I'm sorry. He won't go to rehab?"

"Oh, he'd go, he just doesn't follow through with anything he accomplishes there when he gets out."

"And he calls you when he needs help?"

Was he judging her? She shot him a sideways glance. "Yes."

"How often does that happen?"

"Often enough."

He fell silent, and Grace refused to squirm. It wasn't any of his business. She pressed the gas, and they rode the rest of the way in silence, even though they both kept an eye on the mirrors, looking for a tail. Thankfully, no one seemed to have any interest in them or where they were going.

Which was a part of town she frequented only when she was on a case. What was Bobby doing here?

She slowed as the street came into view and made the sharp right, then pulled into the parking lot. The streetlights had the area well lit. A bouncer sat on a tall stool near the door, checking IDs and stamping hands.

But, of course, Bobby was nowhere in sight. She sighed and texted him.

And waited.

"Could he have left?" Sam asked.

"I guess he could have, but I don't think he would." After another two minutes with no text back, she opened her door and turned to Sam. "Wait here, please?"

He didn't look like he approved of that, but nodded. "Sure."

"I'm used to this, Sam, I promise. I'll be fine."

Her assurances didn't wipe the scowl off his face, but he stayed put. Grace walked to the front door, showed her ID, paid the cover charge, and stepped inside. She could have just flashed her badge and kept the money, but she preferred to keep her law enforcement status under wraps for the moment.

She stood to the side of the door and scanned the place. "Come on, Bobby, where are you?" This was a new low for her brother. He usually stuck to the bars closer to his trailer.

Frustration tugged at her. Why did he have to pull this tonight?

She was exhausted and simply wanted to go home and crawl into bed. After setting her alarm. She had a killer to find and didn't have time for Bobby to pick now to go off the deep end again.

She pulled Bobby's picture up on her phone, walked up to the bar, and slid onto a stool.

"What can I get you?" The bartender looked like she might be sixteen. Her makeup was thick enough to scoop off with a spoon, and her multicolored hair was pulled back in a tight ponytail. Her tiny shirt rode up, showing off her rail-thin midsection, and Grace wanted to take her home, fatten her up, and tell her she could have a better life if she wanted it. Unfortunately, Grace had other priorities at the moment.

She resisted the urge to ask for the girl's ID and simply held her phone up to show the screen. "Have you seen this guy?"

The young woman leaned in, and Grace could see she looked a little older up close. "Oh, yeah. Bobby, I think he said his name was. He's been in here a lot lately."

"He called me to come pick him up. You see where he went?"

"Yeah. He said he felt sick and took off for the bathroom."

"Thanks." She slid a five-dollar bill in front of the girl, then twisted herself off the seat and headed for the bathrooms in the far-right corner.

At the men's door, she knocked.

Nothing.

"Bobby? You in there?"

"Need me to go in?" She turned to see Sam standing behind her, hands in his pockets, a slightly sheepish look on his face. "You were taking a while so I thought I'd come check on you." He waved at the door. "So . . . should I?"

"Sure."

One eyebrow lifted, but he stepped past her and pushed inside the men's room. "Bobby?"

The door started to swing shut behind him, but she placed a foot in the crack so she could hear.

"Hey! Grace, get in here!"

■ ■ ■ ■

Sam knelt beside the unconscious man and placed two fingers against his neck. Grace dropped to her knees to cup the face that was turning an alarming shade of gray.

"Bobby!" She lifted his eyelid and Sam could see the pinpoint pupil.

He grabbed the guy's hand. "Fingernails are blue," he said. "He's OD'd. Call an ambulance."

"You call." She dug into her pocket, pulled out a device, and shoved it up Bobby's nose, then sprayed.

Narcan.

Sam dialed 911.

Bobby gasped. Sam rolled him to his side when the guy heaved, threw up, then drew in another shuddering breath.

"911, what's your emergency?"

"Overdose. I need an ambulance. Narcan has been adminis- tered. Patient is conscious. At the moment." He gave the address and tucked the phone under his chin while he checked Bobby's pulse. It was racing. He looked up to catch Grace's eye. "He's withdrawing but might need another dose."

"I've got it," she said. "Bobby? Can you hear me?"

Bobby shuddered again and pressed a hand to his head. "Hurts."

"Yeah." Grace squeezed her brother's hand. "Help is on the way."

She moved her brother away from the vomit, and it was all Sam could do not to gag. He'd never been one to handle puke very well. Even with his own kids. "How far away are they?" he asked into the phone.

"Three minutes out."

He nodded to the door. "I'm going to let the bartender know what's going on. You good?"

"Yeah."

Bobby groaned, but at least his color was better. Sam slipped out of the bathroom and walked to the bar. The bartender had her back to him, pouring a drink. "Hey, ma'am?"

She turned. "Name's Carly."

"Carly, an ambulance is on the way. Bobby OD'd. Might want to break out the mop and bucket too."

She shuddered. "Not me, but I'll send the paramedics that way when they get here." She set the drink in front of the customer and wiped the counter next to him.

The fact that she didn't seem terribly concerned told Sam a lot. "This happen on a regular basis?"

"Regular enough. Sometimes they're alive when the ambulance gets here. Sometimes not."

"Right."

She moved on to the next customer, and Sam shook his head. He walked back to the bathroom to check on Grace and Bobby. "Well?"

"He's hanging in there. Where's that ambulance?"

"Should be pulling in any second now."

As though they heard him, the paramedics pushed into the bathroom, leaving the stretcher right outside the door.

Grace gave them the facts while they got the IV running. Bobby let out another groan, and Grace stepped back to let them work. Finally, they got him on the stretcher and rolled him out of the bar to the back of the ambulance.

Grace turned to Sam. "I'm going to the hospital."

"Of course. I'm coming with you."

She looked so tired, she was ready to fall over, but she'd push through and do what she had to do for her brother, just like she must have done multiple times for the job. Like they both had.

He met her gaze. "It's been a day, hasn't it?"

She shot him a weary smile. "And it's not over yet."

Instead of following the ambulance, she headed to her house where she changed for the coming day and grabbed her things to wait out the rest of the night at the hospital. Sam followed her back to the hospital in his truck, and they pulled into law enforcement parking spots.

"Feels a little like déjà vu at this point, doesn't it?" She sighed and aimed herself at the emergency entrance, and they walked inside. They let the woman at the desk know who they were there for and took a seat in the corner of the waiting area. It was mostly empty except for a woman and a toddler in the opposite corner of the room.

Sam glanced at her. "What led Bobby down this path and you to the FBI?"

"It's a pretty sordid story, and you'll think I'm a terrible person if I tell you."

She was dead serious. "No, I won't," he said. "We all have our pasts, our mistakes. Our shame. I'm no one to judge."

Grace lifted her chin and her eyes locked on his, studying, searching. "You really mean that, don't you?"

"Wouldn't have said it if I didn't."

"I'm the reason Bobby's an addict. When I was seventeen and he was fifteen, I introduced him to his first joint."

"Oh, man. I'm sorry."

"Yeah. I smoked it occasionally when things were stressful at my house." She hesitated. "Okay, full disclosure. I smoked it because I knew it would make my parents mad." She rolled her eyes toward him. "Back then I was one angry young woman, thanks to my parents uprooting us my junior year to move across the country away from my friends, my school, everything I loved." She sighed. "I fell in with the wrong crowd, even ended up in juvie twice."

"What? You? What for?"

"First time was truancy. I hated school and ditched it every chance I got. The second time . . . well . . . in the middle of that wrong crowd I mentioned was a guy, Cole, who introduced me to weed. One day, a cop stopped us and spotted a blunt I didn't realize was there. We were both arrested, but I was a minor, my parents had money, and they made the charges go away. Only the judge sent me to juvie. I graduated high school while in there, thanks to a woman named Mrs. Gibbs. She was the psychiatrist who helped me turn my life around and let go of the anger. Find God."

"She's the reason you went into psychiatry?"

"Yeah." She smiled. "A big part of it anyway. But about a week before all that, Bobby followed me one day and caught me. I made him smoke it so he couldn't rat on me. Only, he liked it. A lot. And from there, he moved on to stronger, harder stuff." She sniffed and swiped a hand under her eyes. "My parents know this and blame me for his current situation."

"And you feel responsible."

"Of course." She shrugged. "I mean, in my head, I know I'm not. Not really. It was one joint, not even a full one. He had two hits before I came to my senses and snuffed it out, knowing that I couldn't encourage him. But his curiosity sent him exploring, and he wound up finding more than he could deal with."

"Still not your fault. He made his choices."

"Like I said, my head knows that. Convincing my heart—and my parents—is another story. Putting all that aside and moving on has been more difficult that I would have ever imagined."

"But you're working on it."

"Moving forward? Living my life? Yes. Finally. Which is why I allowed myself to say yes to dinner with you."

"Oh." They fell silent and he pursed his lips. "You know, after Mark's insinuation that I was like my father and could have had something to do with the killings, I wasn't going to ask you out again."

"I got that impression."

He glanced at her. "I kind of thought you did. With that one look and one comment, he sent me right back into the past. All of the speculation, the questioning. Did I know what my father was doing before I decided to turn him in? The side-eyed looks that silently wondered if I was a killer like him." He shook his head. "It sent me running."

"From me."

"From everything."

"And yet, you came to my house even after you knew I was safe and the killer was gone."

"I knew I would have to give a statement."

"And that's the only reason?"

He shot her a small smile. "No. I had to see for myself you were okay." Sam wanted to squirm under her assessing gaze but forced himself to stay still. "I was worried. And . . . I knew that if I reverted to old behavior patterns, then the road back to baseline would be harder."

"Very self-aware of you."

"I've had a lot of practice." He paused. "I'm glad you're okay."

She reached out and squeezed his hand. "Thank you, Sam."

His gaze lingered on hers. She was so incredibly beautiful, with her expressive brown eyes. Eyes so bright, yet filled with a pain he wanted to help take away. "I think you're a pretty incredible person, Grace Billingsley."

She swallowed. "You know how you asked me if I'd ever been wrong about being able to discern a lie from the truth?"

"Yes, I remember."

"I believed Bobby's lies. Even though I knew better. I had no discernment when it came to him. So, I let him move in with me. I came home one day, and he was high, hallucinating. He was holding my landlord at knifepoint, convinced the man was a snake and he needed to cut off his head."

"Whoa."

"I talked Bobby down, then tackled him and got him cuffed. I begged my landlord not to press charges."

"He agreed?"

"Only if I would show proof that Bobby was in rehab. When I presented Bobby with his options—jail or rehab—well, he went back to rehab."

"Mighty understanding landlord."

"He had a sister who was a junkie living on the streets with her mental illness. He knew what it was like, and that's the only reason Bobby wasn't arrested, I'm sure." She ran a hand over her eyes. "I see now I wasn't doing him any favors. Maybe he would have gotten clean in prison."

"Or not."

"Yeah," she whispered. "Or not."

Sam leaned closer and let his lips hover over hers. She didn't move or take her gaze from his. "I've wanted to kiss you since the night we met."

"Wow."

He slid an arm around her shoulders and closed the distance. With her soft lips under his, everything in his world was suddenly right. Until it hit him he was kissing her in a hospital waiting room. He pulled back. "Um, I'm not going to apologize for the kiss, just the timing of it."

"Why?"

"Well, your brother is fighting for his life and I . . ."

"Offered me comfort." She smiled and stroked his cheek. "It's okay, Sam. I appreciate that you want to make the pain go away."

"Yes . . . well . . ." He cleared his throat. "You want some coffee? And I'm not talking about that vending-machine stuff in the corner over there. I'm going to run across the street. Shouldn't take me more than ten minutes or so."

"Sure, thanks."

He headed for the exit, planning to make it a fast errand. She needed coffee and he needed to figure out what he was going to do. Not kiss her again, that was for sure. *Really, Sam? You know better than that.* But like he'd told her, he didn't regret it one little bit.

He truly didn't want to leave her alone, but the sun was going to be coming up in a few hours and he still needed to talk to Eleni. Not to mention, he should probably grab a catnap first, if at all possible. At the door, he glanced back at Grace. But he wouldn't leave her if she needed him.

He mentally slapped his head. What had happened to keeping his distance? She'd gotten along just fine without him up to this point.

But . . . she knew about his father and it hadn't seemed to faze her.

But . . . once the press found out he was dating someone . . . *Stop it.*

He wasn't dating *anyone* and was getting way ahead of himself. Grace had agreed to have dinner with him and that was it. A dinner that hadn't even happened yet, no less.

But he knew himself pretty well, and no matter how much he might deny or fight it, he had to admit he wanted to spend time with Grace outside of chasing a serial killer. He just had to keep her alive long enough to make that happen.

CHAPTER
TEN

After Sam took off, aiming himself toward the exit, Grace pressed her fingers to her lips and regretted that Sam had ended the kiss so soon. She'd enjoyed it. But he was right. This wasn't the place or time.

She rose to pace. What was she going to do about Bobby? He was escalating, and if she didn't figure out a solution, he was going to wind up dead. A shudder rippled through her, and she clamped her arms around her midsection.

The door opened and a doctor spoke to the woman at the desk, who pointed at Grace. Grace met him halfway. "I'm Bobby Billingsley's sister. How is he?"

"I'm Dr. Jim Ellsworth." He shoved his hands in his coat pockets and shook his head. "Your brother's in rough shape. You got to him fast—and the fact that you had Narcan saved him to get him to this point—but . . ."

She always had Narcan with her just in case Bobby called. "But he'll live?"

He sighed. "That's still to be determined. We're trying to keep him stable. He's on oxygen, but stops breathing every so often, which means immediate attention. We'll keep him in ICU."

Not the news she wanted. "Of course. I'll be in the waiting room. Will you come get me if there's any change?"

"Someone will."

"Thanks." He left and Grace pulled her phone from her pocket. Returned it to her pocket and paced for five minutes.

"Come on, Bobby, don't be a dork. It's just weed."

Bobby held the blunt between his thumb and forefinger, then lifted it to his lips.

Grace dropped her head into her hands. "I'm sorry, God," she whispered, "I'm so sorry. I don't know how to undo that day. Nothing is working." And now, she had to call her parents.

Or should she?

What was the point in waking them when they couldn't do anything? Maybe she should just wait and call them closer to sunrise.

She leaned her head back against the wall and closed her eyes.

Grace wasn't sure how much time had passed before she roused to the sound of a baby crying. Two cups of coffee sat on the small table next to her, and she picked up the one that had a G written on the white top. One sip told her the cups had been there a while, but where was Sam?

With a short sigh, she picked up her phone, dreading the call she had to make, but it was time.

She breathed a short prayer, then dialed her father's number.

Just when she thought it was going to go to voice mail, her father answered. "Hello?" She ignored his cranky "you pulled me out of a sound sleep" greeting.

"Hi, Dad."

"Do you know what time it is?"

Basically, the very question she'd asked Bobby a couple of short hours ago. "I know it's early, and I'm sorry, but Bobby's in the hospital." She left off the word "again."

Silence. Then a heavy sigh that contained all the grief a parent can carry over a wayward child. A sigh that sent daggers straight through her heart and deep into her very soul.

"Let me guess," her father said. "He OD'd."

"Yes." She hated that was the first thought he had. But with past experience . . .

"Great. Is he alive?"

"He is." At the moment.

"You're at the hospital?"

"I am." She told him which one.

He hesitated, and she let him think. "Your mother and I will be there when we can get there," he finally said.

Grace closed her eyes and drew in a steadying breath. "I'll be here." She'd leave a message with her ASAC and let him know the situation. Hopefully, Bobby would turn the corner in the next little bit and she'd feel more comfortable leaving him. "Bye, Dad."

"Bye." She turned to find Sam coming toward her from the bathroom.

"You okay?" he asked.

"Just peachy. I called my parents."

He raised a brow. "Why does your tone make that sound . . . uh . . ."

"Like a death sentence?"

He choked. "I wasn't going to put it quite like that."

She shot him a sad smile. "It's a slight exaggeration, but my parents and I don't have the best relationship for the reasons I explained earlier."

"I'm sorry."

"I am, too, actually." She just didn't know what else to do to make it better.

"Well, if anyone knows how hard it can be to deal with difficult parents, it's me," he said. "So, you have my sympathies."

She blinked at him and frowned. "I honestly don't know whether to laugh or apologize when you say stuff like that."

He chuckled, then shook his head. "Laugh. It's what I have to do. You know us law enforcement types and our morbid sense of humor."

"We're also psychiatrists. Are we supposed to fall into that habit?"

"Are you saying you don't?"

"I should probably plead the Fifth, but I'll admit I might be familiar with the coping mechanism." She sighed. Again.

Sam sipped his coffee and grimaced.

Grace wrinkled her nose. "Yeah, those are old, but thank you for getting it. It's cold, but at least it's good."

"Just needs a microwave." He glanced at his phone. "I'll heat these up at the nurse's station then I need to check in with my mother-in-law."

She placed a hand on his arm. "Hey, there's not a good reason for you to stay. Go home to your family." He hesitated a fraction, and she tilted her head. "Sam. Go."

"I guess I will if you're sure? I really hate to leave you alone."

"I won't be alone for long. My parents will be here shortly."

"And the way you say that makes me feel like I'm leaving you at the mercy of wolves."

She snickered. "No. You're not. I must be more tired than I realized. I usually hide my family issues a little better." She lifted a hand before he could speak. "And the fact that your family issues are exponentially more complicated than mine probably allows me to subconsciously relax my guard around you." Which could be a not-so-great thing.

"All right," he said, "I'll catch up with you in a few hours. I'm going to check in on Hal, then catch an Uber to get my car and head home."

"Let me know how he's doing?"

"Of course. I'll text you."

"Thanks for everything, Sam. I really do appreciate it."

He nodded, and soon she was left alone with her thoughts and her worries about her brother, a serial killer on the loose, and who his next victim could possibly be. Fatigue still gripped her and she craved just a few more minutes of rest. She said a prayer for the possible victim, then sank on the chair and closed her eyes. She'd take a thirty-minute nap, then get to work on putting together a profile of this killer.

She jerked awake from a dreamless slumber, glanced at the clock on the wall, and gasped. She'd slept for three hours. She'd needed it, but she needed to catch a killer more. And quickly.

She stretched and frowned. Her parents still hadn't shown up. And no one had come to give her an update on Bobby. Or if they had, they hadn't wanted to wake her. She entered the ICU area and found the nurse's desk.

The nearest person looked up. "Can I help you?"

"I'm Bobby Billingsley's sister. Could I get an update?"

"Sure, just a sec." She went to her computer, and while she tapped the keys, Grace rubbed her eyes. Flecks of mascara dotted her fingers and she figured she probably looked like a raccoon. "Okay, the doctor asked me to let him know when you woke up. Let me call him so he can talk to you in person."

"Is Bobby still alive? Just tell me that much."

"Yes, ma'am, he is."

Some of the tension left her. "Okay, thanks."

She returned to her seat in the waiting room and called Mark. "Hey, Grace."

"Hey." She filled him in on Bobby. "I'm still waiting to talk to the doctor and for my parents to get here. If they don't come soon, I'm going to call my sister." Lucy wouldn't be thrilled to get that call, but if she blamed Grace for their brother's issues, she didn't let that be known. "Any update on the search for the killer?"

"We've been digging into the victims' pasts and trying to find a connection. So far, the killings look to be completely random."

"They're not."

"Yeah, I agree. I know you've been dealing with your family emergency, but when are you going to get us that profile? Or should we pull in someone else?"

Pull in someone else? Absolutely not. "Come on. Stop being ridiculous. You know this takes time. I'm working on it. I hope to be in the office shortly. Have you set up a task force?"

"Putting it together now."

"Give me until lunchtime. Send me whatever you have, and I'll read through it while I'm waiting. Once I'm done here, I'll bring sandwiches and we can start putting the profile together."

"That works. I'd like ham on wheat."

"I know. Text me any other orders." Dr. Ellsworth appeared in the doorway. "Hey, Mark, I've got to go. See you in a few hours." She hung up and strode toward the doctor. "How is he?"

"Let's sit down."

"This is a sit-down conversation? That can't be good."

"No, it's not."

She followed him to a private corner and slipped into the nearest chair. He sat across from her, linked his hands, and rested his elbows on his knees.

"Bobby's lung function has been affected for the present. I have no idea if it's permanent or not, but since he aspirated with the OD, it's very likely he'll develop pneumonia. We've already started him on antibiotics in an effort to ward that off. He's fortunate you found him when you did. He wouldn't have lasted much longer. And if he continues down this path, he's going to die."

"I know."

"I'm sorry. I know you do, and I'm probably too blunt, but it's just—" He let out a low sigh. "I'm just seeing a lot of this right now and I want to save them all. Unfortunately, not everyone winds up with a happy ending."

"I can deal with blunt. And I know what you mean about not everyone getting their happy ending." She thought about the three victims of the serial killer she needed to profile. Those victims sure hadn't gotten their happy ending, and if she didn't get busy, someone else was going to die—possibly the fourth victim if the killer kept his word. She rubbed a hand over her eyes and did her best to squash the guilt that wanted to rise up and strangle her. "All right, thank you. How long do you expect him to be here?"

"A while. Assuming he pulls through, when he's released from here, he's going to need rehab."

"He needs a lot of things. Should he make it, how long is your best educated guess of his time here?"

He hesitated, then sighed. "He's in ICU. It's still touch and go with his breathing, so . . . definitely for several days, maybe several weeks. I honestly don't know. All I'll say is, he's here for a while."

"Fabulous." She was going to need help with this. As much as she hated to ask, she was going to have to force herself to do it. "Thank you."

He nodded and stood. "He's unconscious for now. You don't have to stay here. Go home and take care of yourself. If anything changes, you'll be the first one we call."

He walked out, and her parents still hadn't arrived, but her phone dinged with information from Mark. She settled herself in the chair, glanced at the time, and realized the sandwich shop wouldn't open for another three hours, so she started to read.

■ ■ ■ ■

Sam blinked and rubbed his eyes, wondering how long he'd slept. A glance at the clock said it had been just a few hours since he'd crashed. Memories of Grace and Bobby rushed in and he groaned. All the way home from the hospital, Sam had wrestled with leaving Grace alone, but figured his family needed him more than she did. Or *would* need him first thing in the morning. When he'd walked in the door, the house had been quiet and he'd needed sleep.

Hence the face-plant on the couch.

Noise from the kitchen pried his eyes open once more, and he rolled to his feet, running a hand through his hair. "Morning, Vanessa."

She shot him a glance over her shoulder. "Morning. It must have been a rough night if you didn't even make it to your bed."

"Yeah. I'll tell you about it sometime. I'm going to get the kids up."

"Xander already left. They had an early-morning practice. Eleni spiked a fever last night. I suspect strep. Already have a call in to the doctor, and I've got the time to take her, so shouldn't throw your day off."

He blinked. "Wait a minute, I'm a doctor. I can check her out."

Not that he specialized in pediatrics, but he *had* done a rotation in the area. Before his life fell apart.

"That's what I told her. She said she needed a real doctor."

"Ouch."

"I called Connor. He said he'd see her as soon as I could get her over to him."

"Connor?"

"A friend I met at church."

"The one you have a date with Friday night?"

She gave him a sideways look. "Maybe."

"And he's a medical doctor? With a degree and a license to practice?"

"Well, duh. I'm not going to take her to the vet. Or some quack. Seriously, Sam?" She planted her hands on her hips. "What kind of grandmother do you think I am?"

"Right, right. Sorry. Okay, then. If that's what she wants."

"Said she did."

He raked a hand over his head. "I'm guessing she wasn't feeling well yesterday. Maybe that's why she was so emotional."

Vanessa choked on her laugh. "Honey, she's almost thirteen. That's the reason she's *emotional* right now." She shrugged. "Not saying being sick with something couldn't add to it, but right now, you're just going to have to practice patience."

"Something I feel like I'm in short supply of lately." He sighed. "When will this stage pass?"

"You'll be dead by then."

He laughed, then frowned when she didn't. "What?"

"I mean, she's a female, Sam. There's no way to calculate how many years this stage lasts. No one's ever lived that long."

He winced. There were so many things wrong with that statement.

"And don't think I don't know what you're thinking. Men don't get off the hook. They're just as bad in different ways."

What? A headache started behind his eyes. "Moving on to another topic, please?"

"Sure."

"Should I fight her mother on this whole phone thing and let Eleni have one? I mean, El's right in some ways. All of her friends, and I do mean *all*, have one. So, honestly, she has access to one just about any time she might need one. She certainly manages to text me whenever she wants to. But I get that it's not *hers*."

"Have you sat her down and told her all the reasons you don't want her to have one?"

"Of course." Sort of.

"In detail?"

"No. I don't want to give her nightmares." Like the ones he dealt with on a regular basis. "And since Claire seems to think El's old enough to stay by herself for a couple of hours, I don't want her to be afraid to do so."

Vanessa shook her head and opened the cabinet to grab a K-Cup pod. "It's a fine line, isn't it?"

"Yes. And every time I think I might have a handle on this female preteen thing, someone moves the line."

After she popped it into the machine, she turned back to him. "That's the way it's been since the beginning of time. All you can do is your best. Stop trying to figure it out and just pray. As a father, that's your best line of defense."

"I'm on the prayer thing."

She smiled. "I know. I am too." She grabbed four eggs from the refrigerator and cracked them into the frying pan, then zapped bacon in the microwave.

"If she has strep, the bacon is going to hurt."

"That's what I told her."

All righty then. "Let me guess . . . she insisted."

"She did. Some people just have to learn things the hard way."

There was so much truth in that statement, but he wasn't touching it. "Is there enough for me?"

"Absolutely. You want to take the rest of it up to your daughter?"

"Happy to do so."

"Liar."

"Okay, so maybe happy is stretching it, but yeah, I want to talk to her."

His phone rang and he glanced at the screen. The prison number his father used. He let it go to voice mail like he'd done with the other hundreds of calls.

"He won't give up, huh?" Vanessa asked, her brows pinched over the bridge of her nose.

"What do you mean?"

"Your father's calling."

He raised a brow. "How did you know it was him?"

"You have that look on your face."

"What look?"

"Like you smell something that's a cross between a dead body and spoiled milk."

"Oh, that look." He paused. "How do you know what a dead body smells like?" She lasered him with a "don't mess with me" stare and he grimaced. "Yes, it was him. I thought about blocking the number, but it's possible another prisoner may get permission to use that phone to reach me, so . . . I can call in to check or listen to voice mail."

She blew a raspberry. "That's about the silliest thing I've ever heard, son. Who do you think you're kidding? You could stop those calls from him if you really wanted to."

Him. His *father*. The serial killer. The man who'd spoken to him in the prison. He groaned. "I suppose. So what does that say about me?"

"Only you know the answer to that."

"You should have been a shrink."

She snorted. "I live with one. Close enough."

He heard the water running upstairs. "Sounds like someone's up."

"Five more minutes and this will be ready."

Soon, Sam had a plate of bacon, eggs, and toast with grape jelly, and a glass of apple juice in his possession and made his way up the stairs to Eleni's room. She had the door open and was sitting on the side of the bed looking miserable. "Hey," he said.

"Hey."

"Brought you something to eat. Can I come in?"

She nodded and he stepped through the door. The subtle scent of a perfume hit him along with toothpaste and the soap she'd used to wash her face. It all added up to a scent that was uniquely Eleni's, and he breathed it in while he tried to figure out what to say to her. He set the plate and glass on her nightstand.

"Throat hurts," she mumbled.

"The eggs and juice should slide down pretty easy. Might leave the bacon and toast for another day."

She nodded, but looked longingly at the bacon. "I really wanted it."

"You can try it, but . . ."

She sipped the juice and pulled her legs beneath her.

"The Motrin working?" he asked.

"Yes. I think the fever is gone. I feel a little better. Not as hot."

"I hear you want a real doctor to look at you."

She shrugged but didn't offer an explanation.

"You know I'm a real doctor, right?"

Another shrug.

He sighed. "Can I at least look in your throat?"

"I guess." She set the juice aside and opened her mouth.

He used the light on his phone to take a look at the red tissue with white patches. "Ouch. That looks painful. I'm sorry."

She sighed. "It's not that I don't think you're a real doctor. I'm just still mad at you and . . ." She trailed off with another shrug.

"Look, Eleni, as much as it pains me, I get that you're growing up and I'm going to have to come to the realization that things are going to change because of that."

She looked at him, a spark in her otherwise sick-dull gaze. "So, you're going to let me have a phone?"

"I'm . . . considering it."

"Oh, Dad, really?" Tears filled her eyes, and he was struck at how beautiful his dark-haired, dark-eyed daughter was.

"It really means that much to you?"

"It really does." She chewed on her bottom lip. "But I know it costs money and your monthly bill would go up on your plan. I can do some extra chores or something around the house to help pay for it."

And just like that, she convinced him. "That's very mature of you."

"More mature than running to my room and slamming the door?"

"Just a bit."

A smile played around the corners of her mouth. "Thanks, Dad."

"I'm not promising anything, but I'll talk to your mother about it. Now, eat if you can. I'm going to let Nessie take you to her doctor so he can do a swab just to make sure it's strep. And prescribe you some antibiotics since that's not my usual realm."

"Okay."

He kissed the top of her head and handed her the fork. "I have one more question for you."

"What's that?" she mumbled around a bite of the egg.

"I hear your mom and Brett are leaving you alone sometimes. Are you okay with that?"

She shrugged and looked away.

"El?"

"I've thought about it, and if I'm old enough to have a phone, I guess I should be old enough to stay alone for a couple of hours, huh?"

He sighed. "I don't know. Those are two different things entirely. Do you want me to talk to your mom? Let her know you don't want her to do that?"

"No. I'll talk to her if I decide I'm not comfortable with it." She hesitated. "I'd be more comfortable if I had a phone to use if I needed one. Not just to text friends—although, I'm not going to lie and say I don't want it for that reason—but I would feel safer if I had one."

He studied her, trying to see any hint that she was playing on his dad emotions, working to manipulate him. But it just wasn't there. She meant every word she said.

"I can understand that." He tried to wrap his mind around her newfound maturity. "All right, then. I'll talk with your mom about it and see if we can come to an agreeable solution. Do you want me to bring the television in here for you?"

"Please."

"Be right back."

"Thanks, Dad."

Once he had her all set, he texted Grace.

> How are you? How's Bobby? Anything I can do?

He strode to his room, showered, and got ready for the day even though he could use a few more hours of sleep. By the time he was ready to leave the house, Grace still hadn't texted him back. Worried, he aimed his Bucar toward the hospital. He'd just stop in and see if Grace was still there and get a report on Bobby and Hal. Then he'd head toward HQ because he had clients to see and some investigating to do. He wanted to know the connection his father might have to the killer of the women. Because while it wasn't obvious, it was there.

And he was going to find it.

CHAPTER
ELEVEN

Grace checked on Hal to find the man still in his medically induced coma, then moved on to her secure email account. She'd purchased a notepad and pen from the gift shop and made notes as she read through everything Mark had sent.

Lost in her musings, working through everything she knew about the victims and the crime scenes, she was almost surprised when her parents stepped into view. Then she glanced at the wall clock, stunned at the time that had passed. It had taken them six hours to get there. Granted, they lived twenty minutes away and she'd woken them from a sound sleep, but still . . .

She had to leave in thirty minutes. She rose and went to them. "Hi."

"How is he?" her mother asked. Her red-rimmed eyes nearly ripped Grace's heart to shreds.

"He's still alive, but the drugs damaged his respiratory system, so they're monitoring that. He's going to be in ICU for the time being."

Her father nodded. "So . . . once again, we wait."

"Yes, Dad, I'm sorry." More sorry than she'd ever be able to express. "I guess you really didn't need to rush over here." Not that they'd rushed, but . . . "Come sit down."

She returned to her chair and gestured to the seats opposite her. "How'd you find him?" her father asked.

"He called me to come get him. When I got there, he'd disappeared, but someone saw him go into the bathroom."

"To shoot up," her mother said, the bitterness in her tone hitting Grace right in the guilt meter.

"Pretty sure it was pills this time, Mom," she said, her voice low.

The waiting room doors swished open once more and she spotted Sam standing just inside. He met her gaze and she waved him over. "Sam, I didn't expect you to come back this morning."

"You weren't answering your texts, so I decided to drop by and check on you."

"Oh, sorry." How many times was she going to say that word today? She cleared her throat. "I was so lost in what I was doing that I didn't hear the notification, I guess. But these are my parents. Hugo and Maria Billingsley." Sam shook hands with them both. "This is Sam Monroe. He's another psychiatrist with the Bureau."

"Nice to meet you both," Sam said. "Sorry it's under these circumstances." He turned to Grace. "And I don't mean to intrude. We can catch up later if necessary."

"Not necessary," she said. "Mom, Dad, if you'll excuse us for just a minute?" She placed a hand on Sam's bicep and led him to the corner where she and the doctor had discussed Bobby just a few hours earlier. "I've been talking to the ASAC and Mark. They've put together a task force," she told him. "I asked him to include you on it."

"Yeah, I think that's a good idea."

"Having you on the force can only be beneficial in figuring out what your father's involvement is."

He nodded. "How's Bobby?"

"No change. My parents just got here. I hate to leave them, but I can't miss this first task force meeting, and I've just gotten to work on the profile a little bit. I'm nowhere near ready to present any findings." She raked a hand over her hair. "Once I get my parents settled and get another update on Bobby, I'm grabbing sandwiches and heading that way."

"I can follow you. I'm parked not too far from the entrance."

"Perfect. My car is still where I parked it last night. Meet you there in ten? I need to tell them goodbye and make sure the nurses have my number in case they need to get in touch with me."

"I'll bring the car around and wait on you."

He left, and Grace drew in a steadying breath before she pulled out her phone and dialed her sister's number.

Lucy answered on the first ring. "Hi, Grace."

"Hey, I've got news about Bobby and it's not good. He's alive, but—"

"Wait, what? Slow down."

"Bobby. He's in the hospital."

"Oh. He OD'd again, huh?" Her sister's sadness reached through the phone line.

"Yes." She filled her in. "Mom and Dad are here, and I need to leave. Can you—"

"Wait a minute, you're actually asking for help? What's going on? You never let anyone help."

Grace sighed. "I have a big case that I need to be working, especially while Bobby is still unconscious. But Mom and Dad . . . I just can't leave them alone . . ."

"I can come. I can be there in about thirty minutes."

"Thank you, Luce."

"Yeah."

She hung up and walked back over to her parents.

"Hey, I have to leave, but—"

"Of course you do," her mother muttered.

Grace suppressed a flinch. "Mama, I would stay if I could, but I have to work."

"Work is good," her father said. "It keeps people out of trouble. If Bobby had been working, he wouldn't be in this spot." But Bobby couldn't hold down a job because he couldn't kick the drugs. And he couldn't kick the drugs because Grace had gotten him hooked.

"Come on, Bobby, don't be a dork. It's just weed."

She shuddered and wondered if she'd ever be forgiven for her tragic teen choices. "I'm going to talk to him when he wakes up," she said. "I want to see if he'll be willing to go back to rehab."

"For what?"

"I know, Mama, but I have to try."

"You try a lot, but all your trying doesn't get us anywhere, does it?" she said.

Okay. She was done. "I'll check in with you when I can. I love you both." She walked toward the door, fighting the guilt and tears, and made her way to the exit. When she stepped outside, a blur of movement to her left caught her attention. A lime-green-colored van pulled to a stop in the wrong lane. The driver's door opened, and a man pointed a gun in her face. "Get in or I start shooting anyone I can find."

From the corner of her eye, she saw Sam pull to the curb. He jumped out of his Bucar. "Grace!"

The man turned and pulled the trigger. The sharp crack sent a bullet winging Sam's way. The side mirror on his Bucar shattered. Sam ducked, people screamed and scattered.

Grace sucked in a hard breath while her hand went for her weapon. "Sam!"

Before she could blink or move in Sam's direction, the shooter turned the weapon back on her. "Don't do it." She lifted her hands where the man could see them. "Drop your bags fast and get in," he said, "and go to the back or my aim is more accurate next time."

Leaving her shoulder bag and laptop on the sidewalk, Grace climbed in and maneuvered her way between the front seats into the back. Her heart pounded and she stared at the man who scrambled in after her and slapped the lock on the door, mentally recording his features. Caucasian, five o'clock shadow, green eyes, wide nose, white teeth with a slight chip in the front left tooth.

Favoring his left arm, but still able to use it. She must have just grazed him.

He motioned with the gun. "Get over to the side and cuff yourself to the bar."

The van's interior held two horizontal bars, one on each side of the van. Three pairs of handcuffs hung from the one on the left. She studied him, debating for a brief second whether she could take him. He lashed out with his left hand and gave her a hard shove, sending her to the metal floor. Pain arced through her knee and she ignored it, launching up to plant a fist under his left eye. In a flash, he punched her in the side of the head. While pain and stars were still dancing behind her eyes, he leaned over, snagged her weapon from the shoulder holster, and stuck it in the back of his jeans.

Grace held on to her racing pulse, gasping and working to control the raging ache in her head—and the fury that he'd gotten ahold of her gun. The only thing that gave her hope was that Sam had seen everything go down. He was already calling for backup, security was racing toward the scene, and this guy thought he was going to get away with it. All she had to do was play it cool. "What do you want?"

"I told you what I want. Cuff your wrist."

She did so. He threw himself into the driver's seat and gunned the engine.

■ ■ ■ ■

Sam pressed the gas, staying with the green van, shouting at the dispatcher that the kidnapping of a federal agent was in progress. "I'm turning west on Howard. We need air support now!"

The van rocked around another turn and Sam stayed on its tail. He could see the driver in the side mirror and noted the blond hair and pale skin.

And darting eyes.

"Officers en route," the dispatcher said.

Sam didn't bother to reply. He was too busy making sure that the guy didn't run someone down in his desperation to escape. He hit a back road and Sam stayed right with him, relaying his new direction. "Wait, he's heading toward the marina." That would be a dead end. He'd be trapped. Or would he? "What are you doing?" He whispered the words aloud.

"Officers are on the way there as well," the woman's voice echoed through his Bucar.

"There's a kidnap victim in that van who's a federal agent. They'd better not do anything stupid."

"They're well trained."

He grunted and stayed on the man's tail. He had to realize this was a futile effort and still he pressed on. Finally, he slowed, turned toward the marina, and pressed the gas. Sam had a bad feeling. "He's going to drive into the water!"

"Notifying the Water Police now," she said.

The van blasted through the marina gate and headed for the pier. Sam stayed with him, grateful that the place was basically deserted at the moment. Marina security gave chase as well while the van continued its journey straight for the water. It hit the pier, bouncing on the wooden dock, hit the end, and nose-dived into the water.

Sam screeched to a halt, threw open the door, and raced for the pier. He spotted the Water Police vessel in the distance, but Sam wasn't waiting. Without hesitation, he jumped feet first into the frigid, dark water, the breath nearly freezing in his lungs. He kicked back to the surface and swam over to the bobbing, sinking van, then dove under. With outstretched hands, Sam aimed himself toward the van, touched metal, and made his way to the driver's side front window. The driver was gone but had lowered the front windows, allowing the water to pour in. The hind end of the van still stuck up above the surface, but with the front windows down, it was going under fast. He kicked to the surface, grabbed a breath, and dove back under to swim through the van's driver's side window. Through the murkiness, he could make out an air pocket in the back and aimed for that. He made his way past the front seat to the belly of the vehicle and broke through the water to grab a breath. Grace had her back to him. "Grace!"

She spun, handcuff key gripped between her shaking fingers, eyes flashing with barely held-in-check panic. "Sam! Get out of here."

"Not without you!"

"The water keeps pushing me away and I can't see what I'm doing. H-here." She shoved the key at him and he snagged it, lifting his head above the rising water. "I'm going to wrap my legs around yours to keep you anchored," she said. "Go under and get these off me. P-please." She clamped her legs around his knees.

They were going to be underwater in about ten seconds, then they were going to have to fight their way out. "The front windows are open," he said. "Once you're free, swim for it."

She nodded, he sucked in a lungful of air and ducked under, bending at the waist while her legs held him in place. The water rocked around them, pushing and pulling at the van. He kept his focus, using his fingers to trace the cuff. He finally found the hole, shoved the key into the lock, and twisted.

The cuff released and she grabbed his hand, pulling him up for one last gasp of air. Then the water closed over their heads and they were under. He pushed her toward the front, following behind her, one hand on her back in order not to lose her. She slipped out the window and he was right behind her.

She kicked and headed for the surface, which wasn't that far. The water was probably about twelve feet deep, but deep enough to do what the killer had intended. He joined Grace, bobbing in the waves, teeth chattering, lungs aching.

"There they are!" A boat pulled next to them and lowered a ladder, then a man leaned over the side with a hand held out. "Grab on."

Helicopters hovered above. Low enough to see what was happening, but high enough not to churn the water too much. Grace grasped the rung of the ladder and hauled herself up so that the officer was able to snag her hand and help her the rest of the way into the boat.

Sam was next. He rolled over the side of the boat, sides heaving, shivering, the wind cutting through his wet clothing. A blanket settled over his shoulders and someone passed one to Grace. He scooted over next to her and wrapped an arm around her, then pulled her to his side. "Come on, Grace. Body heat."

"Yeah." She shuddered and didn't hesitate to snuggle up next to him. The fact that he didn't mind one bit didn't come as a surprise.

An officer handed them a mug. "Hot coffee. It's black, but it's warm."

Sam took his, his hands shaking, but he managed to hold it without sloshing it. Grace did the same. "Thank you," she said.

"Hold on. We'll have you back on land in a few minutes. It's going to get windy, so I'm going to tuck your heads under this blanket." He pulled it from where he'd clasped it under his right arm and spread it over the two of them.

Sam blinked in the sudden darkness, then carefully lifted the mug to his lips and sipped, thankful it didn't burn all the way down but was warm enough to thaw his throat a fraction. "That was scary," he murmured.

"Terrifying."

"Let's not do that again."

She went silent and he wished he could see her face. "I would have drowned if you hadn't come along," she said.

"You would have gotten it."

"No," she said, her voice low. "I don't think I would have."

He fell silent and gripped the mug in his left hand while he hugged her tighter with his right.

The boat engine rumbled, and soon they were speeding toward the dock. The wind was cold, but without the blanket, it would have been miserable.

"Was it him?" he asked.

"Yes."

"He say anything to you?"

"Just that he'd kill innocent people if I didn't get in the van with him."

Well, that explained a lot.

"I don't think he meant for this to happen," she said. "You saw everything go down and called in reinforcements while you chased us, right?"

"Yeah, pretty much."

"The only way for him to escape was to make sure that someone had to come after me."

He nodded. "Which is why his van is now at the bottom of the marina."

"Yeah." She hesitated. "He wanted me alive. He shoved that key in my hand before he swam out the window."

"Whoa, what? I thought that was your key."

"No, and I'm not sure I could have gotten mine out of my vest pocket in time to get the cuffs off." Grace pressed a hand to her eyes. "I think he realized that."

"So, you're saying he kidnapped you, dunked you into the marina, then made sure you at least had the possibility of escaping?"

She nodded. "Crazy, huh?"

"Definitely one of the weirder things I've heard of."

She sighed. "Maybe once they pull the van up and CSU goes over it, they'll find something to lead us to him."

"I'm sure you'll have something to add to whatever they find."

"I'm going to need extra paper in the printer for this report."

■ ■ ■ ■

Dumb. He was so *dumb*. He gripped his cheeks and pressed, warding off the scream once more. He'd been holding it in since he'd climbed out of the lake, shaking, freezing, teeth chattering, fingers turning numb.

Now, he stayed hidden, huddled under a tarp he found at the back of the yacht. When he surfaced, he hid under the pier until he could move without being seen. Once everyone was distracted and getting Grace back to shore, he swam to the nearest yacht that had a ladder next to the motor. He climbed up and into the stern. The tarp had been lying right there and he'd slipped under it.

The fact that he'd escaped the van and authorities was nothing short of miraculous. Just another sign that he was doing what he was supposed to be doing. But he had to be more careful. Plan better. If the Water Police hadn't been so focused on getting to Grace, he'd be in custody right now.

"Gotta be careful, you idiot."

He'd been watching the hospital for hours before she'd stepped outside, and he'd reacted, not realizing the other agent was waiting for her. The ensuing chase and escape of Grace Billingsley had him tied up in knots and in need of . . . of . . . something.

He pressed his cheeks harder, silencing the scream once more, and soothed himself that Grace had survived. That was a relief. At least he'd have another chance to find out what she said. The chopper blades beat the air and churned the water. They'd probably search the shoreline first, then start on the vessels. If they had enough manpower, they might do both at the same time. Which meant he needed to act quickly and figure out how to get off the boat and out of the area without getting caught.

He lifted the edge of the tarp and peered out. The Water Police were still in the vicinity, their motors rumbling, cruising along the shore. Definitely looking for him. He waited for the chopper to make another pass, then rolled out from under the tarp and army crawled to the glass door. He gave it a push and breathed a relieved sigh when it opened.

Now, he could only hope no one was inside.

From his position on the floor, he glanced around. The place was lived in, indicating it was a year-round residence for someone. Which meant there would be some dry clothes somewhere.

He stood, walked into the kitchen, and wrapped his fingers around the hilt of the biggest knife he could find. He stepped over to the window and glanced out. Yep, they were clearing the boats. Moving quickly, he searched the boat, looking for anyone aboard.

Finding no one, he carried the knife to the main bedroom and tossed it onto the bed. Then turned to the closet and opened it.

And laughed. "Ah, the gods are smiling on me today."

He pulled the police officer's uniform from the hanger, stripped out of his wet clothes, and quickly changed.

CHAPTER
TWELVE

WEDNESDAY MORNING

Grace sat on her bed and dried her hair with the towel while she thought about the fact that she'd almost died less than twenty-four hours ago—and her kidnapper had gotten away. Unbelievable.

She'd missed the task force meeting yesterday—ordered to take care of herself after the whole ordeal—so she'd come home, showered, fixed a hot pot of coffee, then written her report over the next three hours, pulling every detail she could remember from her tired brain. Once that was done, she'd crashed into a deep sleep for four hours, checked on Bobby, who was still unconscious but showing some slight improvement, and was now ready to get to work on her profile of the killer. Somewhere in the midst of all of that, Mark had texted that the van had been pulled up and a team was already working on it.

Two agents watched her house, one in front, one in the back. She felt slightly guilty for refusing to go to a safe house, but that was going to have to be a last resort. If she hid out, the guy would just lie low and everything would be dragged out even longer. If he showed up at her house again, she'd know it.

Sam had checked on her twice since she'd said goodbye to him from the back of the ambulance. He'd finished his report and headed to the prison to meet with several patients.

And she was going to be at the task force meeting to share everything she'd learned. As she'd told Jerry and Mark, it could take up to two weeks to gather the information, but with everything she'd just gone through with the man, she had some things to add to her profile. And once she talked to the families of the victims, she'd add that and send off her report. If the killer hadn't been lying when he said he had another victim, the faster she put everything together, the faster they could get started finding this guy.

Finally, Grace changed into work clothes, grabbed a banana and a container of yogurt from the fridge, and headed for her Bucar. With an agent in front of her and one behind her, she made her way to her office and parked.

When she stepped into the conference room, all eyes turned on her. Jerry frowned. "Grace. What are you doing here?"

"Heard there was a task force meeting."

Frank Boggs, her unit chief, raised a brow. "Come on, Grace, you've had a pretty traumatic couple of days. You need some time off."

"No, sir, that's exactly what I don't need. I need to find this killer and I need to do it now." She took a seat and placed her notebook in front of her. "I've gone through all the reports and my own notes—" Movement at the door stopped her.

Sam stepped inside and shot them a tight smile. "Sorry I'm late."

Frank nodded. "Have a seat. We're just getting started." Everyone murmured their greetings. Everyone except Mark, whose nostrils flared.

Grace shook her head. "Okay, as I was saying, I've gone over the crime scene notes, photos, the first two autopsies—and of course, my two encounters with the man." She gave them her description. "I've got an appointment with Josey set up."

"Josey?" Sam asked.

"One of our forensic artists. She and I are going to see if we can put this guy's face on paper and get it on the news. On the way here, I set up appointments to speak with Gina Baker's and Carol Upton's husbands, and Sonya Griffith's daughter. Sonya was widowed last year, and her daughter and grandson moved in with her shortly after her husband died. I'm hoping after I talk to them, we'll have some idea of a connection between the three ladies—at least geographically. I know that Gina and Sonya lived about thirty minutes apart from one another. Gina in Manassas and Sonya in West Springfield. Carol also lived in Springfield. Gina was a homemaker when she wasn't working as an X-ray technician at Prince William Medical. Sonya was a high school teacher, and Carol, a local real estate agent."

"That's a pretty big geographical radius," Mark said.

"I know. I'm working on narrowing it down. The two Springfield locations help."

For the next two hours, they discussed possible suspects, then Grace checked her phone. "I need to go," she said. "Josey's ready for me. Send me the notes on whatever else I need to know, please?"

Frank nodded, and Grace gathered her things. She shot a look at Sam and found him watching her, eyes thoughtful, but the rest of his expression hooded and closed off. She had no idea what he was thinking. Her phone buzzed again. A text from Lucy.

She hurried from the room and pulled up the text.

> Bobby still the same. Mom and Dad are too.
> When are you coming back?

Grace swallowed a groan just as her phone went off again. This time Julianna was the sender.

> Can you meet on Saturday? Penny, Raina, and I
> will fly up in Penny's chopper. We'll have lunch
> then come home.

She texted Julianna first.

> Yes, plan on it. Of course, plans may change.

That's the nature of the job. You know we all understand.

Because they all lived it too.

> Pray for Bobby. He OD'd and is in ICU. Holding on right now. Don't know if he'll make it.

Grace!!!! So sorry. I'll alert the others to crank up the prayers.

> Thanks. Talk more later.

A heart emoji flashed back, and a wave of gratitude washed over her. She headed to find Josey while contemplating the answer to her sister's text. No one in her family was aware of anything that had happened with the serial killer, and she wasn't about to tell them. While her parents held her responsible for Bobby's actions, they still loved her—whether they wanted to or not. Knowing she was the target of a serial killer, that another one of their children was in danger of dying, would send them over the edge.

Yeah, they didn't need to know about all of that.

She found Josey in the cubicle she used whenever she was in the building. The woman was tall, graceful, and full of joy in spite of her occupation. Grace rapped her knuckles on the fake wooden wall. "Hey."

Josey looked up from her laptop. "Hey."

"Thanks for coming so quick. I know this wasn't on your list of things to do when you woke up."

"Not a problem. I want this guy's face out there too. Have a seat." Grace dropped into the chair beside the woman who already had her program running. Josey flicked a glance at her. "How are you doing?"

"I'm not shaking anymore, and I didn't have any nightmares when I slept, but I suspect that they'll hit me at some point."

"Having this guy in custody will go a long way toward giving you some peace of mind."

"Yeah."

"All right. Tell me about the shape of his face."

For the next hour, they worked together, Grace pulling from her memory and Josey using her art skills. Grace watched her attacker come to life. "Stop," she said. "That's him."

"You're sure? Nothing you would change?"

She shook her head and rubbed her sore knuckles. "Wait, yes. I punched him."

"Where?"

"Got him on the left cheek, I think. Can you do one with a bruise and one without?" The bruise would fade eventually.

"Sure." She shadowed in a bruise, then pulled the two pictures up side by side.

Grace shuddered. "Yeah, that's good. That's exactly how I remember him. If you could send those to my phone, I would appreciate it." Josey's fingers flew over the keyboard, and a second later, Grace's phone pinged. She took a second to forward it to the case agents so they could send it to the task force and media spokesperson for the Washington Field Office. "Thank you."

"Of course."

Grace rose. She still had more work to do. First things first. Talk to Gina Baker's husband. She ran her thumb over her knuckles once more and Josey frowned. "You okay?"

"I'm fine. Something's nagging at me, but I can't place it."

"The sketch?"

"Maybe." She shrugged. "I'll figure it out. See you later."

"Bye."

Grace stepped out of the office, considering the task ahead of her. She'd already asked Jerry and Mark if they would go with her. Mark had agreed. Jerry had a family obligation he didn't want to cancel if at all possible.

"Do you mind if I take a look?"

Sam's voice jerked her head up. "What?"

"The composite," he said from his position against the wall. "I'd like to see it."

"Sure."

She pulled it up on her phone and showed it to him. He blinked. "Wow. That's incredible."

"I wondered if you got a good look at him too."

"I got mostly a glimpse. Not good enough to give details like you did. But looking at that, yeah, if he was in a lineup, that's who I'd pick." He paused. "Are you an artist?"

"No, I took Carrie Parks's forensic art class last year. She taught us the basics of what we needed to know to describe a suspect in order for someone to draw it." She blew out a low breath. "Didn't think I'd need it for this kind of situation." She frowned. "What are you doing here? Don't you have clients to see?"

"I've rearranged my schedule a bit. I thought I'd hang out with you if that's all right. See what the victims' families have to say. There's a link to my father, I just have to figure it out."

She raised a brow. "You get clearance for that?"

"I did."

"You got your weapon?"

"Always."

"All right, I'll call Mark and let him know that you and I are getting some lunch, then we can meet up with him to go talk to Adam Baker about Gina and what she could have possibly done to attract a killer's attention."

■   ■   ■

With escort in tow, Sam and Grace wound up at the pizza place that Xander's football team frequented on a weekly basis located three miles from his home. Once they were seated at the table with two agents watching the door and the parking lot, Sam leaned back and studied the woman in front of him. "What kind of pizza do you like? Maybe we could split one?"

"I can eat pretty much anything. I even like anchovies." He grimaced and she laughed. "Why don't you order what you like, and I'll eat a couple of slices and a salad? Seriously, I'm not that picky."

Sam let his gaze roam the restaurant, noting there were only five occupied tables. Their busiest times were lunch and evenings, but they were early. It would be jammed in about an hour.

"Dad?"

Sam turned to see Vanessa and Eleni in a booth behind them. "Oh, hey, I didn't realize you guys were going to be here." He frowned at his daughter. "Shouldn't you be at home in bed?"

Eleni shrugged. "I promised not to breathe on anyone in case I'm still contagious, but I wanted pizza and Nessie said it was early enough that there wouldn't be a lot of people in here. And, yes, I know we could have ordered in, but I wanted out of the house, so she said she'd bring me."

"Of course she did. How's the throat?"

"It's okay. The Motrin helps."

Sam smothered a grin at how old and knowledgeable she sounded.

Eleni's gaze slid to Grace. Sam made introductions all around, then raised a brow at Grace. "You mind if they join us as long as she promises not to breathe on you? She's been fever-free for the past twenty-four hours, so. . ." He shrugged.

"I don't mind. I'm not worried about a few germs." Grace smiled at Eleni and slid over in the booth. "You're welcome to sit by me or—"

Eleni moved so fast to join Grace that Sam blinked. "Hi," his daughter said with a grin, no sign of illness in sight, "so you work with my dad?"

"I do. On some things."

"Cases dealing with serial killers?"

"El . . ." Sam shot her a look that she ignored.

"He thinks he can figure them out and help them," Eleni said, "but I did some research and, honestly, I'm not so sure. Most of them don't seem like they're sorry for what they did, just sorry they got caught. What do you think?"

Vanessa slid next to Sam with a long-suffering shrug.

Grace's eyes darted between him and his mother-in-law, who

bit her lip. "Well, I think it all goes back to the beginning of time when there was good and evil."

"You mean the serpent in the garden?"

"Exactly. He was very self-centered and selfish and was only interested in having his own way. As a result, he ignored God's command to love others and submit to the authority of God. But, not only that, he hated God and wanted to do whatever it took to hurt God, so he went after those who loved God. And he still does that to this day."

Sam stayed quiet, wondering where Grace was going. Eleni—and even Vanessa—looked captivated, the moment broken only by the arrival of the waitress.

Once they'd ordered and received their drinks, Eleni turned back to Grace. "Is there more?"

"Of course. So, if you go to church, then you know about how the enemy deceived Eve into eating from the Tree of Life."

Eleni nodded.

"Well, that's when things went south. At that point, separation from God happened and all that was perfect became imperfect and broken—the earth, our bodies, everything, including our minds. And the minds of some people are more imperfect than others."

"So, you're saying the serial killers that Dad works with are broken?"

"Yeah. I think so."

"Can they be fixed?"

She sighed. "I think God can do anything, but I also believe he gives us a choice. If the people your dad works with can acknowledge that what they did was wrong and they're truly remorseful, then yes, I believe God can 'fix' them. Or at least forgive them." She smiled. "So, with that hope, I think your dad's work is really important. Because they all have souls, and if your dad can reach just one, then that's a victory for the good guys."

"And a defeat for the enemy," Eleni said, her voice soft, thoughtful.

Grace raised a brow. "Exactly."

"That's cool. I like that." She turned to Sam. "Can I play the arcade game while you guys talk?"

He dug four quarters out of his pocket, and Vanessa passed her four more, then looked at Grace after Eleni walked over to the game area. "That was a very good explanation."

"Well, thank you. I've done a lot of thinking about it and praying, of course. To put it in simple terms, there are so many broken and hurting people in the world who need God's touch to heal and fix that brokenness. Not all of them are serial killers, thank goodness, but if I can be a part of the healing process, then I count myself blessed." Her gaze connected with Sam's. "I'm sure you feel the same way."

Did he? Or was he so focused on simply figuring out the "broken" brains that he'd let his original goal of helping others fall to the back burner?

The fact that he questioned himself bothered him. He cleared his throat. "Yeah. Of course I want to help."

Grace gave a little laugh that faded fast and pain flashed in her eyes. She was thinking about Bobby, no doubt. "But I'm sure there are less serious topics we could talk about."

"I had no idea El really even thought about what I did or who I worked with."

His mother-in-law narrowed her eyes at him. "Seriously?"

"I mean, I know she knows what I do. We've talked about it some, but she just never really seemed that interested."

"She's interested."

"Apparently."

Eleni slid back into her seat just as their food arrived. For the next thirty minutes, they ate and chatted, with Grace promising Eleni not to be a stranger.

Sam finally nodded to his phone. "We need to head out."

Vanessa took another swig of her tea, then rose. "And I think this one could probably use a nap."

"I'm not five, Nessie."

"No, but you're stubborn."

Eleni rolled her eyes, but the fact that she didn't argue said a lot about how she felt.

Grace nodded. "I'm ready when you are."

■ ■ ■ ■

The killer watched Grace and the others leave the restaurant. He'd done his homework to know that Sam Monroe had become a good friend to her. And now she was hanging out with his family? Interesting. It was also intriguing to see that the child had instantly bonded with her, clinging to Grace's words with unwavering attention.

And Sam . . . well, it was obvious to anyone that he was smitten with Grace. The older woman looked like she would be a handful, spunky and in good shape for her age. She'd be trouble for anyone. Trouble he didn't need, for sure.

But that was okay. There were other ways to achieve his goals. The other two agents had sat separate from the little family and Grace, but they didn't even try to hide the fact that they were playing bodyguard.

The whole almost-drowning thing must have really done a number on her. He'd been worried she wouldn't get out in time and had almost taken her with him, but the odds were that he would have been caught if he'd done that. So, he'd provided her as good a chance as any and given her the key to the cuffs.

And so, his quest to learn what she'd said at the scene would continue because he needed to know. He would be *expected* to know. He glanced at his watch. It was time for him to head to work, but when he finished his shift, he'd have time to devise another plan. One that might have to include a little incentive to get Grace to cooperate with him.

He smiled.

If she had bodyguards, he had her scared.

And that suited him just fine.

CHAPTER
THIRTEEN

Following Grace on the way to the Bakers' home, Sam's father called him three times within five minutes. And all three times, he declined the calls. He finally called the prison and spoke to Nate about his father's phone privileges. "We need to come up with some other positive reinforcement for him. I need him not to call this number anymore. Please."

The line went silent, and Sam could almost see the man's eyebrow reaching into his hairline. "Okay," Nate finally said. "I'll see what I can do."

"I know it's been a little over a year. I don't have time to analyze my reasons for allowing it to go on this long. But as of this moment, I need it to stop."

"All right," Nate said. "Sure. Any thoughts on what he might be willing to replace this reward with?"

Sam had lots of thoughts, but none he was willing to voice. "Just ask him and see what he says." A thought occurred to him. "And while I have you on the phone, I'd like a list of numbers he's called for the entire time that he's been there." Maybe it wasn't just Sam he was calling.

More silence. "Sam, I—"

"I'm working this serial killer case. There are some similarities to my father's killings. I just need to run down every angle."

"They're letting you be a part of the investigation?"

"Yes. I have the unit chief's okay. And there's no actual evidence that my father's involved. In fact, they're pretty sure he's not."

"But?"

"But I'm not completely convinced and want to cover all the bases. And since they're letting me . . ."

He thought the man might refuse. "I'll get that pulled for you," Nate finally said.

"Thank you."

When he hung up, he couldn't help but wonder if he was leading himself on a wild-goose chase. Every word he'd said to Nate was true. There was absolutely no evidence that his father was involved. But the fact that the killer took their phones . . .

He simply couldn't shake the idea that it meant something.

Something no one had put together yet.

Because he was the only one who could.

Grace pulled into an upper-middle-class neighborhood with homes that had been built in the last five years. The lawns were meticulously well-kept even in the middle of November. The sod would turn bright green in the spring, but today it was a dull brown that still looked good. Mark parked behind him, and they all climbed out of their sedans at the same time. Mark walked past him without meeting his gaze and joined Grace to walk up the front steps.

Don't let it get to you.

Sam trailed behind and waited at the bottom of the steps while Grace rang the bell.

The door opened a few seconds later. "Hi," the man said. "Right on time."

Mark held out a hand. "Mr. Baker."

"Special Agent Davis." He eyed Grace and Sam. Grace introduced herself and Sam.

"Come on in." He led the way into a formal living room and

gestured for them to take a seat. "Don't know what you think I can tell you, but you're welcome to ask your questions."

"I'm a behavioral analyst," Grace said, "and I may have some different questions than those of the investigating agents."

The man was in his late fifties, fit, and held himself like he had some military in his background. Then Sam spotted the Navy insignia on the wall and mentally patted himself on the back for the observation.

Grace leaned forward. "I know the words 'I'm so very sorry for your loss' are inadequate and offer no comfort, but I truly am sorry. And I want to find the person who did this so we can put him away forever."

He nodded, his throat working. "Those are the best words I've heard since she died. Thank you." He pulled in a deep breath. "Ask your questions while I still have some composure."

"Of course. Can you tell me what Gina did the day she disappeared? Who she saw, where she went, what she did. Any little detail is important."

"I've already gone over all that with the other agents." His gaze flicked to Mark.

"Yes, sir, I understand that, but sometimes when people tell something more than once, they add things they might not have in the original version. New memories or observations."

He sighed and raked a hand down his face before gripping his thighs and clearing his throat. "She got up that morning, and like we always do, we had breakfast. She talked to our oldest daughter, Leslie, and agreed to pick up our granddaughter from day care since Leslie had a meeting after school where she teaches and was afraid she would run late. I'm retired Navy, but I do some real estate on the side. I've got to have something to do with my time. Anyway, I had three showings that day, so I left shortly after breakfast. Around eight o'clock." His jaw quivered. "That was the last time I saw Gina. She never showed up to get Gabby, and three days later, I got a call she'd been found in the park and she was . . . dead."

"The day she disappeared, did you talk to her at all after you left the house?"

He blinked. "Ah, yes, we exchanged a text."

Grace straightened. "What did she say?"

"Just that she was having lunch with a friend and getting her hair done at the salon."

"I don't remember reading about the friend in the report. What's her name?"

"Pamela McGraw. Hold on and I'll get you her number." He rose to snag a pen and notepad from the small table in the corner of the room, wrote on it, then passed the paper to Grace. "She lives four houses up from here."

"Okay, I'll definitely want to talk to her and the hairdresser, but other than that, was there anything Gina may have said that indicated she thought someone had targeted her?"

He shrugged. "No. Nothing." His jaw hardened. "I saw a lot of stuff during my stint in the military. Served in Iraq and Germany. But this . . ." He drew in a shaky breath and blew it out between pursed lips. "I can't wrap my head around it. It just makes absolutely no sense whatsoever."

Sam raised a brow. It did to the killer, they just had to figure out how.

"So, Gina had her phone with her," Grace said. "Did she ever say she was having any issues with it?"

"Her phone? No. I just know they couldn't find it at the scene. Guess he must have tossed it."

"Did Gina and Pamela meet often?" Grace asked, a smooth segue away from what happened with the phone.

"Yeah, every Tuesday."

"At the same place?" Again, Grace's interest seemed to spike, and Sam had to admit, he enjoyed watching her work.

"No," Adam said, "they had a variety of restaurants they liked to meet at."

"But no pattern? Like the first Tuesday of the month they met at Jackson's Hole Diner, then the second was Logan's Roadhouse, and the third, something else. Nothing like that?"

He thought for a moment, then shook his head. "No. They usually texted the morning they were going to meet and decided then."

It could have been the killer knew the routine of the Tuesday lunch, followed Gina to it, waited until she was done, then managed to get her alone. It wouldn't have been hard.

"Could we get the footage from your doorbell camera for the week preceding Gina's disappearance?" Grace asked.

The man blinked. "The doorbell camera? But I didn't get any suspicious notifications."

"I'm not looking for suspicious, just notifications."

He gave a slow nod. "All right, I can get you that."

Grace handed him her card. "Email it to that address, please."

"Sure."

For the next thirty minutes, Grace asked question after question, building a detailed background victimology of Gina to go with the timeline of the woman's movements just before her death.

"The report said she had a doctor's appointment scheduled the day before she was found," Grace said.

"Right. She has—had—asthma and needed a prescription filled. In order to get that, she was required to see the doctor."

"Okay, thanks." She made more notes, her pen scratching across the page.

Mark listened for the most part, interjecting with his own questions occasionally. Good questions, Sam admitted silently. Grudgingly.

His phone rang, and he glanced at the screen before rejecting the call once more. Apparently, Nate hadn't yet taken care of the issue.

■ ■ ■ ■

Grace stepped out of the Baker home, her mind spinning while she reached for her phone. The thing had buzzed three times while she'd been questioning Adam Baker, and even though she desperately wanted to look at it in case it was about Bobby, she'd forced herself to get through the interview.

She glanced at the screen. A text from Lucy.

Bobby doing better. More later.

A sigh of relief filtered through her lips. With that bit of information, she could switch back to the case.

She had so much new information to sift through and put into her profile. So far—after her run-ins with the man—she knew it was a Caucasian male. He was thin, well-groomed, green or blue eyes, probably contacts, between five foot ten inches and six feet tall, and had a compulsive need to know what she'd said about him. He fell into the organized criminal category. Very little evidence was found at the scene. Which meant he was probably above-average intelligence. It was possible he was educated, married, gainfully employed, and more. He was most likely well-liked by friends and charming, not to mention cunning and controlled.

But was he? The attack at the hospital seemed brazen. Then again, if Sam hadn't been there waiting for her, the killer would have very likely taken her to whatever destination he'd had in mind and gotten away with it. He clearly knew he couldn't charm her into the vehicle since he carried the gun. The van was outfitted with bars and cuffs—another sign of organization.

He was familiar with the area, probably even lived nearby one of the victims.

But which one?

"Grace?"

Sam's voice pulled her out of her thoughts. He and Mark were watching her with matching frowns. "Oh. Sorry. I was just thinking."

"Can you think in the car?" Mark asked. "It's warmer there."

"Yes, of course."

"We heading to the Griffith home?" Mark asked.

She glanced at her phone once more. Bobby was okay, but . . .

"Grace?" Mark wasn't hiding his impatience well, and Grace raised a brow at him.

"Get in your car and get warm, Mark. You lead and I'm right behind you."

"And I'll be behind you," Sam said.

Grace thought Mark might say something sharp, but apparently he changed his mind at the last second and strode to his vehicle, climbed behind the wheel, and started the engine.

Grace met Sam's gaze and shook her head. "Ready?"

"Yeah."

Once in the car, her phone rang and she sent it to the Bluetooth speakers. "Hello?"

"Hey, it's Carmen in the lab. I've already sent the results to Mark and Jerry, but since it was your house and you, I wanted to call you. I ran the DNA sample from your house and there's no match in the CODIS system."

Grace blinked. "Seriously?"

"Yes, sorry."

"It's . . . okay, I think. I mean, I'm really surprised, but thanks for letting me know." She hung up and frowned. How was that possible? This guy was not a newbie killer.

If he wasn't in the system, it was only because he hadn't been caught.

When they got to Sonya Griffith's home, her daughter was waiting on the porch. She invited them in, and for the next hour and a half, Grace asked her the same questions she'd gone over with Adam Baker. "And there's nothing you can think of that was out of the ordinary?"

"No. Nothing."

"And she didn't know Gina Baker or Carol Upton?"

"No." She raked her hand through her reddish-blond hair. "I told the other agents that there's not a connection."

"Did she have lunch with friends on a regular basis?" Sam asked. "Like at any particular restaurant?"

The woman blinked at him. "Uh, no. I mean, yes, occasionally when she's not working. She's a teacher—or *was* a teacher"— her eyes filled, and she swiped the tears away with a motion that said it was becoming a habit—"so her lunch break was always at the school. She got together with friends on her days off and the weekends every so often."

Grace nodded. "Okay, thank you." She closed her notebook and tucked her pen into her pocket. She'd recorded the conversation, but still liked to write notes as she went. Mark had once again contributed by asking a question occasionally but, for the most part, had let her take the lead. "I appreciate it. Once again, I'm so sorry for your loss."

She showed them out, and Mark turned to them. "I'm heading back to the office." He looked at Sam. "Don't you have a job to do?"

"Look," Sam said, "I don't know what your problem is with me, but could you just please share so we can move past it?"

"My problem is your father."

"Well, I'm not my father."

Grace was tempted to intervene, but they were big boys, and this had been needing to happen for a while now. Maybe not in front of her or in the street here, but . . .

"Maybe not, but my parents are divorced because of your father, so I got no love for any of you."

"Wait a minute, I thought you didn't like me because I proved you wrong on a case."

Mark snorted. "I don't care about that. I care that my father was married to your father's case and my mother left as a result."

Sam glowered. "I'm not responsible for my father's actions—or your parents', for that matter—and if you can't see that, then you're a blind man."

"And you're the son of a killer. I really don't understand how they let you work here."

Sam's jaw tightened, and Grace had had enough. "Okay, you guys. I get there are issues here, but this isn't the time or place to continue this."

Sam's phone buzzed and he glanced at it, then sighed. "I've

got to go make a call." He seared Mark with a hard look. "We're not done."

"Yeah, I think we are." He glanced at Grace. "You good with me heading back to the office?"

"Yes, fine."

Mark climbed into his vehicle and took off, leaving her and Sam still standing in the street. Sam nearly vibrated with the effort he was making to hold in his emotions. She didn't blame him.

"I should have known who he was," he said. "I've studied the case files over and over. I know all the agent names who worked the case—cases—but I didn't put it together that James Davis was Mark's father. His name is Marcus in my file. I guess I just didn't connect it."

"It's a common last name. No reason you should have connected the two."

"Every reason I should. And it was that case that set Mark's parents on the course to divorce because his father let it consume his every waking hour. No wonder he hates me."

"He doesn't hate you. He hates what the case did to his parents, and you're a convenient target for his anger. You know that as well as I do." She sighed. "Come on, I'll buy you a cup of coffee on the way back to CIRG."

"I can't come with you. I'm going to head to the hospital. Brenna texted me and said Hal has taken a turn for the worse."

"Oh no. I'll follow you. I can check in on Bobby and work from the hospital."

He nodded. "But let me follow you instead. I want to keep an eye out for anyone who might decide to tail you. Not that I need to tell you this, but be careful and watch your mirrors."

"It's becoming a habit, trust me."

"Good."

He climbed into his car, and Grace led the way, keeping an eye on her mirrors as she'd promised. When they arrived at the hospital, she was almost surprised that nothing had happened en route. She and Sam met in the lobby.

"You want to check on Hal?" she asked. "I'm going to see how Bobby's doing, okay? You can fill me in on what Brenna has to say when I'm done? My family will probably be in the same waiting room. Then I'm going to find a place to work on this profile. I have enough, I think, to make it worthwhile to send them what I've got. I can always add to it later if something comes up."

"Sure. That's fine."

When they walked in, she spotted Brenna in a chair near the window. When Brenna looked up and saw them, she burst into tears.

Grace met Sam's gaze. Okay then. Bobby was going to have to wait a few minutes.

CHAPTER
FOURTEEN

Sam hurried to Brenna's side. She stood and threw herself at him, burying her face in his chest. For a moment, he froze, then patted her back while she cried. His eyes met Grace's, and she grabbed a tissue from the box on the end table, then handed it to Brenna, who pulled back and swiped her eyes.

"Thank you." She looked at Sam and flushed. "I'm so sorry. I didn't mean to fall apart all over you."

"It's okay. Things are hard right now, but what is it? Is Hal—" He really didn't want to ask, but she was shaking her head.

"No, he's still alive, but he threw a clot and they almost lost him."

"But he's okay now?"

"Well, not okay exactly, but yeah, they said he's stable."

"Stable is good. Did the doctors say when he might wake up?" She shook her head. "They're still keeping him in the coma."

"Do you have someone who can sit with you?"

She glanced at the door. "My boyfriend should be here soon. He said he was coming, but he owns a restaurant and sometimes it's hard for him to get away." A sigh slipped from her and she waved a dismissing hand. "I had my little breakdown, but I'll be fine now. Thank you."

"Do you want us to wait for him to get here?"

"No, that's okay." Strands of hair had escaped her messy bun, and she tucked them behind her ear. "Really. I'll call you if they let me know anything more. Seriously, Grant will be here any minute now."

"Okay. If you're sure." Sam caught Grace's eye. "Want to check on Bobby? I'll hang here for a few minutes and give you some time with your family."

"Thanks." She headed for the far corner. Grace's parents stood to greet her with hard faces and sad eyes.

Sam turned away so as not to intrude on the moment, but the stiffness in Grace's shoulders said a lot about her internal turmoil.

"You don't have to wait with me," Brenna said. "Please. I think I just want to be alone."

Feeling like he should obey her wishes, he walked to the table along the back wall, poured a cup of coffee, then pulled out his phone to check his schedule. He needed to get to the prison for an appointment with one of his clients. One he didn't feel right about rescheduling.

"No," someone from Grace's family circle said. "Absolutely not. You can't ask her to do that. Why would you even think that's a good idea?"

Sam turned. Grace planted her hands on her hips and tilted her face to the ceiling with eyes closed. He didn't know if she was praying or counting. Maybe both. Finally, she drew in a deep breath. "Lucy, it's okay."

"Are you kidding me? No, it's not okay." The young woman Grace had called Lucy mimicked Grace's stance with hands on her hips, chin jutted, eyes narrowed. She had to be Grace's sister. The two looked enough alike to be twins. Their mother had gray-streaked brown hair and their father had a full head of the same. His dark face had a plethora of wrinkles that suggested a lot of time in the sun.

Grace pressed a hand to her eyes and shook her head. "I can't do this right now, I'm sorry." She turned on her heel and headed for the door. Sam's gaze bounced between Grace and Brenna. Grace never looked at him, just walked past him and out the door. "Grace?"

She held up a hand. "Just give me a minute, Sam. Please. Then we can head to the office."

"Yeah. Sure."

He frowned and tossed his coffee in the trash. He hated to waste it, but it wasn't that good anyway. He followed Grace out of the waiting room and into the hallway in time to see her enter the bathroom. While he waited, his phone buzzed. Jerry. "Hello?"

"Hey, Grace isn't answering her phone, but I thought you could pass on a message. I just wanted to let her know that the guy in the video department examined the doorbell footage. There's a green van that sat on the curb of the Baker residence for three days. Someone actually reported it to the police, but no one seemed to care."

"Great. What are the chances it's the same lime-green van that CSU is now going over with a fine-tooth comb?"

"Hard to tell, but could be. Unfortunately, I can't get a plate off it to compare, but I think this is a dead end. Once the van leaves, it doesn't return."

"Thanks. I'll pass that on to her."

Five minutes later, Grace came out, but he could tell she'd been crying. "Can I do anything?" he asked.

"No, it's just family stuff. It got to me today more so than usual."

"Because you're tired and have a serial killer after you, so your defenses are lower?"

She stilled, then gave him a small smile. "That probably has something to do with it." A sigh slipped from her and her shoulders bowed a fraction. "My mother said something about Bobby coming to live with me. My sister jumped in before I could respond. Which earns her the biggest hug and the best Christmas present I can find."

"Let me guess. They want Bobby to move in with you so you can keep an eye on him."

"Yeah."

"You wouldn't be able to do that and your job, would you?"

"No. Or keep my sanity, either, but I'll have to deal with all of that later. Bobby's not ready to go anywhere for a while, so I've got time to procrastinate—on that issue anyway." She drew in a deep breath and let it out slowly. "I really need to head to the office to work up this profile—at least get back on it. Mark and Jerry and the others are going to have me fired if I don't get busy."

"They do understand you almost died, right?"

She gave a humorless laugh. "Yes, they do. But I've also declared that I'm fine. So, now I have to prove it."

"Are you fine?"

She rubbed her head. "I'm . . . I don't know, Sam. Right now, I'm okay. When I go home, I may not be. I'll keep you updated."

"Please do." He paused, then filled her in on the call about the doorbell footage.

She groaned. "I was really hoping that would lead to something else."

"Yeah. Sorry." He studied her, then went for it. "Want to try for that dinner again tonight?"

"Only if you bring the steaks to my house and we cook them there. Maybe doing something like that—something normal—will chase away the sense of darkness still lingering there."

He nodded. "If they're still in the refrigerator. I do have a seventeen-year-old son who enjoys grilling. And steak."

Finally, her eyes lightened, and her lips curved in a real smile this time. "Sounds like a kid after my own heart."

"Yeah." He glanced at his phone. "Speaking of kids, I need to check on Eleni."

"Sure. You do that. I'm going to head to the office."

"I'll walk with you to your car."

"Sam—"

"Just let me do it."

He thought she might continue to protest, but she finally nodded. A young man with hair tied up in a man bun, a five o'clock shadow, and an old blue-jean jacket passed them and walked into the ICU waiting room. Through the window, Sam watched the guy go straight for Brenna and pull her into a hug. "I'm glad he's finally here," he said. "I was beginning to think he was a figment of her imagination." And he felt better about leaving her.

Grace headed for the elevator and he followed her. Just as she pressed the button, his phone rang. A glance at the screen had him biting back a groan. His father. Talking to Nate again had just moved to the top of his priority list.

■ ■ ■ ■

After Sam had left to climb into his own vehicle, Grace sat behind the wheel of her Bucar, gripping the steering wheel while her mother's words played in her head. *"Bobby needs more than we can give him. He listens to you, Grace. If he lived with you, he wouldn't do this kind of thing."*

Really? Did they honestly believe that living with her would somehow magically allow Bobby to control his addiction? That she could do her job and take care of Bobby at the same time? And if he died "on her watch"? What then? They'd blame her. If she refused to let him live with her and he died on a sleazy bathroom floor of the bar on the outskirts of town, they'd blame her. He'd lived with her once, and it had been a disaster. Of course, they didn't know that, but still . . .

God, please tell me what to do.

With her eyes on the mirrors, she cranked the car and backed out of the parking spot. Thirty minutes later, she arrived at CIRG and pulled into her assigned slot. The tension headache eased and the muscles across the back of her shoulders and lower neck loosened. She hadn't realized how tight she'd been holding her body until she didn't have to anymore.

Once she was through security and at her desk, she opened her laptop and went to work on the profile. Two blessed uninterrupted hours later, she hit Send on the email and sat back.

There. It was done. Mark, Jerry, and everyone on the task force now had it in their inboxes with the full knowledge that she was working with what she had, and as soon as she learned something more, she'd update the document.

But for now, it was off her plate.

A knock on her door pulled her gaze from the computer screen to see Frank there. "The shooting was ruled good." He stepped inside and placed her weapon on her desk. "You're back to full speed ahead." He paused. "Not that you ever weren't full speed ahead."

"That was faster than normal."

"It was a no-brainer. I encouraged them not to dillydally. They didn't." His gaze held hers. "How are you doing? Be honest. Don't gloss over what you've been through. The break-in at your house, the kidnapping, and the dunk in the marina . . . that's all terrifying. It's going to have a lasting effect on you."

She was actually able to pull up a smile for him. "I know. I studied that stuff in med school, remember?"

He didn't return the smile, and she sighed. "Okay, honest answer. As long as I stay busy, I do all right. I can push it to the corner of my mind, and while I know it's there, it's not consuming me. Last night was also okay because when I finally crashed, I didn't dream. Surprisingly. Tonight might be a different story." She shrugged. "I guess we'll find out."

He studied her for a moment, then shook his head. "Take time now if you need it. I don't want to see you have a breakdown because you didn't deal with this immediately."

Grace started to respond, then stopped. He had a valid argument. She nodded. "I promise to self-evaluate often. If I feel like I'm pushing too hard, I'll take the time off. I won't deny the experience was terrifying. It was. I was scared out of my mind. But . . . I'm also angry. So, I'm channeling that."

"As long as you're not in denial."

"No. I'm really not."

He could require her to talk with someone in the Employee Assistance Program or a member of the peer support group who had survived a shooting, but he just nodded. "All right, then. Stay in touch with me on a more regular basis. We'll take it one day at a time."

She suppressed a sigh. He was just concerned about her mental state and she couldn't blame him one bit. "Sure. Any word on a missing woman who might be the person the killer was talking about at my house?"

"No. Nothing." He paused. "You think there's really another victim?"

She flashed to the scene in her home. The killer in her kitchen. His face. "Yes. I do."

Frank rubbed his eyes and nodded. "We need to find this guy."

"I know. I had one more observation."

"What's that?"

"He didn't seem to care that I could identify him. He didn't wear a mask or . . . anything."

"Well, a guy in a mask sitting in a van would draw way too much attention."

"True."

"And he probably didn't expect you to be able to walk away from him, either. He planned to kill you once you told him what he wanted to know."

"I know that too."

Frank shrugged. "Which is why he had no reason to hide his face from you."

She got it. "I know, Frank."

"I know you do. You just gave us all a scare." He cleared his throat. "Change of subject. I need to catch you up on a few things."

Grace sat up straighter. "You want to take a seat?" She waved a hand at the lone chair near the door.

"No, I've only got a few minutes before I have to head into a meeting. Jerry said he'd email you the Griffith report, but in a nutshell, they checked the footage at the entrance to the park and landed on a stolen vehicle right off the bat. It was the first car through the gate that morning. The owner reported it missing that morning when he went out to go to work. No home or street cameras so no footage there. Agents are questioning neighbors to see if they saw anything. It's probably not a stretch to think it's the car the killer used to transport the body to the location where he finally left her."

"Right." She paused. "Wait. The park opened at sunrise. Did you get the car leaving?"

He nodded. "Yeah. It left two hours later."

"He needed time to get the phone in place," she said.

"Probably. We've got a BOLO out on the car, so we'll see if someone spots it. Most likely, it'll be abandoned somewhere."

She leaned forward, clasping her hands in front of her on the desk. "He scoped the place out, Frank. He knew exactly what tree he was going to put the phone in and where he was going to leave her. He had the little phone camouflage thing built and ready to simply put into place. He was there before Monday."

"I would agree with that, but there's no way to know when. Then again, it could've been in the last couple of days."

Grace wove her pen through her fingers while she thought. "Even if you figured out what day it was and saw the vehicle, it was probably stolen too." She sighed. "He's going around stealing cars like they're candy. I think we need to keep an eye on any vehicles stolen until we catch this guy. And then post a BOLO for it as soon as the report comes in. Who knows? We may catch a break and someone will see the car, call it in, and we'll catch this guy. And all sleep easier at night." It never hurt to dream a little, right?

Frank raised a brow. "That's actually not a bad idea."

She shot him a tight smile. "I have good ones occasionally. Any word on the van?"

"They've pulled it from the lake and it's in the crime scene unit's lab. I'll let you know if they find anything."

She nodded. "Thanks."

"One other thing the ME said. All three victims' hands were messed up, but so were their knees, and he found some concrete residue under one of Sonya's toenails. He said it was just a faint speck and he almost missed it."

"Concrete?"

"Yeah. And the guy isn't killing them right away. They go missing, then three days later, they show up dead. I don't know where he's keeping them or what he's doing with them in the interim, but with this current victim, we're on a time clock."

"We don't even know who she is," Grace said.

"I know. It's a needle in a haystack. Mark and Jerry are going through all of the missing persons reports looking for anyone who matches the first three victims."

"Let me know what they find?"

"Absolutely." He glanced at his watch. "I've got to go. See you later."

Frank left, and Grace turned back to her computer to pull up Hal's information, a copy of his visitor list, and the log of those who'd actually come to see him. Grace started reading. By the time she'd reached the end, she'd learned absolutely nothing new, so she moved on, thinking, her brain searching for another avenue of investigation. She tapped a quick text to Sam.

> Can I get a list of every prisoner in proximity to Hal Brown? If that's possible, can you send it to this email addy?

She typed in her bureau address.

Thirty seconds later, her computer dinged, indicating an email. He'd sent her the list. She texted him.

> That was fast. Thanks.

I'd already requested it and I've already been through it. Figured you'd want it at some point. We can talk about each person if you need information.

I need to know if Hal and any of the other inmates had been communicating with each other on a regular basis. If there were any patterns to the communication, etc.

I'll look into it. Mitch would probably be the one to talk to about that.

And I'll pass this on to Jerry and Mark. I know they'll want it too.

Thanks.

How's Eleni?

Better. Thanks for asking.

I'm glad. She's a sweet girl.

Most of the time.

Grace laughed.

Talk later?

Yep.

She set her phone aside and pulled up the list of inmates that Hal could possibly have been in contact with.

One name jumped out at her immediately.

Peter Romanos. Well, that was no surprise. They were housed in the same area. But it did bear closer investigation. Because if it was just a coincidence that Peter's name was on the list, she'd eat her badge.

CHAPTER
FIFTEEN

WEDNESDAY LATE AFTERNOON

Sam sat back in his chair and rubbed his eyes. He had a small but comfortable office in the prison on the first floor, two doors down from the warden's more spacious one. Since Sam met clients in a designated area with a glass partition between him and the inmate, he didn't spend a lot of time in his office, but mostly used it for writing reports, making phone calls, and eating lunch occasionally when he needed to be alone.

And sometimes, he used it for research.

This afternoon when he'd sat down, he pulled every name of every serial killer incarcerated at the prison and populated the list by number of known victims. Then he culled it to those who could possibly, in some way, have contact with Hal. From there, he looked at every name on the visitor list, how often they visited, and when.

When his father's name appeared as someone who had contact with Hal, he nearly had a coronary, but it made sense. The man had been in the cell two doors from the hostage situation, watching the whole thing go down. Watching and smiling. An uncomfortable tingle started at the base of Sam's skull. The kind of tingle that said he was going to have to do something he didn't want to do.

His phone buzzed, cutting off the feeling for the moment. His mother-in-law. Sam swiped the screen. "Hi, Vanessa, thanks for calling me back."

"Sorry it took me so long. El's fine. Connor came over and checked on her a bit ago."

"He did?"

"Yes." She paused. "You're okay with that, right?"

"If you trust him, I'm okay with it, I'm just . . ."

"What?"

A wave of guilt washed over him. Eleni was his child, and he or Claire should be the ones caring for her. "I can probably come home in a couple of hours. I just have one other client to see."

"Why would you come home? We're fine. She goes back to school tomorrow as long as she's fever-free for twenty-four hours—and she has been, so we're good."

"I know, but I'm her father."

"And I'm her grandmother. Let go of the guilt and do your job. This is one reason I moved in, remember?"

He remembered. "Well, I know how yucky you can feel with strep, so I'm glad this appears to be a milder case."

"Yep, he gave her a shot yesterday to get the meds in her system and I think that's made a huge difference. Right now, she's in bed with the television watching some teen sitcom. I checked and it's age appropriate."

Once again, Sam was overwhelmed with gratitude for the woman. "I know I've said it before, but I'll say it again. I really don't know what I'd do without you."

"I've told you before, Sam. You'd manage. And—"

"And what?" He frowned.

"If it helps with the whole father-guilt thing, I'll admit that I have some guilt myself. It's my daughter who bailed on you and her family when you needed her most."

Sam blinked. *Bailed* was one way of looking at it, he supposed.

"So, while I would help you and my grandchildren regardless, I guess it also helps me feel a little less of my own guilt," she said.

"Not that I don't love doing it, but it does help me manage my anger with Claire."

He'd never thought of it that way.

His intercom buzzed.

"Well, if I can steal the words of a wise woman, let it go. Claire did what she did and we've moved on. It's been eight years. I'm not angry with her anymore." In fact, he felt pretty much nothing towards his ex. Not anger, betrayal, hurt, lingering affection. Just . . . nothing.

Which probably was something he should address, but he simply didn't have the time or energy to go there right now.

His intercom buzzed once more. "Hey, Vanessa, I have to go. I have a patient who's ready to see me."

"Bye, son." She hung up and Sam smiled. She didn't call him "son" often, but when she did, it . . . warmed him. Even after all these years, he still missed his mother. A lot.

But she'd made her choice and walked out on him and her family. Much like Claire had done to him and their kids.

The intercom buzzed once more, and he sighed.

He walked out of his office to find his administrative assistant, Janice Myers, at her desk, a frown on her face and Mitch Zimmerman seated in the chair opposite her desk. "About time," he thought he heard her mutter. Janice had a sour personality and didn't care who she offended with it. Some days were better than others. Today wasn't one of those.

He bit his lip on a response and nodded to Mitch. "Hi, Mitch."

"I'm here for our appointment."

Sam frowned and turned to Janice. "Have a seat in my office. I'll be right in." Mitch swept past him, and Sam looked at Janice with a raised brow.

She shrugged. "I moved him up so you could get out of here at a decent time."

"Oh. All right then. Thanks." And that was why he kept her around. She might be a pain sometimes, but she was good at what she did and she knew how to prioritize. Sam could learn from that.

He shut the door behind him and walked around to sit behind his desk once more, then leaned forward and clasped his hands in front of him. "How are you doing?"

Mitch shrugged. "I'm fine."

Sam studied him. He actually did look fine. "So, no nightmares?"

"No." Mitch ran a hand over his head. "Look, Hal's been on edge since he got here, but he's been basically well behaved. Not a problem." His eyes locked on Sam's. "I know talking to you always put him in a better frame of mind."

That was good to hear. "But still no idea what set him off?"

"Not a clue. He'd just finished his shift in the library delivering books and collecting ones people were done with. He returned the cart and the books to the library, and I put him back in his cell. Thirty minutes later, he went ballistic." He paused. "I have no idea where the shiv came from or why he even had it unless he was feeling threatened in some way, which—" He shrugged. "Totally possible, of course. I hadn't heard any murmurings that anyone was out to get him, but . . ." Another shrug, but the man's eyes darkened. "When he was holding that thing against my throat, not knowing if he would just snap and use it? Let's just say, all I could think of was getting away from him no matter what it took."

"Understandable," Sam said.

Mitch paused and sighed. "Should I have tried to take him down another way? Maybe. I don't know. I'm not sure I should have stabbed him with the shiv, but . . ." He raised a hand to rub the area still bandaged from Hal's pressure with the weapon. "It was instinct, I guess, from my days overseas."

"I can't answer that, Mitch, I'm sorry. I think you did what you thought you had to do to survive. No one can fault you for that." Would Sam have done the same thing? Maybe.

"I wasn't aiming for his neck," Mitch said. "He moved and . . . I just . . . I don't know. I'll admit I was scared."

"I'd be worried about you if you hadn't been."

Mitch laughed. A low, husky sound that didn't hold any humor.

"I just hate that I didn't see he was ready to snap. I mean, I'm with the guy every day."

"You can't read minds. We all miss stuff." *Like the fact that your mother doesn't love her family enough to stay and that your father's a serial killer.* The thought popped into his head and he quickly shoved it out. This case was affecting him more than he'd counted on. "Do you like your job, Mitch?"

"*Like* it?" He tilted his head and looked at Sam. "I don't *hate* it, but it wasn't what I'd planned on doing with the rest of my life."

"What'd you want to do?"

"Play in the NFL." He laughed. "But doesn't every kid?" He rubbed a hand down his cheek. "I'm fine with the job. Most days. If a better offer came along, I'd probably take it."

Most probably would. "Right." He paused. "Do you have much to do with Peter Romanos?"

Mitch's eyes narrowed. "I mean, he's on my block so I see him every day. Why?"

"Has he caused any trouble lately?"

"Him? No. He's one of the lifers that I actually like. He's polite, does what he's told to do, and never causes any trouble at all. Knowing who he is and the way those guys think, I figure there's some motive behind it—like not losing his yard privileges, but as long as he's not causing any issues, I don't care. Why?"

"Just . . ." Sam stopped. What was he doing? "Never mind. It's not important. Let's circle back to Hal." For the next forty minutes, they talked about the incident and what Mitch might expect when he returned to work. "You might experience some PTSD symptoms," Sam said. "Don't be surprised to find yourself jumping at the slightest thing an inmate does."

Mitch nodded and Sam's phone buzzed. He glanced at the screen, noting their time was up and that Grace was texting. He stood. "That's it for today. Do you think you need to come back?"

Mitch stood too. "I don't think so." He hesitated. "Can I let you know how I'm doing in a couple of days?"

"Of course."

"Thanks, Doc. I appreciate the time."

Sam ushered the man out, waved to Janice, who pretended she didn't see him, then returned to grab his phone to read the text from Grace.

We still on for an early dinner?

Absolutely. I'm leaving now.

■ ■ ■ ■

Grace smiled when Sam's text popped up, and she rose to grab her things.

"Grace?"

She'd almost made it. She turned to see Frank standing at her door. The look on his face sent her stomach to the floor. "Another one?"

"Yeah."

"You want Sam there?"

"Absolutely. He thinks Peter Romanos has something to do with this, and I'm inclined to listen. I want him to see everything first-hand. He's just not officially involved in the investigation."

"Of course. I'll call him."

"Thanks. I'll text you the address."

She'd just buckled her seat belt when Frank's text came across her screen.

Fountainhead Regional Park

His next text was directions.

She groaned, then copied and pasted the texts to Sam.

Dinner is going to have to wait again, I'm afraid.
Can you meet me there?

You've got to be kidding

came his instant response.

I wish. I'm headed there now.

Right behind you.

It would take her at least thirty minutes, if not more, to get to the park. Jerry and Mark would leave from the Washington Field Office and Sam would be leaving from the prison. Local officers and park security would keep the scene contained until they could get there.

When she pulled up to the park's entrance, security checked her credentials and motioned her in. Once she got to the scene, she parked next to another Bucar and climbed out. Voices filtered to her through the trees, and she spotted a path that cut through them. Grace followed it to the edge of a clearing. A woman's body lay in the center of it. Crime scene tape had already been put up around the perimeter to keep the surprisingly large crowd behind it. Mark and Jerry must have just arrived seconds before she did, because they'd already ducked under the tape, heading toward the body. They'd have to work fast to beat the sun sinking toward the treetops.

She stopped at the edge of the tape and scanned. The killer had chosen an area near enough to a campsite that it would ensure a pretty quick discovery, but isolated enough he didn't risk being seen too soon. Clever. Thoughtful. Well organized and executed without a hitch.

She looked for the phone. It would be well-hidden. Even more so than the last two. While agents worked the scene, she searched.

Sam walked up to stand beside her. "Hey."

"Hey."

"You spot it?"

"No, not yet." She wasn't even surprised he knew what she was doing.

"What about the rubberneckers?" He nodded to the onlookers behind the tape.

"I've been scanning the ones I can see, and no one jumps out at me as a potential killer. If he's here, he's very good at blending in—or I just haven't spotted him."

"One thing I've been thinking about," Sam said, "is, how does he get these women to go with him? I mean, I guess the presence of the gun would do it, but according to the autopsy report, there aren't any drugs in their systems."

"All three fought back, but no DNA under their nails because he took those. No DNA on any of the clothing. But there was a fleck of concrete under a toenail on the third victim, so he's probably keeping them somewhere like a basement or . . . something."

"Okay. And he keeps them a while. Could be the drugs are just out of their systems by the time he kills them."

"There is that."

She scanned the area once more. Where could the phone be? She ducked under the tape and aimed herself toward Mark and Jerry. The ME had covered the body with the familiar black tarp out of respect for the victim. There was no way to hide her from the onlookers, not in this situation.

Had that been one of the reasons the killer had chosen this spot?

She wouldn't put it past him. Everything he did seemed well-thought-out and planned.

Even the break-in at her house. He'd come with a plan for when her alarm system went off. He'd come with a plan when he'd snatched her from the hospital parking lot.

She stopped a few feet from the body and watched the ME write something in his notebook.

"I want to know where he's meeting them," Jerry said, looking up at her. "What is it that they say or do that triggers his desire to silence them? And where are they disappearing from? It doesn't appear to be their homes. What were their last known locations again?"

Grace dug into her memory. "Um . . . Gina Baker was last seen at the salon. She got her hair done, then left. Cameras show her getting into her car and leaving the parking lot, then nothing. She just disappeared. The ME said he kept her alive for at least three days because she'd only been dead a few hours."

"And Sonya Griffith and Carol Upton?"

"Pretty much the same story for both ladies. Except Sonya disappeared from a pharmacy. Had a car full of groceries that were on the verge of spoiling when they found her car in another parking lot where it appears she ran in to grab a prescription. Cameras show her going in, but not coming out. Nothing on the register camera—the only one inside the store. We have to assume she left through the back entrance. The camera out there was broken, so we don't know exactly what time she left or was *taken* out that way. We may be assuming a lot, but that was the only other exit, so . . ." She shrugged. "The cameras picked her up at six p.m. near the pharmacy. A man spoke to her and walked away. We thought we had something when we were able to get his plate, but when we tracked him down, he was at work. He'd stopped in to grab some snacks for a meeting and batteries for a mic. He asked her if she knew where he could find batteries and off he went. No way was he involved. After that, she walked into the pharmacy and out of view of a camera, and we never could pick her up again."

"And Carol?"

"Same story, different channel." Grace sighed. "So, what's her name?" she asked, indicating the tarp.

Mark consulted his little black book. "Kristin Davenport."

Sam rubbed a hand down his cheek, his frown deeper than she'd ever seen it.

"What if they're just random?" Mark asked.

Jerry raised a brow. "You mean you think we're wasting our time looking for a link between the victims?"

"Yes."

Grace shook her head. "The attacks are too personal. I mean, cutting someone's tongue out is an act of rage—or perceived justice. But it's also a message."

Sam nodded. "Agreed."

Mark's nostrils flared, and Grace thought he might say something snarky, but he just looked away, his gloved hands fisting at his sides. The ME stood and Mark nodded to the body. "Fingernails?"

"Gone."

"Figured."

Grace once again perused the area. "Is anyone recording the crowd? It's a nice size, but not so big we couldn't send the faces through the facial recognition software." Her eyes scanned and she stopped on one particular man.

"Yeah," Jerry said, "Val's got it."

Valerie Page, another agent.

The man at the edge of the tape met her gaze briefly, then his eyes swept past her to the body under the tarp. He was close enough she could see the camera and press badge looped around his neck. He had a goatee, glasses, and short dark-brown hair. Not her killer. She let her eyes move on.

"He didn't leave a phone out here," Mark said. "Or if he did, it's so well-hidden, we're not going to find it."

"Then let's get a K-9 team out here to get a whiff of something the woman touched," Jerry said. "A dog can find it."

Mark nodded. "Good idea." He pulled his phone from the clip on his belt. "I'll get one on the way." He stepped away and Sam sighed.

She looked at him. "What?"

"I still think my father's behind all this in some form or fashion," he murmured loud enough for her to hear, but too low for Mark and Jerry to pick up on his words. "I just can't figure out how to . . . figure it out."

"Well, the more this guy kills," she said, "the more chances he has to leave something behind to lead us to him." But that meant more people had to die first, and frankly, that just wasn't acceptable. "We have to think harder, Sam."

"I know."

Grace spotted the reporter over Jerry's shoulder, camera to his eyes, snapping pictures of the transfer of the body to the back of the coroner's vehicle. For some reason, it angered her. Who had let him get this close anyway?

"Hey!" she called.

He ignored her. Mark looked up from his conversation and Jerry turned.

"What is it?" Sam asked.

"That reporter. He's out of line with the pictures." She strode toward the man. "Hey, you! Stop with the pictures. Have some respect."

He met her gaze briefly and she frowned. He looked slightly familiar, but she couldn't place him. Probably from seeing him around crime scenes? He lowered the camera and stepped back, then turned and darted into the still-gathered crowd.

Grace went after him. There was something—

"Grace!"

Sam's shout echoed around her, but she ducked under the crime scene tape and gave chase.

CHAPTER
SIXTEEN

"Grace!"

His second shout went about as well as his first. She ignored him and kept going after the reporter. Sam bolted after the two of them. Not that Grace needed his help when it came to confronting a reporter. Then again, if she lost him, Sam might be able to help find him, since it was obvious she really wanted to talk to the man.

Grace disappeared along another trail that led deeper into the woods. She zigged and zagged, and he lost sight of her several times before catching a peek of her once more. Then she veered off the trail, scrambling through the underbrush, fighting tree limbs and vines that tried to trip her up. Sam stayed after her, but she was fast, nimble as a jackrabbit, and he . . . wasn't.

He leapt over a rotting trunk, only to catch his left foot on part of a root when he came down. His ankle twisted, sharp pain shooting through it and up the side of his left calf. He fell to the forest floor with a sharp cry he couldn't bite off. He rolled and shot to his feet once more. As soon as he put weight on the ankle, he hissed, but it wasn't broken, so he clamped his teeth together and pressed on.

Unfortunately, his clumsy tumble cost him too much time and

distance, and he lost sight of both Grace and the man she was chasing.

■　■　■　■

Grace had never been so grateful to be in good physical shape, but the guy in front of her was in as good a shape as she was . . . or better. And he'd just disappeared into a thick copse of trees. She kept going, but slowed, not wanting to follow him too closely lest he try to get the drop on her. What was wrong with the man? She'd just wanted to talk to him, but his obvious desire to avoid her simply made her that much more determined to confront him.

She kept her hand on her weapon and glanced over her shoulder to see nothing. She'd thought Sam was right behind her. Grace spun back to scan the trees, trying to see through them as she approached. The fading daylight wasn't helping. With her weapon clutched in her right hand, her heart pulsing the blood through her veins at a faster than normal rate, she reached for her phone with her left hand. Where was Sam?

Something slammed into her back. The breath whooshed from her lungs, her weapon flew from her fingers, and she barely managed to get her hands in front of her before she hit the wooded ground. Grunting, she bucked backward, and the weight slid from her for a brief second before returning with more force. He trapped her hands behind her.

"Hello, Grace, we meet again."

Him? "Get off me," she managed to gasp through gritted teeth. He was heavy and strong. And she wasn't going anywhere unless he let her or help arrived. And neither one of those appeared to be happening anytime soon.

"What did you say, Special Agent Grace Billingsley? Word for word, what did you say?"

"Why?" It was the only word she could get out while her shoulders burned with the pressure of the awkward position. He eased up a fraction and she sucked in a gasp of air.

"Grace!"

Sam's voice reached her and the man on top of her froze. She lowered her nose to the ground, then brought her head up as hard as she could into his face.

Pain ricocheted through her skull, but his scream echoed, mingling with a flash of satisfaction and the second call of her name from Sam.

Her attacker—the killer—shot to his feet, and Grace kicked out, bringing him back down next to her while she rolled to her knees. He did the same, shooting his fist out, aiming for her head. She ducked, spinning her face away. His hand shot past her and she grabbed it, twisting. He yelled and pulled, scrambling to his feet and losing his glove in the process. The glove in her hand distracted her for a brief second. Long enough for him to kick out and catch her in the ribs. She gasped and listed sideways, trying to drag in a breath.

He bolted. Ignoring the pain in her shoulders and ribs, Grace dove for her gun, snagged it and rolled, aiming it in the direction he went. Panting, she scrambled to stand, taking a second to get her balance, then took off after the man once more.

"Grace!"

Sam's voice was closer, but she couldn't stop to acknowledge it. She had a gut feeling who she was chasing—and it wasn't a reporter. Five steps later, she pulled to a halt and spun in a circle. He was gone. Her fingers tightened around the grip of her weapon, and she let out a low groan while resisting the urge to stomp her feet even while she grabbed her phone and dialed Mark's number.

"Grace?" Mark's shout made her wince. "Where'd you go?"

"The killer's in the woods. He was watching." She gave him an approximate location. "We need air support and dogs out here ASAP. I'll ping you with my exact location as soon as we hang up."

"On it." He clicked off and she sent him the location, then tucked her phone back into her pocket, wincing with the effort. Her shoulders weren't dislocated, but the muscles had been strained to the point that she was going to be sore for a few days. And she was probably going to have a lovely bruise on the left side of her rib cage. She took a deep breath, gauging the pain and whether or not anything was cracked. She didn't think so. The vest had protected her from that at least.

She turned and spotted Sam limping toward her. With one last look over her aching left shoulder, she hurried toward Sam. "What happened?"

"I twisted my ankle." Sweat beaded his pale face.

"Broken?" she asked.

"No." He dipped his head in the direction the killer had gone. "Who was that?"

"It was him."

She wouldn't have thought it possible, but his jaw tightened further. "*Him?* As in serial-killer him?"

"Yeah."

"How did you know?" He tilted his head back toward the crime scene. "Why didn't you tell someone? Chasing him by yourself was a stupid thing to do."

He was furious with her, eyes blazing. She frowned and held up a hand. "Hold up. I didn't know it was him until he tackled me and spoke. If I'd known it was him, I would have called for backup. I just thought he was some nosy reporter who didn't mind stepping over the boundaries."

At her explanation, the fire dimmed in his gaze. "You didn't recognize him?"

She pressed fingers to her eyes. "No. He looked different. He had on some kind of disguise. A really good, sophisticated one. A mask." Grace dropped her hand and listened. Helicopter blades beat the air, approaching fast. "Good. They're looking for him. And now I need to give another description to Josey so we can get his new face circulating."

"He had on a mask? Didn't look like one."

"I know. It was one of those realistic silicone things, I'd wager." She rubbed her knuckles. "That's what was bothering me at my house. When I punched him, his skin felt weird. It was too smooth."

She sighed and raked a hand over her disheveled hair, tucking strands back into the ponytail. The action hurt her shoulders and pulled at her bruised ribs, but she ignored the pain—just like she'd been doing most of her life.

Pain was pain. It was annoying, but it had never stopped her from doing what needed doing. She looked at Sam. "I'm not in the least superstitious, but I don't think we should schedule any more dinners until this guy is caught."

"No kidding."

She held up the glove she'd managed to pull from the killer. "Let's get this to the K-9 handler and see what they can do."

CHAPTER
SEVENTEEN

Sam leaned against his Bucar, thinking. He knew what he had to do, he just didn't want to do it. But that tingle at the base of his neck was persistent—and insistent. He resisted the urge to slap at the spot while he listened to Grace, who was sitting in the back of the ambulance, buck against the paramedic's advice to get X-rays. "I'm a doctor," she said. "I think I'd know if I needed X-rays. Nothing's broken, just bruised and possibly torn."

Sam heard a dog bark and looked toward the trees. The handler and the dog walked at a fast pace, but the tight look on her face said the killer had once more gotten away. They were really going to have to step up their game if they were going to catch this guy. Not that this was a game. Not in the slightest.

Grace stepped out of the back of the ambulance, quickly hiding a wince, but not before he saw it. He walked over to her. "You need to rest."

"I'll rest when he's caught. How's the ankle?"

"Throbbing. I'll get the paramedics to wrap it."

"Good idea."

Sam's phone dinged and he glanced at the screen. Eleni. On his mother-in-law's phone.

It's El. Call me when you can, please. Thank you.

He raised a brow at the polite words. But at least they weren't indicative of an emergency. He limped to the ambulance. "Got an Ace bandage?"

The paramedic pulled one out. "Want me to wrap it?"

"Sure."

Sam slid his shoe and sock off and got his first glimpse of the damage. He swallowed a groan at the sight of the various shades of purple starting to appear beneath the skin. The ankle was swollen and would take a few weeks to heal. "Great." He'd just have to prop it up as much as possible.

"You need to ice that," Grace said, looking at his ankle.

"I know."

The paramedic wrapped the ankle with a professional skill that even Sam had to admire. Then he pulled his sock on and tried to stuff his foot in his shoe. With a sigh, he gave up and let his heel rest on the back of the department-issued sneaker. At least it was his left foot, so he could still drive.

Mark and Jerry approached, matching frowns on their faces. "You two all right?" Jerry asked.

"Fine," Grace said.

Sam nodded.

Mark skewered Grace with a glare. "What were you thinking chasing him like that?"

Grace held her own and glared right back. "Didn't know he was a killer, Mark. Thought he was a reporter. But when he ran . . ." She shrugged. "I had to find out why." She glanced at Sam. "And I knew Sam was right behind me."

Mark snorted. "Fat lot of good that did, huh?"

"Shut up, Mark," Grace said, her voice mild but the warning clear behind the words.

Mark shot her a scowl but clamped his lips together.

Sam smothered a smile, wondered if he should let everyone know that he could stand up for himself, then swallowed the words and cleared his throat. "I don't suppose anyone found the phone?"

Jerry shook his head and Grace sighed. "He either didn't need it," she said, "or was using it to record everything from where he stood in the crowd. Or he just wanted to watch. Which he got to do for the most part."

"Until you ruined it for him," Sam murmured.

"Think he'll hold that against me?"

"Probably."

Mark rolled his eyes. "You two need a keeper."

"It's called protective custody," Jerry said with a sharp look at his partner. "Seriously."

"Wait a minute," Grace said, "he didn't come after me today. I went after him. I mean, I didn't *know* it was him, but—" She waved a hand. "Never mind. I'm going to call Josey and see if she can meet me so we can do another sketch."

"Don't need it," Jerry said. "We got him on video." He held out his phone and Sam looked over Grace's shoulder. A man in his midthirties with a goatee, glasses, heavy coat, and short dark-brown hair had been captured in the frame.

She leaned in. "That's about as good a description as I could give, so that will save us some time in getting his picture out there."

"And he might not have been *chasing* you," Jerry said, "but he was definitely *watching* you." He showed her more footage, and it was obvious the killer was tracking her movements. "You need to go into protective custody."

She grimaced, and Sam raised a hand to touch the back of her arm. "Grace, maybe you should listen to them."

"I'm fine with having someone watch my house and follow me around, but I'm not hiding out. It doesn't use any more agent manpower to give me an escort than it would to cover a safehouse. Which, by the way, does nothing but delay the inevitable. And, I mean, think about it. If he's coming after me, he's not hurting someone else, right?"

They fell silent. Sam searched for a response and came up blank.

Grace looked at them one by one. "But I might know how to end this and catch him at the same time."

Sam stilled, and Mark and Jerry stared at her with narrowed eyes. Once again, she'd rendered them speechless.

"How?" Mark finally asked.

"We figure out how to get word to him that I'll meet him and tell him what he wants to know. The deal is once he knows, he leaves me alone. We set up the meeting and you guys catch him. Preferably before he kills me or anyone else."

A sound escaped Mark, and Sam couldn't decide if it was a scoff or a cough. "Are you insane?" the man asked. Sam was going with scoff. "He'll know it's a trap."

"Of course he will, but if he agrees . . ." She shrugged. "At least we may have his attention focused on something besides killing more people."

The three of them fell silent, each looking at the other. Sam finally shook his head. "That's a really, really bad idea."

"But it might work," Mark murmured.

Jerry sighed. "Grace, you've done some crazy things in the past in order to catch a killer, but this one moves to the top of the list."

"I'll agree with that," she said, "but he's targeted me. Let's use it."

Sam shook his head. "No way."

"How are you going to get word to him that you want to talk to him?" Mark asked, ignoring Sam.

"Put it in a press conference." Apparently, Grace was going to ignore him too.

"There's no way Frank will go for that," Jerry said. "You know it and we know it. It's simply too risky."

Sam sure hoped he was right.

Grace's lips tightened like she wanted to argue, then she sighed and let out a low groan. "He'd flip, wouldn't he?"

"Faster than an Olympic gymnast," Jerry said.

Sam let his gaze bounce between the three of them and finally landed it on Jerry. "Just to be clear, using Grace as bait is off the table, right?"

"It is."

"But—"

"No," Jerry said, cutting Grace's protest off. "Absolutely not." She sighed but stuck her chin out.

Sam's phone buzzed once more. This time from a number he didn't recognize.

Hi Dad, it's me, Eleni. I'm just texting you to tell you that I got my own phone!!!! Brett got it for me as an early surprise birthday gift!!! I love you!!! Thank you for saying yes!!!

Brett? *Brett* got her a phone? What was her stepfather thinking? He was going to kill the man.

"Sam?"

He realized he'd let out an audible sound. "What?"

"You growled," Grace said.

"No, I didn't."

"You actually did," Jerry said.

Grace shot a frown at the agent, then raised her brows at Sam. "What is it? You okay?"

"No." He tucked the phone into his back pocket. "Sorry. It's a family thing that's going to have to wait. What now?"

"We eat while we wait for a report from the coroner," Jerry said. "I'm starving."

Well, if they were going to eat, he could deal with Claire and Brett. "I'm going to make a phone call. I'll follow you wherever you decide to eat." He wanted the privacy of his car for this conversation.

Grace nodded, and Sam pulled his phone from his pocket and climbed into his vehicle. He used voice commands to call Claire, dreading the upcoming conversation, but it had to be done.

"You're actually calling me?" she said in greeting.

He couldn't fault her for being surprised, as they rarely talked on the phone. It was either text or via Vanessa as a messenger. Then again, she probably should have been expecting him to call about *this* situation. "I felt like this was important enough to discuss. I hear Brett paid a visit to Eleni this afternoon."

Silence.

He sighed. "I'm not trying to start a fight, Claire, I just want to know what he was thinking. I'd barely said something to Eleni about the fact that maybe we could get her a phone and then he's over there giving her one."

"He bought it a few weeks ago. I talked to Eleni just after lunchtime and she told me that you'd given her the green light."

"Um, not exactly, but what happened to you saying she should not have one?" He followed the others out onto the highway.

She groaned. "I was just acting like I didn't want her to have it and then we were going to surprise her, but then you didn't want her to have it, so we were kind of hanging on until one of us could convince you. But her birthday is coming up in just a few days, so we decided to go ahead and give it to her once she said you were good with it."

Sam clung to his patience. "Wow. Why didn't you just tell me all that?"

"Because we wanted it to be a *surprise* and . . . I thought if I told you, you would ruin it."

He wanted to close his eyes and pray. Instead, he kept his gaze focused on the road and Grace's vehicle just in front of him. "No, you just didn't want to have to discuss it. It's easier to ask forgiveness than permission, right?" She'd said those words more than once during their marriage.

"Look, Sam . . ." At her tone, he knew the conversation was over. The two words she'd used as an intro to tell him she was leaving. *"Look, Sam, our marriage isn't working . . ."*

"Okay?" Claire asked, pulling him back to the present.

"Sorry," he said, "I missed that last part. What?"

"I *said*, I don't have time for this. Brett's running late and I have paperwork to finish. I've got to go, all right?"

What was the point? "Yeah, sure, but we're not done with this topic. You can't just—"

"Talk to you later. Bye."

"Claire! Don't hang—" He saved his breath. She'd already disconnected the call.

He tossed his phone into the cupholder and pulled into the parking place at a diner that looked like a hole in the wall but served delicious food.

A big juicy burger wouldn't do much to settle his anger at his ex, but at least it would taste good and give him a chance to figure out what he was going to say to Eleni and his mother-in-law when he got home.

■ ■ ■ ■

Grace was thankful for the two agents willing to watch her house tonight. Mark and another agent she'd worked with, Jade Carpenter, volunteered to take shifts. Mark said he'd stay until one in the morning and Jade would take over from there until Grace was ready to leave for work. Grace had offered for Mark to stay inside, but he'd chosen to stay in the car.

Probably because Sam had followed her home and now sat on her sofa, his eyes on the far wall, lost in thought.

Since she was starving, not having eaten much at dinner with her stomach in knots, she rummaged through her refrigerator and came up with two apples, a chicken breast, an old bag of salad, and a bottle of expired ranch dressing.

She shut the door and picked up her phone. "Sam?"

"Yeah?"

"You like Italian food?" He started to get up and she waved him back into his seat. "Stay put and keep that ice on your ankle. You can answer me from there."

He settled back with a grunt. "I'm not used to being grounded, but yes, I like Italian, why?"

"Because it's going to be a long night and I'm ordering delivery. There's a little place around the corner that's pretty fast."

He nodded. "That works. If they have chicken marsala, I'll take that."

He was saying all the right things, but she had the sense that his mind was on something else. She made the call to order the food, getting Mark his favorite dish of chicken Parmesan, since the least she could do was feed him, then walked back into her den to settle into the recliner next to the sofa.

"You okay?" she asked Sam.

He rubbed his chin, his eyes still on her fireplace. "Mm-hmm. Yeah. Why?"

"Because you don't seem okay. What's going on with you? Something to do with that family thing that could wait?"

Sam sighed and leaned his head back, transferring his gaze to the ceiling. "My daughter's stepfather bought her a phone."

"And that's a bad thing?"

"He did it without asking me about it." He looked at his phone. "And Eleni's mother didn't really have an explanation other than they wanted to surprise Eleni and thought I'd ruin the surprise if they told me."

"Oh. That's definitely a bad thing." She paused. "Should you be at home with your family right now?"

"No, I'll have to deal with it later, but for now, it's fine." He set his phone on the end table. "Eleni, who, as you know, has strep, is at home with my mother-in-law, who texted and said she was sleeping. Xander's been at football practice and will be out with the team for pizza." He rubbed a hand across his chin. "It'll be nine o'clock before he gets home. Which is why it was a good night to do dinner—which I was really looking forward to and am disappointed it didn't happen. But I enjoyed eating with you even if Mark and Jerry were there."

"At least Mark kept his snarkiness to himself."

"Yeah, there is that." He shot her a soft smile and Grace swallowed at the look. It was amazing how much his eyes said without his lips moving. They were saying, "I like you. I'm attracted to you. I want to spend time with you." Which was good because she felt the same, but it also meant she was going to have to open up and be vulnerable if they were going to have any kind of relationship.

Which was *not* good.

Not good at all.

Simply because she was really bad at that kind of thing. But she definitely would like to kiss him again if that short peck in the hospital was anything to go by.

And that probably was not good either. "Sam, I—"

Her phone buzzed, crashing into the moment. She snagged the device from her pocket and frowned. "It's the hospital." She swiped the screen. "Hello?"

"Is this Grace Billingsley?"

"It is."

"This is Yvonne Sims, one of your brother's nurses. I couldn't find anyone in the waiting room, but your number was the emergency contact."

Grace sucked in a breath. "Okay, what's going on?"

"Bobby took a turn for the worse and we've had to put him on a ventilator."

"Wait. What? I thought he was doing better."

"He was, but sometimes these things happen. I just wanted to let you know."

"Of course," she said. "Thank you. Please call me and let me know if there's any change. I'll be by to see him as soon as I can get there." She hung up and pressed a hand to her forehead. "Okay, I'm going to work some more on this profile, go over everything I've got, and—"

"What's going on with Bobby?"

Grace closed her eyes and filled him in.

"Aw, Grace, I'm sorry. Do we need to go?"

"No, not right now. Maybe if something changes." She clenched her fingers around the phone. "My parents left and didn't bother to let me know."

"What about your sister?"

"Lucy. I guess I should call her and see what's what. Give me a minute?"

"Of course."

Grace dialed the number and got Lucy's voice mail. "Hey, Luce, call me when you get this, please." She hung up and pressed her palms to her eyes, drew in a steadying breath, then let it out slowly through pursed lips. She repeated that four times, then lifted her head to find Sam watching her, concern in his eyes. "I'm okay," she said. "Working will help." She grabbed her laptop and opened up a maps page. "Let's look at this geographically." She put the four locations into the program and studied it. "I've had some training in the area—got to play with the software and everything—but I'm not an expert by any means. I'll see what I can do, then call in a real geographic profiler and have him double-check my work. But for now . . ." She pointed. "Well, they're all parks, and if the picture means anything, it looks like a Y."

"Any common areas?"

"Nothing that I could put my finger on and say this is where he lives or works." She tapped a few more keys. "Let's see what the software says. So, distance decay and the buffer zone put him here." She pointed at Dale City Baptist Church. "This area."

"Lots of houses in that area."

"Yeah, but maybe with the sketch, we'll get a hit. Where was the van stolen from?"

"Uh . . ." He looked at his phone. "The IKEA parking lot right off Potomac Mills Circle."

"Right." She entered that information into the program. "It's still saying right around the church area. I'll let Mark and Jerry know. This is just a preliminary profile, so . . . we'll see." She sent them the information and sat back to find Sam studying her. "What?"

"I like watching you work. You're amazing."

Heat rose from her neck into her cheeks. Maybe her dark skin would keep him from noticing. She cleared her throat. "Well, um, thank you." The doorbell rang, saving her from having to say anything further. She beelined for it. Mark was coming up behind the delivery man, and she handed him a takeout bag, then joined Sam in the kitchen. After a quick prayer of thanks for the food and a plea to catch the killer soon, Grace looked up. "So . . ."

Sam looked up. "Yes?"

"Tell me something."

"Okay." He jabbed the food with his fork.

"What do you do for fun?"

He paused mid-bite, chewed, then swallowed. "Fun?"

"Yeah, you know. That thing that isn't related to work and you smile while doing it. Bowling? Skydiving? Thrift store shopping?" She smiled at his grimace. "Okay, not thrift store shopping. So . . . what?"

"I like old movies, playing pick-up football games on the weekends with some buddies I go to church with. I like camping and hiking and cooking over an open flame." He shrugged. "Mostly, I get a kick out of cheering for my son, who plays football on Friday nights, or watching Eleni win spelling bees or land a double axel."

"Spelling bees?"

"She's crazy smart like that. Can spell words I never knew were in the dictionary."

"Wow. And a double axel?"

"Yes, she's been skating since she was three. And Xander has colleges looking at him." He rubbed a thumb over his lips, looking thoughtful. "I don't know how I got such great kids, but I'm grateful—especially considering who their grandfather is." He shifted and grimaced.

"Your ankle is bothering you." She stood. "I've got some ibuprofen in the cabinet. I have some pain meds from a migraine a little over a year ago if you want that, but you can't drive with it."

"I'll take the ibuprofen."

She got it and returned to slip the pills into his hand.

He took them, his gaze locking with hers. "You get migraines?"

"Every so often. As long as I eat right, get enough sleep, and don't stress about stuff, I'm fine."

He raised a brow. "Then you must get a migraine every day."

"I know, right?" She shrugged. "I take a daily pill to ward off the worst of them. I really do try to keep my stress level under control with various tactics, but right now, it's kind of through the roof." She pressed on the spot sending warning signals in her temple.

"Looks like you might need the painkiller more than I do."

"Naw, it'll pass." She turned back to her food. Catching a killer would make it pass faster.

CHAPTER
EIGHTEEN

An hour later, Grace had added more to the profile, including ex-cons with violent pasts who lived in the area. She sent that information to Mark and Jerry, then shut her laptop and pressed a hand to her rib cage. "I think I'm done for the day."

Sam checked the time and nodded. "Yeah, same here."

"But we made progress, I think."

"Yeah. It's a process, for sure."

He stood and took her hands. "Grace . . ."

"Sam . . ."

"I enjoyed kissing you."

She blinked, then smiled. "Do you need to hear that the feeling was mutual?"

"Yes, please."

She stood on tiptoe, cupped his cheeks, and pulled his lips to hers. This time the kiss lingered, deepened. He slid his hands around her waist—gently in deference to her bruised ribs—and settled her against him. He lost track of time while he immersed himself fully in the amazing experience of kissing Grace. Then it was time to stop.

And catch his breath.

He lifted his head, and she opened her eyes. "I think it's safe to say that I feel the same," she said.

He smiled. "And with that, I'd better wish you a good night and go home."

She nodded and he stepped away, his heart full of hope for the first time in years. Right now, he planned to ignore the little voice that wanted to tell him he wasn't right for her, that he came with too much baggage and she deserved someone who wasn't so messed up.

Because deep down, he knew that letting Grace in, being vulnerable with her, would change his life forever.

For the better.

And he desperately wanted that. He just prayed he could be the man she needed.

After a wave to Mark—who openly ignored him—he climbed into his car and headed home, hoping for a chance to catch up with Eleni. Surely, she had to wake up at some point before going back to bed.

Twenty minutes into his drive, with the kiss still lingering in his mind and on his lips, he noticed the car behind him coming up fast, his high beams on. Sam kept an eye on the mirrors, wondering why people didn't realize riding someone's tail usually didn't make them go faster. He finally turned into his neighborhood— and the person followed him, the lights blinding him once more. He frowned, his mental alarms going off. There was no way he was going home and leading this person to his residence. Then again, it could be a neighbor who wasn't being very neighborly. He pulled to the side of the road and waved the driver around him.

But the other car pulled to a stop behind him.

A chill crawled up his spine and his hand crept toward his weapon. Then the car slammed into reverse and backed up, swerved into the drive next to it, then sped back out of the subdivision.

Sam was tempted to follow, but he'd caught the license plate in the rearview mirror. Whispering it to himself, he grabbed a pen from the console and wrote it on his hand.

He called the terminal operator at the office and requested the info.

"The car is registered to a Douglas Mason."

"Reported stolen?"

"No. Not yet."

"Thanks."

Douglas Mason. Why was that name familiar? "Anything on him?"

"Nothing that I can find."

"Okay, thank you." Sam hung up and wracked his brain. The name was pretty generic. "Douglas Mason. Doug. Doug Mason. Dougie." Saying the name and the variations out loud didn't bring anything to mind either.

With a loud sigh, he drove home, then pulled into the garage next to Vanessa's car. Xander wasn't home yet. He sent a text to his son, asking him to check in with him, then let his finger hover over the app that would tell him his son's location. He tapped it and saw that the kid was still at the pizza restaurant.

Xander responded.

Be home in about thirty minutes.

Sam smiled, his fingers typing his response.

Great. Be careful.

Duh.

With a shake of his head, grateful that he could trust his son, Sam climbed out of the car, wincing when he put weight on his ankle, but at least it held him. When he limped into the kitchen, the lights were off, but a warm glow came from the den, and he found Vanessa curled up in a chair in front of the fire.

She looked up. "Hey there."

"Hey." He dropped onto the couch and propped his foot up on the coffee table.

She raised a brow. "That's legal now?" She referred to his rule of no feet on the furniture.

"Exigent circumstances."

Now she frowned and leaned closer. "Your shoe isn't all the way on. What did you do?"

Her powers of observation never failed to make him smile. "Jumped over a tree trunk chasing a guy and came down on a root."

"Ouch. Guess you're not as young as you used to be."

He snorted. "Didn't have a thing to do with age. Just a stupid root."

She rose. "Let me get some ice for that."

"Vanessa, I can do that."

"I know you can, but I also know you probably won't. You need some ibuprofen too?"

"No, I had some at Grace's."

When she came back with the ice pack, he slid his shoe the rest of the way off and settled the pack on the ankle. "Thanks. How's Eleni?"

"Better."

"I hear she had a visitor this afternoon. And I don't mean your friend."

Vanessa sighed. "She did."

"And no one thought I needed to know about that?" He kept his tone even, as he didn't want her to think he was throwing any accusations her way. He wasn't.

"Oh, I definitely thought you should know."

"Why didn't you text or call me?"

She chewed on the corner of her lip. A sure sign she was stressed. He waited.

"Claire asked me not to."

He huffed a short laugh. "She thought I wouldn't find out?"

"No." Her smile was wry. "I think she was just wanting to delay the inevitable confrontation she knew was coming with you." She shrugged. "And besides, I knew as soon as they left, Eleni was going to text you and you'd know."

"She did."

"I figured." She rubbed a hand down her cheek. "Do I need to apologize?"

"No. You're walking a fine line. Living with me, but not wanting to completely alienate your daughter. I get it."

"Well, I drew the line, so . . ."

"Yeah." He hesitated, then changed the subject. "So, how's your doctor friend?"

She met his gaze and smiled. "He's a nice man. You'd like him."

"Am I going to get to meet him anytime soon?"

"Maybe."

"Does he have a last name?"

"He does."

Sam laughed. "Are you going to tell me?"

"Only if you promise not to do a background check on him or something."

"Oh, come on, Vanessa, that would be abusing my position. I'd never do that."

She studied him. "Hmm. Okay then. His name is Connor Jackson. He's fifty-nine years old, loves the Lord, and rides a Harley."

"A Harley? As in motorcycle?"

"Yes."

"Please tell me you don't ride it."

"Of course I do." Her eyes lit up. "It's exhilarating."

Sam groaned. "I think I need to go to bed."

They fell silent once more, and he closed his eyes while fatigue washed over him.

"How's Grace?" she asked, breaking into the quiet. "I liked her. And so did Eleni."

He smiled. He couldn't help it. Then he frowned. There was so much he needed to process when it came to Grace Billingsley that he didn't know where to start. "She's fine. She was attacked today, and I followed her home to make sure she got there safe."

Vanessa gasped. "Attacked?"

He opened his eyes at the horrified word. "Uh yeah. Sorry. I must be more tired than I thought." He didn't usually just let those words bypass the filters. "It's a long story, but it ended well, so it's all good."

"And that's how you hurt your ankle?"

"It is." He drew in a deep breath, slid his foot off the table, and leaned forward, clasping his hands between his knees. "Forget that for a minute. I need to ask you a question."

"Sure."

"What would you think if I answered the phone the next time my father called?"

He wouldn't have thought it possible, but her eyes went wider. "Why would you do that?"

"Because I may need his help to catch a killer."

She gaped, then snapped her lips together and shook her head. "Oh, son, I don't know if you want to open that can of worms."

"I know I don't *want* to," he said, "but he's called every day since they moved him to his current *local address*." He framed the last two words with air quotes. "I have no idea what he wants because I don't listen to his messages, I delete them."

"But?"

He rose and paced to the French doors that led out to the deck. The deck he'd built last year with every intention of entertaining, barbecuing, hanging out with his kids . . .

"But I wonder if I should. Maybe it would bring closure."

"Can you actually have closure in this kind of situation?"

A valid question. "I have no idea, but I think I have to find out."

"Well, hon, that's your decision, of course. I'm not sure I'm in favor of it."

"I'm not sure I am either."

The garage door opened, then shut, and Xander's familiar gait echoed from the kitchen. Sam waited for the sound of the refrigerator opening. It came a mere second later. The teen was so predictable. "Thought you just came from the pizza place?" he called.

"I did. Now I want ice cream."

"You didn't have a milkshake?" That particular restaurant made the best on the planet.

"Of course." His son stepped into the den, spoon in one hand, carton of Rocky Road in the other. "But it was a long ride home and now I'm hungry again."

"It was a fifteen-minute drive," Vanessa said.

Xander nodded. "Exactly. An eternity." He dropped onto the couch and opened the ice cream. "How's the munchkin?"

"Better, according to your grandmother," Sam said. "How was practice?"

"Fine. I think we're going to tear it up Friday night. You'll be there, right?" He scooped a huge bite into his mouth.

"Wouldn't miss it. And your sister's party is Saturday night at the Skate Palace."

His son swallowed. "Right. About that. Can I at least ask Bryce to come? I don't think I'm up to hanging out with ten preteens."

A reasonable request. "Of course."

"Thanks." Xander finished off the ice cream and bounded to his feet. "Okay, now I've got to study before I go to bed. See you guys in the morning."

"Night, son. Love you."

"Love you, Xander," Vanessa said. "Leave the carton. I'll throw it away for you."

"Thanks, Nessie."

Xander disappeared up the stairs and Sam grabbed the ice pack, then rose with a pained groan. "I'm going to check in with Eleni."

"She's asleep, Sam."

"I guarantee you she's not."

"You think she's texting her friends?"

"Absolutely." He made his way slowly up the stairs and opened Eleni's door. The nightlight under the window bathed the room in a soft glow. Her phone was plugged in and resting on her nightstand and it looked like she was actually asleep. Huh. "El?" he whispered. "You asleep?"

She drew in a deep breath and blinked. "Dad?" she croaked.

"Yeah, sorry. I didn't mean to wake you."

"S'okay." She rubbed her eyes. "I'm just tired, so trying to sleep a lot. The doctor said it would help me get better faster. I don't want to miss my party."

"Good for you."

She sat up. "I'm sorry if you're mad about the phone. I know you didn't exactly say it was okay."

"But you told your mother I did?"

"No, but I told her you said you were considering it. I guess she took that to mean it was okay."

He picked up the device protected by a pretty pink case that had her name engraved on the back. "Do you mind if I make sure the parental controls are set?"

She frowned. "Okay. What does that mean?"

"It means, I set it so you can't access certain things that can be harmful for girls your age."

"Oh. Okay. But I'll still be able to text my friends? And you?"

"Of course."

She smiled and lay back down. "Okay, then."

"I'm going to be honest with you, too, El. I'll be able to track your location."

"That's fine. I don't go anywhere that would get me yelled at anyway." She yawned. "And don't worry. I won't change the password." She gave it to him while he pondered the fact that his daughter had matured in the time it had taken him to blink.

"Who are you and what did you do with my kid?"

She chuckled.

Working quickly, Sam applied the safety measures, memorized her password, and set the phone back on the table. She'd already fallen back to sleep. He kissed her on the head, grateful her skin felt normal to the touch, then tucked the covers around her. He glanced at the phone once more. He still wasn't sure he liked it, but he'd give it some time. Maybe it would be fine. He had to let her start growing up at some point.

After checking on Xander to find him sprawled on his bed,

books and laptop open, Sam started toward his own room, then stopped. Looked at the door at the end of the hall and headed toward it. He opened it and stepped inside the attic. The chill wrapped around him, but he ignored it and let his gaze land on the large box in the far corner. The label read "Peter's stuff— Box 1."

CHAPTER
NINETEEN

Thursday morning came way too fast for Grace. She felt like she'd just closed her eyes when the alarm sounded. With a groan, she shut off the incessant buzzing and—as carefully as possible—rolled out of bed and into the shower. She checked on Bobby to find that he was doing better but still unconscious. She then called Lucy.

"Hey," her sister said in greeting.

"Hey."

Silence fell and Grace cleared her throat. "So, I checked on Bobby. They said he was doing better."

"Good."

"Mom and Dad aren't there."

"And I'm not either." Lucy sighed. "I know it sounds cold, Grace, but he's got to stop being allowed to disrupt our lives, and the only way that's going to happen is if we do something to stop it."

Grace closed her eyes and pressed her thumb against the left side of her head where it was starting to throb. "It's not cold, Luce. It's . . . reality."

"Exactly." Lucy sounded surprised that Grace agreed. "So, you're not going to let him come live with you?"

"No. I tried that once. It didn't go so well."

Silence. "You did?"

"Mm-hmm." Why had she even mentioned it?

"You never said."

"I know. It was right after he got out of rehab for the first time. I told him he could stay with me until he found a job and built up some savings."

"Whoa."

"Everything was fine for about a month, then he relapsed and ended up stealing the pearl necklace Grandma left me."

Lucy's gasp echoed through the line. "Grace," she whispered, "what?"

"When I realized he was high after coming home from work, I called his boss and found out he'd been fired the week before. I immediately checked my jewelry box, and the necklace was missing. I found it at a pawn shop." It hadn't been hard to track it down. Bobby had gone to the one nearest her home. "Next time it was the diamond earrings Uncle Steve got me on my twenty-first birthday."

And the next time it was the attack on her landlord.

"Why in the world did you let him stay after the necklace theft?"

"You know why." Grace cleared her throat. "Anyway, no. He won't be living here when he gets released from the hospital. I'll help him find a place and—"

"Stop it, Grace. You're not responsible for him."

"Yes," she said, "yes, I am."

"Him being a junkie is his fault, not yours."

Grace wanted to wrap herself up in that statement and let herself accept it, because while her mind knew it was absolutely true, her heart had a hard time believing it. "I don't want to get into it, Lucy. Mom and Dad blame me, and I blame myself, so I guess everything else isn't important." She glanced at the clock and suppressed a groan. An incoming text from Mark sent her phone buzzing in her hand. "Look, I've got to go. Let me know if you or anyone goes up to the hospital and if anything changes with his condition."

For a moment, Lucy didn't say anything, then she blew out another loud sigh. "Fine. Bye, Grace. Be careful catching the bad guys. Love you."

"Love you, too, baby sis. Talk later." She hung up and refused to let the tears fall. Drawing in a deep breath, she opened the text from Mark.

> Hair found in Sonya Griffith's car matches the DNA found at your house. Still no idea who it belongs to.

But at least they had a match. Now to find the person.

> And nothing on the van that would tell us who stole it, but Gina Baker's DNA was in it and so was Carol Upton's. We're definitely on the right track, that's all I've got for now.

> Whoa. Okay. Thanks.

Setting her phone aside, she ignored the pain in her shoulders and ribs and finished drying her hair. She pulled it into a tight ponytail, refusing to think about Bobby and what would come when he was well enough to leave the hospital. Instead, she focused on the case. They really needed Hal to wake up.

When she walked into the kitchen, she stopped short, visions of the killer's attack grabbing at her mind. She saw him at the door, the shears in his hand, the smell of whatever soap he used so strong it triggered a headache. Her heart skipped into overdrive and sweat broke out on her brow while her breathing came in short pants.

"Stop," she whispered. "It's just a panic attack. PTSD. Whatever. He's not there." She pressed a hand to her head and waited. It took a minute, but the feeling finally eased, and she snagged her weapon, then walked to the window to look out. Jade Carpenter was standing beside her vehicle stretching and patting her cheeks.

Guilt hit, then faded. Grace had had her fair share of sleepless nights doing the same thing for other agents and hadn't regretted it one bit. She filled two mugs with coffee, then waved the agent in.

Jade stepped inside with a frown. "Everything okay?"

"I'm fine." She handed her the mug. "Figured you could use this. Cream and sugar are on the counter."

"Oh, bless you. Thank you. I take it black." She sipped and sighed with her eyes closed. "Okay, now I might be able to function a little more efficiently."

A car pulled up outside, and Grace went to the window once more to see Sam stop at the curb. She smiled at Jade. "You're welcome to take off. Sam and I can handle it from here."

"You're sure?"

"Absolutely."

"Okay, I think I'll grab a couple hours of sleep before I head to the office."

Jade poured her remaining coffee in the sink, then headed for the front door. She and Sam exchanged greetings, and Sam stepped inside. "Good morning."

"Hey," she said over the sudden thudding of her heart and a breathlessness that caught her off guard. Her reaction amused her. She'd never been one for the warm fuzzies, but then she'd met Sam . . . "I didn't expect to see you this morning."

"I need to run something by you."

"Sure. Come on in the kitchen. Coffee?"

"Always."

Once they were seated at the kitchen table, she pushed a cinnamon roll in front of him. "Help yourself."

He did.

"How's the ankle?" she asked.

"Swollen and sore, but I've got it wrapped, so I'm doing all right. It was just sprained and not even that bad. It's ugly, though."

"Happy to hear it. Uh, that it's not bad." She wanted to face palm. Why was she all of a sudden so awkward around him? Just because they'd shared a few kisses? She cleared her throat and ordered her pulse—and emotions—to settle down.

After one bite and some longer-than-necessary chewing, he finally set the roll down, took a swig of coffee, and looked at her.

She waited, all awkwardness gone now in the face of his seriousness.

"I need to visit my father," he finally said. "Will you go with me?"

Grace blinked. "I did *not* expect that to come out of your mouth. Why?" Why go see him, and why ask her to go with him?

"I think I need to, but I don't want to go alone and . . ." His voice trailed off and she stayed quiet, letting him figure out what he wanted to say. Finally, he looked away and sighed. "I suppose you think I'm a huge coward."

"What? Not at all. I can't imagine having to confront my serial-killer father. My father didn't kill anyone and I still don't like being around him most days."

He raised a brow and a slight smile curved his lips. "Thanks. So, that means you'll go with me?"

"Of course."

The smile faded. "I have one more request."

"Okay." '

"I have something in my car I'd like your help with if you have the time and don't mind."

"That was an awful formal way to ask."

He chuckled, then turned serious once more. "I have a couple of boxes that belonged to my father. When he asked me to sell the house and put the money into an account with my name on it too, I agreed. I was going to have a moving company come in and pack everything up, but my aunt, Dad's sister, asked to do it. She and my mother were very close, and I suppose she felt she owed it to me and my sister."

Grace straightened. "Wait, you have a sister?"

"I haven't mentioned her?"

Had he? "No, I don't think so."

"Well, I do. We keep in touch a few times a year but otherwise don't have a lot of contact with each other. For various reasons. Anyway, that's not important. Once my aunt Doreen got everything packed, we held an auction for the furniture and some other stuff, but she kept some things she, for whatever reason, thought I might want some day."

"And that's what you've got in your car."

"Yes. There are three boxes."

"And you want my help going through them?"

He nodded. "Last night, something weird happened. Someone followed me into my subdivision. I pulled over and was about to get out and confront them, but they drove off in a hurry. I got the plate and ran it. It came back registered to a guy by the name of Douglas Mason. That ring a bell for you by any chance?"

"No."

"Well, it did me, but I couldn't remember where I'd seen the name. Still can't. But I looked him up. He's not in the system and owns a local restaurant that's been in business for over twenty years."

"Doesn't really raise any red flags, does it?"

"No, but like I said, I've seen his name somewhere, I just can't place it."

"Recently?"

He shrugged. "I don't know. I need to go talk to him, see if I can figure it out. And ask him why he was so rude last night." He paused. "Honestly, if his name didn't spark something, I wouldn't think much else about it."

"Want me to go with you to talk to the guy?"

"Sure."

"Now? Or after we go through the boxes?"

He thought about it. "After."

"You really think you'll find something in them?"

"That's what I'm going to find out."

■ ■ ■ ■

Sam honestly had no idea why he decided Grace should be the one to go through his father's boxes with him. He was just glad she'd said yes.

The first box had held some of his father's favorite shirts and sweaters. He'd tossed those into the get-rid-of pile.

The second box, a file box, held things like Sam's birth certificate, his parents' marriage license, various pictures of him and his sister as babies.

Grace had gotten a kick out of those. He'd rolled his eyes and moved the box to the keep pile. His kids might want them one day. Once they knew the truth about their family tree.

The third box was smaller and not nearly as organized. "It looks like someone just scraped things off the desk, then dumped out the drawers on top." He picked up the first paper. A power bill. Dated the day of his father's arrest. He set it aside.

"I know you were instrumental in stopping your father," Grace said, "that you turned over the evidence needed to have him arrested, but no one knows the facts." She pulled out another bill and set it on top of the other. "How did you work up the courage to do that? Or was it something you even thought twice about? Or is that a dumb question?"

"It's not a dumb question." He rubbed his eyes, then looked at her. "I was twenty-six years old. I had just started my residency and was going into family practice. Eleni was to be born any minute and Xander was four years old. One night, my sister, who was sixteen, had an acute appendicitis attack. My dad, who was actually in town giving the nanny a break, took her to the hospital and called me. I was almost finished with my shift when they came in. She went to surgery pretty quickly and within an hour was in recovery. Thankfully, it was routine. Easy. No rupture, no major infection. But Dad was a mess, refused to leave her side . . ." He sighed. "He really put on a show."

"You don't think he was genuinely concerned?"

"I have no idea. I don't know what he feels—if he feels anything. He wants what he wants, and he's not above using people—or emotion—to get it."

"What did he want that night? What could he gain by being the concerned father?"

Sam shrugged. "I have no idea. I've revisited that night several times, trying to pinpoint what it was he thought he could get from his big show of concern, but the only thing I could come up with was that he really did care." He drew in a deep breath and let it out slowly. "And I know that's a farce because the only person he cares about is himself. At least, I think so. Like I said, I can't distance myself enough to make a proper judgment."

She nodded.

"Anyway," he said, "when Harmony woke up, we got her transferred to her room for the night and she wanted her phone. That, and a few other things that no one grabbed on their way out the door." He cleared his throat. "I volunteered to go get everything, because it was clear Dad didn't want to go anywhere." Sam pulled out more papers and started organizing them absently. "I got to the house—my childhood home—and went straight to her room to find her phone. I didn't see it, so I kept searching. Finally found a phone on Dad's bed, but I didn't recognize it." He swallowed hard. The memories were never very far from the surface when he allowed himself to go there. Which was almost never. "For some reason . . . I don't know . . . I tapped the screen. He either didn't have a passcode on it or it had been removed. Either way, the wallpaper picture came up. It was a selfie of a girl with two of her friends. I recognized the picture from the news. As you remember, the serial killer—the Cell Phone Killer—was the top of every news story at that time. Cell Phone Killer," he muttered. "Such a dumb name. Anyway, the hunt, the plea for tips, the warnings not to let your teens go out alone—all of that. And there I was staring at one of the pictures that had been flashed across national television."

"Oh, Sam."

"It really didn't register for a minute what I was looking at, then the news reports started playing in my head like a broken record. As well as the picture of her holding her phone with the personalized case." He waved a hand at his own phone. "You know, she'd decorated it with stick-on bling . . . jewels and stuff."

"Yeah, I remember that."

"Anyway, I can't tell you the feeling that came over me. I knew my father was the Cell Phone Killer." He shuddered just saying the words. He frowned so hard he could feel his brows protesting. "How horrible is it that I didn't even try to explain it? Like he could have found it and planned to turn it over to the authorities or . . . or . . . whatever. *Something.* But I didn't. I just . . . knew. My father, a man I loved and admired and respected, was killing young girls. I threw up until there was nothing left."

"Sam, you don't have to—"

"No, let me finish. You need to know it all if we're going to be"—he met her gaze—"whatever we're going to be."

She snapped her lips together and nodded.

"So, lying there on the bathroom floor, I knew I had to do something, but it was like my brain was trying to slog through weird mental quicksand."

"Yeah, I can only imagine," Grace said, her voice soft.

He pulled in another steadying breath. "I finally got myself together somewhat and started searching. I found a box in his closet. It had a padlock on it. I knew where he kept a spare set of keys, got them, and the key to it was on there. I opened the box and there were nine more phones in there. One was a flip phone."

"That belonged to Mary Elise," Grace said.

He nodded. "I think she was his first victim. It was the oldest phone, so . . . maybe. Anyway, I called the FBI number that had been flashing across everyone's television screen and asked for the detectives in charge of the case. Told the woman who answered the phone that I knew who the Cell Phone Killer was. The detectives came out to the house, I gave them the phones, and . . . that was that. They arrested my dad at the hospital as he was walking out of Harmony's room to . . ." He spread his hands. "I have no idea why he was in the hall." He shook his head. "But I'm glad Harmony didn't see him get arrested. She slept through the whole thing."

"Did he know it was you?"

He nodded. "I got there right as they were leading him out of the hospital in cuffs. He looked at me and said, 'You found the phone I left on the bed, huh?' I said, 'Yeah.' Then he gave me this weird little smile, told me to take care of Harmony, and let the agents tuck him into the back of the Bucar. The next day, Eleni was born."

"Wow. Sam, I have no words."

"I don't either, to be honest." He pulled an envelope out of the box, noting it had his father's name on it.

In his mother's handwriting.

CHAPTER
TWENTY

Listening to Sam had been heartbreaking. Turning in his father had taken a strength that she really didn't have a name for. Could she have done it? She wasn't sure.

He set aside an envelope and kept going through the box.

"It was shortly after he was arrested," he said, "that I changed my residency to psychiatry. Unfortunately, that extended my residency one more year since I had to kind of backtrack. Claire was *not* happy. In fact, she was downright furious. We got into a screaming match one night, and I asked her why she couldn't just support me and understand that this was what I needed to do."

"And?"

"She said fine. For me to do what I needed to do and that she was going to do what she needed to do. I had no idea what that meant, and honestly, I'm not sure I really cared. I left the house for a while, and when I came back, she was asleep. I figured we'd make up in the morning and crashed on the couch. But morning came and we got busy with the kids. We didn't talk about the fight, and she never again brought up the subject of me being gone all the time while she was trying to raise two kids." He glanced at the envelope, then dug into the box once more. "This is just old bills and stuff that he never got around to paying."

"What's the envelope you keep looking at?"

"Something I'm going to have to read, but I'm not sure I want to just yet. It's my mom's handwriting."

"Oh. I see. Okay."

He studied the envelope, then went on with his story. "On Eleni's third birthday, I found out Claire was sleeping with my best friend, Brett."

Grace sucked in a breath and stared. "I'm sorry, what?"

He pursed his lips and nodded. "Yeah. I know. It sounds terrible. And it was. Xander was seven and asked me why Brett was sleeping on my side of the bed. It didn't take a genius to figure out what that meant. I confronted Claire and she didn't even bother to deny it. Just said that she'd done what she had to do."

"Oh, Sam, I don't even know what to say to that."

He shook his head. "There's nothing *to* say. But while I was beyond furious, betrayed, shattered, devastated . . . pick one—or all—I can't blame Claire for everything. I was just as responsible for the demise of my marriage as she was. More so, probably. I had spiraled into a depression and was doing nothing but residency, coming home to eat and sleep, and then going back to the hospital. And the media . . . it was terrible during the time leading up to the trial, during, and for a long time after."

"That's why you changed your name, of course."

"That and the fact that patients didn't want the son of a serial killer in the same room with them, much less treating them. It was a legit nightmare. But"—he picked up the envelope and eyed it again—"in spite of everything, I managed get through my residency and was even the top resident. I pushed myself to the very limit. To be the absolute best."

"To prove you weren't your father."

He blinked. "Yes. And in the interim, I was still the worst husband and father ever. Well, okay, maybe not quite as bad as *my* father. But, still bad. My wife found someone else, and my kids didn't really know who I was."

"What happened to turn that around?"

"My six-year-old daughter called my best friend Daddy in front of me."

Grace winced.

"It was bad. But it was also the best thing that could have happened. It woke me up. I started seeing a therapist." He laughed. "Can you picture it? The therapist needed a therapist."

"You know as well as I do that's not terribly uncommon."

His smile faded. "I know. It just felt weird. Shameful." He shook his head. "I can't believe I'm telling you all this. But I think I need to. As a reminder."

"For?"

"For when I talk to my father for the first time since he was led out of the courtroom after the judge read the jury's guilty-on-all-charges verdict."

"You really think he knows something?"

He picked up the envelope once more and lifted the flap. "Yes, I do. And now"—he pulled the single sheet of paper from the envelope—"I suppose I should find out what my mother wrote to him."

"How long has she been gone?"

"She left when I was sixteen and Harmony was six. My dad's sister, Doreen, stepped in to help for a couple of months after Mom left, but she had her own family to take care of."

"So, what did you do when your father traveled?"

He shrugged. "I was driving, so I could get Harmony to school. She was in one of those after-school programs, and I picked her up when I got done."

Grace's heart hurt for the teen who'd had so much responsibility dumped on his shoulders way too soon. "I can't imagine how hard that was."

"It was incredibly hard, but when I got into medical school, Dad was so proud. He finally hired a nanny for Harmony and pushed me to excel in school to graduate with honors." He paused. "At least he seemed proud. He was probably trying to figure out how to use that to his advantage as well, though. Honestly, I'm tired of thinking about him. Trying to look back and figure out when he was manipulating me and . . ." He shook his head. "It doesn't matter at this point."

"Where's your mother now?"

"I don't know."

Grace gaped. Then snapped her lips shut. "You don't know?"

"No. She left and never tried to contact us again. My dad was furious. Adamant that we let her go. He said if she didn't want us, we didn't want her and that was that." He looked at the piece of paper he held. "I believed him."

"Of course you did," Grace said, moving closer to place her hand on his. "You were a teenager, grieving the loss of your mother."

"But that's the thing. He's lied about everything my entire life. What if he lied about my mother too?"

■ ■ ■ ■

Sam wasn't sure where the thought came from—or why he hadn't thought it before. Probably because he did his best not to think about anything related to that time in his life. He unfolded the paper with his mother's handwriting. "Well, this wasn't what I was expecting to find in the box, but I suppose I should quit stalling and see what it is."

Grace stood. "I'm going to grab something to drink. You want anything?"

"Sure. I'll take whatever you have."

"Water, tea, soda, or coffee?"

"A soda sounds good." He rarely drank soft drinks because it had been ingrained in him from childhood by his father that they were terrible for the body.

He felt like a soda today.

Grace left, and he had a feeling her timing was deliberate. She was giving him space to read the letter without her sitting there watching him. Taking a deep breath, he focused on his mother's words.

Peter, I can't do this anymore. I've tried. You know I've tried, but you're never going to give up your other women and I've just come to realize that. One day, the children are going to find out. I'm actually shocked Sam hasn't figured it out yet, but I suppose as a traveling photographer, you can hide it from him more so than anyone else would. But he's not stupid. He'll see it one day. And I won't be able to look him in the eye and give him a good reason as to why I stayed. When you get home, we'll be gone. Please don't try to find us. You don't want us and we both know it. There's something wrong with you on a level I can't reach. Something deep inside that needs more help than I can give. I love you—or at least I did. I'm not sure I do anymore. But I love our children enough to be brave for them. Get help, Peter, for yourself. If you do that, then maybe one day our marriage can be restored. Until then . . . Whit.

Whit. Whitney Romanos. His mother.

Sam's throat clogged. His nose ran, and he grabbed a tissue from the box on the end table while he tried to hold the tears back in his burning eyes.

"Sam?"

He stilled, refused to look up. Refused to breathe. Finally, he dragged in a breath. "She didn't leave," he said, forcing the words through his tight throat. "She didn't leave."

"What?" Grace walked over to set the drinks on the coffee table and take her place on the floor beside him once more.

He cleared his throat. "All these years . . ." He passed her the letter and worked on controlling the rage pulsing through him. "He killed her. I know he did."

Grace stayed silent while she read, then her eyes rose to meet his. "Oh, Sam."

The dam broke and he ducked his head to hide his tears. A sob slipped out and then Grace's arms were around him. The brief thought that he should be mortified blipped across his mind, but all he could focus on was the fact that he knew without a doubt his mother was dead. Grace tightened her grip around his shaking body and pulled him to her so his forehead was resting on her shoulder. He squeezed his eyes shut and worked to get a grip on his emotions.

"Let it out," she whispered. "Just let it out, Sam. Don't be embarrassed or ashamed. Cry it out."

So he did.

Finally, he sucked in a breath, wiped his face with the hem of his shirt, and looked up. She met his gaze, the pain in her eyes searing him to the core. She hurt for him and wanted to do whatever she could to take it away from him. Never having had that before from a woman—from anyone, really—he wasn't sure what he was supposed to do with it. She pressed tissues into his hand, and he used them to blow his nose. "Oh man, I'm sorry."

"Don't apologize. Contrary to popular belief, real men *do* cry."

He nodded. "Yeah."

"And most of them use their shirt to mop up."

A watery laugh escaped him, and he shook his head at the fact that he could chuckle. Only with Grace.

She let her arms slide from around him and sat back. He instantly missed her touch.

"She was leaving," Grace said, her voice low, "and she was taking you and Harmony with her."

"But he killed her before she had a chance." He let his mind spin back to the day he came home from school to find his father sitting in the dark den.

"I was sixteen. I stayed late after school that day for a chemistry club meeting." He shot her a glance. "Yeah, I was a nerd."

"That's not nerdy." She gave him a gentle smile that helped him continue.

"Dad was supposed to be on a weeklong photography thing leading a group through some national or state park in Alaska." He paused. "I don't remember which one. I should remember that, but I don't."

Her hand crept over his and squeezed.

"But when I got home, he was sitting in the den, sipping on a scotch. I asked him what he was doing home, and he said the trip had been canceled and that when he'd walked back in the door, Mom had suitcases packed and was leaving. She had a note that she was going to leave, and he showed it to me. It was in her handwriting, but"—he sat up and straightened the one he'd unconsciously crumpled—"it wasn't this one."

"What did the other note say?"

"Something similar, but without the mention of his affairs or taking us with her. And it had the added sting that she didn't want to be a wife and mother anymore, was leaving, and we weren't to try and find her."

He stood and Grace rose to her feet as well.

"I've got to go." He waved a hand at the mess on her floor. "Um, could I get that later? I'm so sorry, I just need to go."

"Wait, Sam, hold on. I'm coming with you."

"You don't even know where I'm going."

"Of course I do. You're going to see your father."

He gave her a short nod. "I am."

"Well, you're not going alone."

Sam stilled, raised a hand to touch her cheek, felt the silky texture under his fingers. His eyes dropped to her lips and he heard her breath hitch.

He dropped his hand.

What was he thinking? *Get it together, man.* He cleared his throat. "Do we take separate cars to the prison? I guess from there, I can track down Mason."

She studied him for a brief moment, and something like sadness flickered in her eyes before she nodded. "Yeah, I may head to the office when we're done. I'm finished with the profile for now, but there are always other cases. Unfortunately."

"I'll follow you and make sure . . ." He waved a hand and decided not to state the obvious.

"Yeah. Thanks."

"Want to hit a drive-thru for something to eat?"

"Please."

After they swung through a local chain drive-thru, Sam called ahead to let them know they were coming. They ate while they drove, his attention on the area around him and his eyes on Grace, ready to alert her to anything that might indicate danger.

Fortunately, they made it to the prison without incident, but he couldn't help wondering if the killer was just biding his time, waiting for the right moment to strike again. He snorted. Of course he was. But he fully expected his father to be able to shed some light on that—whether he would or not was another thing altogether.

Once they were through security, Sam led the way to the interrogation room and stopped next to the guard. "He's in there?"

The man nodded and Sam sucked in a ragged breath. "All right, thanks."

Grace stepped forward and gripped his arm. "Sam, be careful. Don't let him get in your head."

He closed his eyes and soaked in her words. "Yeah. Don't let him get in my head." He blew out a low breath. If only it wasn't too late.

CHAPTER
TWENTY-ONE

Grace stood on the other side of the mirrored glass and watched Sam enter the room. He'd asked her to listen in just in case Peter said something she could use in her profile. Sam sat opposite the father he'd once loved. The man who'd betrayed him and had most likely killed his mother.

Sam's face held no expression, and she wasn't sure if that was a good thing or not.

His father's face, however, was wreathed in smiles.

Sam leaned back in his chair, and she almost expected him to cross his arms, but he linked his hands together and set them in his lap.

"Sam, my son, you finally came."

The door opened and Grace turned to see Mark and Jerry step inside. "Who decided this was a good idea?" Mark snapped.

"Sam did. He's on the list of approved visitors and he has a right to visit his father. The man's been asking him to for a year now."

Mark scowled, and Jerry finished off a protein bar before tossing the wrapper into the trash can near the door. "We miss anything?"

"No, not yet. They're just kind of sitting there staring at each other while Romanos waits for Sam to talk to him."

■ ■ ■ ■

Sam sat on the other side of the table and studied the man he'd come to hate. "Well, you got me here. What do you want?"

"I can't believe it," his father said. His eyes roamed Sam's face like he was drinking in and memorizing every detail.

"You've called nonstop for over a year now."

"Well, you know I've always been persistent. That and good behavior is what got me moved here."

"Hmm. I don't suppose your money hurt."

He shrugged. "Why have it if it doesn't work in your favor?"

"So, Doreen is still distributing it as you see fit?"

"Why have a sister if it doesn't work in your favor?"

"Right. Well, why don't you tell me what's so important that you'd chase me for a year to get me here."

"I want to see my grandchildren."

Sam bit off the instant no that formed on his lips. He leaned forward, unlinked his hands, and dropped them to the seat to clamp the edge. It was the only way he was able to keep himself from bolting across the table to wrap his hands around his father's neck.

"Well," the man said, breaking the extended silence, "at least it wasn't an immediate no. Although, I'd wager that was the first thing that popped in your head."

"Why?" Sam asked, forcing the word out.

His father lifted his hands and scratched his clean-shaven chin while his eyes bored holes into Sam's. It took all of Sam's training to keep his calm facade in place.

"Why?" his father finally said. "You really have to ask why? They're my *grand*children. I have a right to know them."

Sam laughed. A harsh sound that echoed in the small room. "You have a right? You gave up all rights when you decided to kill children."

"They weren't children. I'd never harm an innocent child." He honestly looked put out that Sam would accuse him of such a thing.

"They were all somebody's child." He paused. "Someone's *grandchild*."

He thought his father might have suppressed a slight flinch, but then decided he was imagining things. Seeing things that he might *want* to see. Like remorse or regret.

"The people I killed were bad women," he finally said. "They caused a lot of pain to a lot of people."

"Like Mom?"

The man froze. "What do you mean?"

"Mom left her family. She abandoned us, right? So, that would make her a bad woman."

"Yes, why?"

"Just trying to find some kind of connection, trying to understand your reasoning. You killed those other women because . . . something to do with Mom?"

A low chuckle containing an uneasy edge came from his father. "That doesn't matter, Sam. All of that is water under the bridge."

"I see." Not exactly, but he'd let it go for the moment even though the question "Did you kill my mother?" hovered on the edge of his lips. He swallowed it. First, he needed information about a killer still out there on the streets. "Okay, well, I have a couple more questions if you don't mind."

"Ask them and we'll see if I mind, then we'll circle back to seeing my grandchildren."

Sam didn't acknowledge that statement. "Do you know someone named Douglas Mason?"

The flare of his nostrils and the slight widening of his eyes would have been missed by anyone else, but Sam was watching for it.

"No, don't think I've heard of him."

If Sam didn't know the man as well as he did, if he didn't suspect every word out of his mouth was tainted in some way, he would have believed him. He let it go for the moment. His father didn't want him to know that *he* knew who Douglas Mason was. "All right. Did you ever have conversations with Hal Brown?"

"Pacman? Yeah, sometimes."

"Are you watching the news in here?"

His father's brows dipped. "Yes. It's the one thing I really don't miss. Well, that and all the football they'll let me watch."

"Then you've heard of the serial killer that's out there."

This time the man's brows rose. "Ah . . ." He steepled his fingers under his chin.

"Ah, what?" Sam asked.

"That's why you agreed to see me. You think I can tell you who the killer is."

Sam fell silent. Should he let his father think he'd figured things out or not? *No*, a little voice inside him said, *keep him guessing.* He cleared his throat. "I would appreciate it if you would tell me, but that's not the only reason I agreed to see you."

Frowning, Sam's father leaned forward. "No? Then what else?"

Sam tucked his left hand into his coat pocket and curled his fingers around the paper. Then released it and linked his hands together once more, setting them on the table in front of him. "I'll get to that in a minute. I have a story for you."

That generated a smile. "Oh, I like stories. This should be good. Go on, tell me."

"The FBI asked me to come to a scene to look at a woman's body. She'd been killed. And her phone was missing." He left out the part about the tongue and the verse.

"Oh, how interesting. And you think—the FBI thinks—that because I took the phones of my girls that I might know who is doing these new killings?"

"Something like that."

Another frown formed. "But how would I know that? I'm stuck in here, basically isolated from everyone else except for a few short hours each day . . ."

"You just said you had yard time and that you talked to Hal. I'm sure you managed to communicate with the other inmates as well. I know you know something." Sam clamped down hard on his desire to grab the man and shake the information from him. "And I think you managed to discern Hal's weakness and use it against him."

"Wow. You really think Hal has anything to offer me?" His father clicked his tongue and shook his head. "Such a shame what happened to the man. Did he die yet?"

"No."

"Huh. Really? A shiv to the neck didn't do it for him. Interesting."

"So, you don't know anything about what set him off that day? You don't know anything about the whole incident?"

"Just what I saw play out in front of me, which I have to admit was much more entertaining than the news or football. But, no, one minute the game was playing, the next he was screaming about his sister." He sighed. "Look, I don't want to waste time talking about things like that. I want to see my grandchildren."

"Well, I don't see that happening."

"Why not?"

Sam gave a slight shrug. "They think you're dead."

▪ ▪ ▪ ▪

Grace winced. Sam had told her that, but to hear him relay that information so casually still made her flinch.

Even Mark sucked in an audible breath. "Oh, that was cold."

But it was all an act. If she hadn't been watching Sam's eyes, though, she'd believe he really didn't care what his father thought about that.

Peter Romanos's face hardened, and his eyes chilled to a degree that made Grace shiver just watching.

"They think I'm dead?" the man asked. "Why would they think that?"

"Because I sure wasn't telling them that you were a serial killer."

The chill thawed a fraction. "Hmm. I can see how that would be a problem. Couldn't you just have told them that I lived in Fiji or something?"

Sam raised a brow. "Seriously? And have them want to know why you never visited? Or we never visited you?"

"But to tell them I'm dead?"

"You are. To me. And to them. Don't call me again unless you have information that will help me catch another killer." Sam stood.

"Sit down, Sam, we're not done."

"Oh, I think we are." He headed for the door and Grace held her breath. He was done?

"Then you're not interested in hearing what I know about the killer who cuts out tongues?"

And there it was.

Grace turned to Mark and Jerry, whose eyes had gone wide. "He was right," Jerry said.

Mark leaned forward. "Yes, he was."

Sam had paused at the man's words, but now he turned and crossed his arms. "So, you *do* know something."

"Well, I can't guarantee that it means anything, but I might have overheard something in the yard."

"You get to go into the yard? And mix with other prisoners?" Grace raised a brow at Mark and Jerry. "He does?"

Both men shrugged.

"Of course," Peter said. "There's a fence between those of us out, but we can still chat."

Sam could picture that. Each cell opened into a fenced area behind it. Much like an indoor-outdoor kennel. He suppressed a shudder at the thought. So many protests and lawsuits had been filed against such treatment, calling it inhumane, but so far, it still existed.

"As long as I stay on my best behavior, I get my yard time. I don't do well isolated for long periods of time, and I don't want my privileges revoked. Obeying the rules makes things easier, so I do it." He shrugged. "I'm in here for life. I'm just trying to make the best of it. But people talk and they talk loud." He tapped his ear. "I've learned a lot just by using this."

Mark laughed. "Is he serious? He stays on his best behavior because he's afraid of losing his yard time? Really?"

Grace studied the man, watching his body language, his facial expressions, his eye movements, looking for anything that would indicate he was lying.

"I think he actually is," she said. "I mean, his behavior has definitely been exemplary."

Jerry made a low sound under his breath and Grace didn't blame him. She wasn't quite as sure as she came across. And yet . . .

Sam was saying something. ". . . know something, I'm listening."

"Are you going to let me see my grandchildren?"

"No."

"Oh. Not even if I help you stop a killer?"

Sam pinched the bridge of his nose, turned, and knocked on the door. "I'm ready."

"Wait," Mark said, "what's he doing?"

Grace sighed. "Playing the game." Sam waited by the door, leaving his father staring after him, jaw slack, like the man couldn't believe he didn't rise to the bait. "Come on, Mark, you're familiar with interrogation tactics. Sometimes, you have to cut bait. It may take some time, but he'll get him to come around."

"You're not even going to haggle with me?" Peter asked.

Sam stayed silent, waiting for the door to open. Then he slipped out without another word or a backward glance.

"We don't have time for him to play," Mark said. "Whoever the killer's next victim is *especially* doesn't have time."

"And if he pushes, he'll get nothing." She pulled in a slow breath. "He can't let the man blackmail him. No, he's doing the right thing."

Jerry shook his head. "I want a go at him."

"You won't get anywhere."

"Thanks for the vote of confidence."

She huffed. "It has nothing to do with confidence. It has to do with knowing your client . . . or in this case . . . your father."

CHAPTER
TWENTY-TWO

As soon as Sam stepped out of the room, his phone buzzed. A text from Hal's sister.

> He's awake.

> I'll be there as soon as I can.

He had a feeling Mark, Jerry, and Grace would be too. Douglas Mason was going to have to wait. His mind spun. What was it he should be putting together with all the pieces—

Football.

Hal had been watching football when he'd had his episode.

His father had mentioned football as one of the things he watched in the prison.

He scoffed. It was too much of a long shot.

Then again, long shots had paid off before. But . . . *football*?

Grace, Mark, and Jerry stepped into the hall. Grace's eyes met his and he strode toward them. "Hal's awake."

Mark raised a brow. "To the hospital it is then."

"So, Douglas Mason is on hold," Grace said.

Sam nodded. "For now."

"I'm right behind you."

When the four of them walked into the ICU waiting area, Sam couldn't help noting that none of Grace's family was there. At her sharply indrawn breath, he was sure that was the first thing she noticed too.

Then his gaze landed on Brenna, who was pacing from one end to the other, coffee cup in hand. When she saw them, she paled, but locked eyes with Sam. He stepped forward and took her hands. "Is he still awake?"

"Yes. I just stepped out to get something to drink. But the doctors pulled him out of the coma to see how he'd do, and so far, he's okay. They've got his head stabilized so that he can't turn it or reach the wound, but he can blink. He's not supposed to try to talk, but he knew I was there because he looked at me, smiled, and squeezed my hand slightly."

"Well," Grace said, "we could do the 'blink once for no and twice for yes' thing with him if you can stick to those kinds of questions."

Sam nodded. "Okay, we'll do that. Brenna, were you at a football game the day this all happened? Sunday?"

"Yes, Grant, my boyfriend, and I were there."

"Oh. Wow. Okay, thanks."

"Why?"

"I think Hal saw you and your boyfriend in the stands and that's what set him off."

Her eyes widened. "You're kidding me."

"No."

Brenna grabbed the hair above her temples and groaned. "Unbelievable. Absolutely unbelievable."

"I can't say for sure, of course, but we'll watch the footage and see." He paused. "Or simply just ask him. It's a yes-or-no question as to whether or not he saw you."

"I saw the cameras. Even waved at them. I never thought . . . it never occurred . . . argh! Even from prison he can do this to me?" She pulled in a ragged breath. "I'm done. I'm just . . . done."

She whirled, grabbed her purse from the chair, and stormed from the room.

Sam started to go after her and stopped. She needed time to calm down.

"So, who's going in?" Jerry asked. "Because there's no way they're going to let us all in there at once."

"Hal would want to see Sam," Grace said. "Let him go in first. Maybe it'll give him some comfort and he'll be willing to put forth the effort to communicate. I'll wait out here and you can fill me in."

"I'll hang with Grace," Mark said.

Sam looked at Jerry. "Guess we're up."

"Let's go."

Sam let Jerry lead the way into the room where Hal lay on his back, eyes closed, an assortment of tubes and wires running from his body to the various machines on either side of the bed.

Sam walked up and touched the back of the man's hand. "Hal? You awake?"

Hal's eyes flickered open, and when he saw Sam, a tear leaked from his left eye and ran down his temple. Sam blinked, grabbed a tissue, and wiped it away. "Hal, it's okay, man. You're going to be okay."

His neck was encased in white bandages, but his mouth moved. Jerry leaned in. "He's trying to say something."

"Yeah. Try again, Hal."

"Sorry." No sound came out, but Sam was able to read the word.

"It's okay, Hal. I know you're sorry and you weren't going to hurt Mitch."

The man mouthed "sorry" once more and his eyes drifted shut.

Sam squeezed his hand. "Hal, I need you to stay awake. I need to ask you some questions."

Thankfully, the man's lids fluttered open. "We're going to do the 'blink once for no and twice for yes' thing, okay?"

Two blinks.

Sam glanced at Jerry and the man nodded. "Hal, you were

watching football the day of the . . . incident. Do you remember that?"

Two blinks.

"Good. Did you see Brenna on the television at the game with a man?"

Blink.

No? "Well, I wish you could tell me what set you off that day."

The heart monitor beeps picked up speed.

"You're doing great, Hal. And just so you know, Brenna is fine. She's safe. I just saw her in the waiting room, and she said she saw you and talked to you."

Two blinks and the monitor slowed.

"Do you know who the serial killer is? The one who cuts out tongues?"

The man hesitated, his eyes on Sam's. Then he blinked one time.

"What? You don't?"

One blink.

Before his hope and expectations crashed into his shoes, he narrowed his eyes. "But you know something?"

Blink, blink.

Jerry let out a low breath and met Sam's gaze. "This is going to take a while, isn't it?"

"Yes, I think it is."

Jerry nodded. "I'm going to let Grace and Mark know."

He left the room, and Sam palmed his eyes trying to think of the best way to get information out of Hal's head without having to resort to spelling everything. An idea formed. "Hal, I know you can't talk, but can you form words on your lips like you did with 'Sorry'?"

Two blinks, then a silent "Yes."

"Hal, do you know the name Douglas Mason?"

One blink.

Sam bit back a groan of frustration. Oh well, it had been worth a shot.

Jerry returned. "Grace said to tell you that she's going to check on her brother while we finish up in here."

"Someone going with her?"

"Mark."

He nodded. "What do you think about getting one of our speech readers in here? If Hal can form the words and someone can read them, this would go a lot faster."

"Good idea. I'll call. You keep getting whatever you can get."

While Jerry dialed, Sam leaned in, took a deep breath, and prepared to be there for the duration.

■ ■ ■ ■

Grace stepped into her brother's room and walked to the edge of his bed. The machines beeped and whooshed, filling the small room with sound. She touched Bobby's hand and curled her fingers around his. "Hey, little brother. I don't know if you can hear me or not, but I'm going to assume you can." She pulled the chair from the corner of the room closer so she could sit and hold his hand. "Things are kind of crazy in my world right now. I'm sorry I can't be here more." Her throat clogged and she cleared it and pulled in a steadying breath. "It's weird how life sometimes runs parallel. I'm working a case with a complicated brother-sister relationship, and while you're nothing like her brother in some ways, you are in others. Same with me. I'm a lot like her. She's struggling and earlier today sounded like she'd given up on him, on trying to help him and keep him in her life, but I'm willing to bet she'll be back once she calms down." Grace traced the veins on the back of Bobby's hand. A hand she'd held when he was small to help him learn to walk. Then given him a hand up onto the slide at the park behind their house. So many times, she'd held that hand, and so many times he'd reached for it, trusting her to lead him down the right path. Keep him safe.

And then she'd betrayed him. Tears slid down her cheeks. "Oh, Bobby, if only I could take that day back. Erase it from our existence, I would. I'm so sorry. But"—she sniffed and grabbed a tissue from the end table—"I can't take the blame or responsibility for your actions anymore. I still love you to the moon and back, though, and I'll be here when you wake up to see what I can do to help you." She kissed his cheek, cleaned up her face, then stepped out of the room to find her father in the hallway. "Dad?"

"Hey."

"I didn't expect to see—I mean—"

He shrugged. "He's still my son. I'm going to sit with him if you're done."

"I'm done."

She started to walk away and his hand on her arm stopped her. "Grace?" She met his gaze. "I know you blame yourself. I know your mother and I've blamed you, but . . ." He covered his eyes with a hand for a brief moment, then lowered it and tears shimmered.

What in the world? "What is it, Dad?"

He shook his head. "Lucy really laid into us yesterday."

Grace stilled. "Oh?"

"Said a lot of things that hurt and . . . made sense."

"I . . . don't know what to say to that."

"Just . . ." He let out a low laugh that held no humor. "Your mother and I are processing." He cleared his throat. "Basically, Lucy said we needed to grow up and stop placing blame on our daughter's shoulders for something she did as a teen. She told us how angry you were for me taking that new job your junior year and making you change schools and find new friends . . ." He waved a hand. "You know."

Boy, did she. "It crushed me to move that year," she said, her voice quiet. "I did a lot of things I wish I hadn't done, but that's part of life. Unfortunately, some actions have more severe consequences than others. My introducing Bobby to weed sent him on a path I never even considered."

"I know."

"And you and Mom still hate me for it."

He looked stricken at her words. "*Hate* you? Is that what you think?"

"Okay, maybe *hate* is a little strong, but you definitely haven't ever forgiven me." She closed her eyes and took a moment. When she opened them, her father still stood there, staring at her, obviously searching for words and coming up empty. "But that's okay, Dad. God's forgiven me and I've released my guilt. Bobby is responsible for Bobby and all of Bobby's choices. Not me." She glanced at her phone. "I'm sorry. I've got to go."

He nodded and she headed back toward Hal's room. When she glanced over her shoulder, her father was pushing into Bobby's room. She found Mark talking to Jerry in the hall. "What is it?"

"Hal's not supposed to talk, but he's able to move his lips a little," Jerry said. "We're waiting on a speech reader to get here, but the guy keeps fading in and out. He's on a lot of drugs. Sam's doing a good job getting information, but . . ." He shrugged. "Hal says he doesn't know who the killer is, but admitted he knows *something*. Just can't figure out what."

Grace rubbed her forehead. "All right, I'm going to head to the chapel. I need some quiet time."

Mark frowned at her. "I'll come with you."

"Why don't you get us some coffee and meet me at the chapel door? I won't be too long. I just need to . . . I need to be in a peaceful place for a little bit." And she needed to be alone.

"Of course."

He walked her to the door, and she slipped inside, taking in the details while the quiet stillness calmed her on-edge nerves. She breathed deep, relaxed her muscles, and fixed her eyes on the cross at the altar while she stepped sideways and put her back against the wall.

A man and woman knelt at the front, and Grace just kept her eyes on the cross. *Lord, I'm a mess right now because of this situation with Bobby. I just pray you fix it and reunite my family. I hate this distance between my parents and me. It's been there far too long. Show me how to bridge it. Please. And, God, about this killer—*

The couple at the front stood, walked down the aisle, and out the door.

Alone in the small room, Grace sank onto the back pew and clasped her hands in her lap.

—*about this killer. God, please don't let anyone else die. You know who this person is. Please let us put all the pieces together so we can stop him.*

The door opened again, and she stood, then stepped out of the pew, preparing to put her back against the wall once more, when something sharp jabbed in the vicinity of her right kidney. "Hello, Grace."

Stupid! Why had she thought being alone in here would be—

It didn't matter. "What do you want?" she asked between gritted teeth. One jab and she'd be on the floor, bleeding out.

His arm came around her throat. "I think we've been over that already."

"And I'd really like to know why it's so important to you to know what I said."

"Because it is." The knife dug a little deeper and she gasped. He paused. Then breathed a quick sigh. "Fine. I'm very detailed. Almost to the point of being OCD. Or maybe there's no 'almost' about it. These killings are very personal to me and it's important that I know every single detail about them. *Every single detail.* You spoke to the camera that day. You spoke to *me.* Don't I have the right to know what you said?"

"So, if I tell you, are you going to let me—"

A woman rose from the front pew. She'd been facing it, praying on her knees, and had been invisible from the back. She spotted Grace and the man behind her and a frown formed. "Are you all right?" she asked.

A hard shove sent Grace over the back pew. She bounced on the seat, then crashed to the floor, banging her forehead on the pew in front of her on the way down.

A high-pitched scream from the woman echoed in the room. Grace scrambled to her feet, biting her lip on the fiery pain that seemed to come from every muscle in her body, and hurried out the door to find Mark pushing himself up off the floor, coffee dripping from his shirt.

"That was him," Grace said. "Which way did he go?"

"To the stairwell at the end of the hall."

Ignoring her pounding head, sore shoulders, and screaming ribs, Grace raced in the direction Mark pointed. His footsteps fell in behind her. She thought she heard Sam yell her name but kept going, fighting a feeling of déjà vu. At least they were in a hospital this time.

She hit the stairwell door and pushed through, slowing down long enough to make sure he wasn't waiting for her. He wasn't. She bolted down two flights of steps, then stopped on the landing of the second floor.

Mark caught up with her, Sam and Jerry on his heels. She looked up. "You guys go after him." Mark and Jerry didn't even pause but went on down. She looked up at Sam. "We need CSU here ASAP." She walked to the silicone mask on the landing and knelt. "Wow. That's some quality work right there."

"I'll get them on the way." He pulled his phone from his pocket. "I only have one bar. I'll be right back."

While he was calling it in, she kept the scene secure, turning away several health-conscious stair users. It took a good thirty minutes for the crime scene unit to get on scene, but it didn't take them long to gather the necessary evidence. The security footage was little help—he'd somehow managed to hide his face after leaving the mask behind.

She and Sam exited the stairwell and found Mark just outside. He spotted them and shook his head. "Guy got away, but we've got the dogs and a chopper once more looking for him."

Sam nodded to her with a frown. "What happened to your head?"

"He pushed me over the back of the pew and I didn't have time to catch myself." Grace pressed a hand to the goose egg with a grimace. "Lovely." She noticed the sticky wetness on her lower back and lowered the hand from her head to touch the area. Red covered her fingers. "You've got to be kidding me."

"Turn around," Sam said.

She complied and lifted her shirt so he could see. "How bad is it?" Now that the adrenaline was crashing, the pain hit her full force.

"Probably could use a stitch or two."

"I'll take a butterfly bandage and some wound glue."

Sam sighed. "Wait inside the lobby, and I'll find something to patch you up with."

While she waited just inside the door as instructed, Mark pressed a napkin to the area. "Protective custody sound good yet?"

"No way. And Frank doesn't need to know about this. Yet."

"Grace . . ."

"I know. He'll probably bench me when he finds out—and I know he'll find out because I really do plan to tell him, but I want this guy, and more importantly, he wants me. That's going to be his downfall."

"Frank will read the report, Grace."

"I know that too."

Sam returned and Mark moved out of the way to let him work. When he finished, he stepped back and tossed the leftovers in the trash.

"It's just a scratch, right, Sam?"

"Something like that."

"You're lucky that's all you got," Mark muttered. He brushed at his coffee-stained shirt. "I didn't realize the guy who came busting through the doors was a killer. I just thought it was someone who was upset. I was literally across the hall from you at the coffee machine."

He was obviously beating himself up about leaving her. "You couldn't have known," Grace said. She eyed Sam. "You still interested in tracking down Douglas Mason?"

"Yeah, because I just remembered where I know his name from."

Mark straightened. "Where?"

"It was on the visitors' logs for one of the inmates."

"Which one?" Grace asked. "Why don't I remember that name?"

"I don't know, but that's got to be it."

"I'm more interested than ever in talking to him now." She turned her gaze to Mark. "What about you and Jerry?"

"We're going to be here for a bit. Feel free to talk with him if it will help with your profile."

"I don't know that it will, but it's possible."

"Then go and fill us in when you can."

"All right."

"You sure you're up to it?" Sam asked.

She sighed. "They've got this. I'm ready when you are."

"I'll call the prison and get the name of the inmate. They can find it faster than I can."

"Then once we have that," she said, "Daria can work her magic and get us everything else we need to know."

He nodded. "Why don't you leave your car here and we ride together? I feel like that would be safer than being in separate vehicles."

Grace hesitated. Agents usually drove their own vehicles in case they needed to get somewhere fast, but . . . "Well, since I'm not going anywhere alone right now anyway, yeah, okay."

CHAPTER
TWENTY-THREE

"You know," Sam said, "this guy isn't going to stop until he gets what he wants."

"Which is for me to tell him what I said. Yes, I'm aware."

"He's watching you. Following you." Just saying the words sent his eyes to the mirrors looking for a possible tail.

"I guess he has to be in order to attack me in the chapel, but he won't kill me until I tell him what I said." She paused. "And he doesn't seem to be a threat to those not on his radar."

"I thought about that. He has a specific reason for killing. If you don't meet the criteria, you're not in danger. Is that what you think too?"

"For the most part. There could be outliers, of course, something that would cause him to hurt another person that didn't meet his criteria, but . . . in general? No, he's careful. Methodical. Strikes when he's sure he can get away. He always has a plan and an escape route."

Sam nodded. "So, what's the criteria?"

"Saying something he doesn't like or thinks is wrong?"

"The age range is pretty specific too."

"Definitely."

Her phone pinged and she glanced at it. "Daria sent some info."

"That was fast."

"That's because it's Daria."

They fell silent, with her reading and Sam thinking until he glanced at her. "What *did* you say anyway?"

She looked up from her phone and shrugged. Then winced.

"Your shoulders are still sore."

"Yes. As to what I said, I honestly don't remember it word for word, but it was basically a promise to catch him and make him pay." Her jaw tightened. "A promise I plan to keep."

"Yeah, and I plan to help you." He paused. "Do we want to give Doug a heads-up that we're coming to see him?"

"Let's not. He might not be home anyway. It's a workday and he runs a restaurant. But"—she shifted and pressed a hand to her lower back with a grimace, then sighed—"let's try home first. According to what Daria was able to dig up, his wife does a lot of volunteer work but might be at the house. Her name is Amelia. She and Doug own a restaurant called The Wicked Chicken and he's probably there."

He nodded and pressed the gas.

His phone pinged a message and he passed it to Grace. "What's it say?"

"It's from Jerry. The speech reader is at the hospital."

"Good. Maybe by the time we finish up with Mason, they'll have something for us."

When they arrived at Douglas Mason's home, Sam noted it was in one of the more sought-after neighborhoods in Arlington. He pulled to the curb and climbed out. Grace joined him and together they walked to the door.

He knocked and Grace stood back, watching, her gaze scanning the street. "See anything?" he asked.

"No, but that doesn't necessarily reassure me."

The door opened and a woman in her midsixties eyed them. "Hello. Can I help you?"

Sam held out his badge and Grace did the same. "We'd like to speak to Douglas Mason if he's home."

"He's not. He's at the restaurant."

"I see. Are you Amelia Mason?"

Her hand fluttered to her throat, but she nodded. "I am."

"Nice to meet you, Mrs. Mason," Sam said. "Do you mind answering a few questions for us?"

"What's this about?" the woman asked. "Is Doug in some kind of trouble?"

"No, ma'am. He's just been visiting an inmate at one of the prisons and we'd like to talk to him a little about that."

"Visiting an inmate?" She blinked and her jaw went slack. Then she snapped her lips together. "Who?"

"Ethan Rogers."

Her brows rose. "Well, I'll be. He never said a word."

"You know Ethan?"

"Sure. He and Doug are half brothers. Same mother, different fathers."

Sam nodded. "Okay, well, can you tell me where Doug was last night around eight forty-five p.m.?"

She frowned. "Why?"

"It would just help us a lot to know."

"Um." She rubbed her forehead. "We have church on Wednesday nights until about eight—at least when Doug can get away from the restaurant—then he usually goes back after church to close, but he didn't go last night. There was a leak in one of the bathrooms that he had to take care of."

Easy enough to check that out. "Thank you, we appreciate your help."

"Of course. I'll let Doug know you're coming to talk to him so he can be preparing to take a break."

"Thank you."

She slipped back inside, and Sam looked at Grace. "Take a break or *make* a break?"

"Guess we'll find out."

The restaurant was only about a twenty-minute drive from the residence. When Sam wheeled into the parking lot, the place was packed. He squeezed his Bucar into an end spot and nodded to Grace. "What do you wanna bet that he's going to say he's too busy to talk?"

"That actually might be legit in this case."

He laughed and climbed out of the car with a gaze on the surroundings.

"We weren't followed," she said, leading the way to the door of the restaurant. He noted how she held herself stiff and moved carefully. She needed a soak in a hot tub.

"You sound pretty sure of that."

"As sure as I can be anyway. I was watching too. If neither of us spotted anyone, then I feel like there's a good chance we're in the clear."

She had a point. He opened the door, and she stepped in ahead of him. He took one more glance at the parking lot, then turned his attention to the organized chaos in front of him as the door shut behind him. Three people sat on the bench to his right, waiting on a table. The bar was in the middle of the room and to the left was more seating.

The hostess, dressed all in black, approached. "How many?"

Grace showed her badge. "We'd like to speak with Douglas Mason, please?"

"Oh yeah, he said you'd be coming. I'm Hilary. Follow me."

Grace raised a brow at Sam and he shrugged. "I may have to apologize for my suspicions."

A tall man, dressed in jeans and a long-sleeved black collared shirt with the restaurant's logo on the left shoulder, was filling the ice dispenser behind the bar. Hilary tapped the granite counter to get the man's attention.

"Doug? The agents are here to see you."

Doug turned and wiped his hands on a cloth he'd threaded through his belt. "Hey, thanks, Hil." He turned to the young man next to him, who had his back to Sam and Grace. "Check the drink machine, will you, Zach? The carbonation still isn't working right again. Too much drink, not enough fizz."

"You got it."

Doug met Sam's eyes and tilted his head toward an area behind the bar. "Always something around here. Come on back into my office so we can actually hear each other."

Sam and Grace followed him through the kitchen and into a back office that did not look like any restaurant office he'd ever seen. The place was immaculate. "Have a seat." He gestured to the two chairs facing his desk, then settled himself into the one behind it. "What do you want to know about Ethan?"

Nothing like getting straight to the point. Sam leaned forward. "Your wife said you and Ethan are half brothers."

"That's right."

"So you were close growing up?"

He shrugged. "I'm six years older than he is, so I mostly thought he was a pest once he outgrew the baby stage. But yeah, I love him. Why all the interest in Ethan and me anyway? What's going on?"

"Where were you last night between eight thirty and nine p.m.?"

He studied them as though weighing whether or not he wanted to answer. "Right here at the restaurant. We close at eleven. I was here all day. And trust me, it was a long day. Had a toilet leak in the men's bathroom that wasn't fun to deal with. Got home a little after midnight and then was back here this morning at six a.m."

The man had so many cameras around the building, Sam had no doubt if they asked to see the footage, he'd see exactly what Doug had just told him.

"Anyone else have access to your car?"

"What? No. Why?"

"What kind of car is it?"

"A silver BMW. Now what's going on?"

Sam cleared his throat. "Last night, someone played tag with my bumper. It was dark, they had the brights on and pulled into my subdivision right behind me, right on my tail. When I pulled over, the person drove away. I got the plate and it was registered to you."

"Follow me." He rose, pulled out the top right-hand drawer of his desk, grabbed his keys, and opened the back door. A silver BMW was parked in the spot to the right. Douglas tapped the key remote and the lights flashed. "I don't know whose car you saw last night, but it wasn't mine."

Sam walked to the rear of the car. "That's the plate and that's the car. Someone was driving it." He scanned the roof of the building. "You have cameras. Any chance we could look at the footage?"

"Absolutely."

He led them back inside, took his seat behind the desk, and pulled up the footage on the screen. "Okay, last night. We'll start at six o'clock and fast-forward. Will that work?"

"Perfect."

Sam leaned in while the man let the footage scroll at a fast rate. All the way up until midnight when the door opened and they could see Douglas getting in his car and driving away.

Sam met Grace's eyes. She'd been quiet up to this point. Now, she frowned. "They looped the footage."

■ ■ ■ ■

Douglas blinked at her. "What?"

"It's just a guess, but I'd say whoever took your car doctored the footage to make sure if you looked at it, you wouldn't see anything odd."

"That's crazy. No one took my car. No one messed with the footage. We done here?"

"Would you mind giving us the original? Our lab can figure out if it was looped, spliced, or whatnot. If not, then I'll apologize."

Doug studied them for a moment, then sighed. "Sure. What's your email address?"

Sam gave him one and the man worked over the keyboard a

few more minutes, then turned back to them. "You should have it in your inbox."

Sam stood and held out a hand. "Thank you for your cooperation. I'm sorry for the intrusion and all the trouble, but you made our job a little easier, so thank you for that."

Douglas offered them a small smile. "Aw, you're welcome. Come back and have a meal sometime, okay?"

Grace raised a brow. "That's sounds lovely. Thank you."

"And we'll be sure to let you know if we find that your car had been 'borrowed.'"

"I'll be interested to hear what you find out."

Once they were back in his Bucar, Sam looked at her. "What do you think?"

"Good question." She frowned. "I think someone took his car and looped the video, but he doesn't want to believe someone would betray his trust like that."

"Yeah. His keys were in the drawer. It would be easy to lift them and go if you knew they were there."

"Let's get a list of his employees. Might not be someone who works there, but you never know."

Sam tapped the screen of his phone, then rubbed his eyes. "I sent the video to Chris, Jerry, and Mark. We'll see what Chris says."

Chris Benning. Video forensics analyst. He'd tear it apart and figure out what was going on. Probably very easily.

"I also told Mark and Jerry that they might want to look at the employees of the restaurant. Ball is in their court now."

"Then, until we hear back from Chris," Grace said, "I think it's time to head back to the office. I want to go over a few things."

Sam nodded. "And I need to check in with my mother-in-law. Thankfully, El's back at school so everything should return to normal."

While he drove to the hospital for her to pick up her car, she pulled up the phone records for Gina, Sonya, and Carol on the laptop attached to the dash. Mark and Jerry had already been through them and found nothing, so she didn't expect to find anything either, but like always, she wanted to be thorough.

"What are you looking for?" Sam asked.

"Anything I can find. I keep thinking we're missing a crucial piece of information that would tie everything up for us. These ladies all had something in common. Credit and debit cards showed they visited the same grocery store occasionally, but that angle didn't pan out."

"Living in basically the same area, that's bound to happen occasionally, so not surprising that didn't pan out."

She went back to the phone records and added the list of Kristin Davenport, the fourth victim, to the screen. One by one she went through the numbers while Sam drove. When he pulled in next to her car, she looked up, her head aching and eyes burning. "I need a bigger screen," she muttered, but something had captured her attention. Something that needed more investigation.

"You have that look. What is it?"

She raised a brow. "I have a look?"

He laughed. "You do. What'd you find?"

They would have to revisit that look thing. "I'm not sure. So many numbers and they're all starting to blur, but Kristin and Gina have a matching number." Excitement built, fatigue fled. "And so does Carol Upton. My, my . . . I think we may be on to something."

"For who?"

"Let's find out." She dialed the number.

"Virginia Child Protective Services. How may I help you?"

Grace identified herself. "What is this number for?"

"This is the Virginia CPS hotline to report cases of child abuse or neglect."

"I see. Thank you so much." Grace hung up and passed on the information to Sam.

"Interesting."

"So, my mind immediately goes to someone who reported an incident to CPS and the killer found out who it was. But the number isn't in Sonya's records. However, that doesn't mean she didn't use a different phone." She tapped her lips with a forefinger. "Maybe she called from the school where she worked? Now that we know the number, it should be easy enough to find out."

"It's possible," Sam said with a nod. "But to kill four different people over . . . what? Four different reports? And how did he even find out or get access to those reports?"

She shook her head. "I'm going to let Mark and Jerry work that angle—and find out if Sonya made a report as well—while we head back to the office so I can work on the profile a little more."

Sam's phone rang and he hit the Bluetooth. "Hello?"

"Hey, man, it's Jerry. The speech reader got here and it took us a while to get Hal coherent again, but he mouthed a few things."

"What?"

"His sister's name mostly. We kept reassuring him she was safe, but he seems to think she's still in danger."

"Why?"

"Well, that's just it. He didn't seem to be able to make that clear, but he was still agitated. He also said a name. Rogers."

Sam's eyes met Grace's, the surprise on his face mirroring hers.

"The doctor sedated him and slapped our hands for upsetting him. We're running down the Rogers angle. He ever mention someone by that name in one of your sessions?"

"There's an *Ethan* Rogers in a cell near him. Could he mean him?"

"We'll talk to him. Thanks."

"Yeah. Will you keep me updated?"

"Of course." He hung up and Grace sighed.

"I'm hungry," she said. "Want to grab some dinner?"

"Sure. Where are we going?"

"Wherever you pick."

His phone rang and he froze. "Tell me that didn't just happen."

Grace didn't know whether to laugh or groan. "It's getting a bit ridiculous."

He sighed and answered on his Bluetooth. "This is Sam."

"This is Nate. Sorry to bother you, but I promised JC that I'd call you and tell you he needs to see you ASAP."

"What's going on with JC?"

"Says it's a private matter, but he needs to talk to you when you get here tomorrow first thing."

Relief whipped through Sam. They weren't going to have to cancel their dinner plans. "That's fine. I'll call Janice and have her work him into the morning schedule."

"Excellent, I'll pass that on."

Sam hung up and Grace let out a low breath. "So, dinner's still on?"

"Still on. And I know where I want to go."

"Where?"

"To the place that has the greasiest, juiciest burger on the planet."

"Sullivan's?"

"I see you're familiar with it."

"Oh yes, but their fried flounder is not to be beat." She paused. "I think we should order it to go."

He nodded. "You call it in, and I'll run inside and get it." He hesitated. "We'll take it back to your office. That work?"

"Sure."

Two hours later, they were settled in the CIRG conference room surrounded by files and two open laptops. Grace stared at the screen. "I've finished the profile but feel like I need to add to it, and this has me tied all up in knots."

"You think you can still be objective with this?"

"Objective? Hmm. I don't know that I have to be. I do know that I'm in this guy's head more so than anyone else can be. I've seen him. I've felt his hands on me." A shudder rippled through her. "I've heard his voice." Her fingers curled into a fist and Sam leaned forward to cover it with his warm hand.

"Hey," he said, "don't let him do this to you."

She drew in a shuddering breath, and he scooted closer. "What if the next time he comes after me, he succeeds?"

"We won't let that happen."

She turned her hand to grasp his. "I'm mad," she said, "but I'll admit, I'm scared too."

He touched her cheek. "Of course you are. I'm scared *for* you. But you've got agents on you, and we're not letting you out of our sight."

"I know. And I'm grateful." She pursed her lips and narrowed her eyes at him. "I can't let him have this much control, this much influence on what I do or where I go." She scoffed. "I wouldn't even eat in a restaurant tonight because I'm worried about him trying something. That's not living, Sam. That's letting him win. And yet . . ."

"And yet?"

"I can't do anything that's going to get someone else hurt either."

He hesitated. "What do you think about coming to the football game with me tomorrow night?"

"What? Did you not just hear what I said?"

"It's a huge crowd. He won't try anything. He might be watching, but there will be a big police presence and we'll have a number of agents."

"Sam, as much as I'd love to go, I have a killer's attention on me. And as mad at him as I am for the havoc he's wreaking in my life, and as much as I'd love to defy him and pretend he doesn't exist, well, I can't risk that."

He sighed. "Yeah, I guess you're right."

"But I'll be cheering Xander on."

"He'll appreciate it." Sam leaned forward. "Okay, so any word back on whether Sonya Griffith called CPS?"

"Mark and Jerry are running with that information, but I've got a call in to her daughter too. Hopefully, she'll call one of us back soon." She stood. "In the meantime, I'm calling it a day." She glanced at her phone. Penny, Raina, and Julianna had all called and texted. It was time to return messages and reassure her friends she was still alive.

For now anyway.

"Want some company?"

She smiled. "I'd love some, but I'm going to run by the hospital before I head home."

"I'll come with you. Is Jade still your shadow?"

Grace waved to the agent who'd just stepped inside. "She is."

"You ready?" the woman asked.

"We're heading to the hospital," Grace said.

"I'll be right behind you."

Thankfully, even though she watched her mirrors, prepared to act should the killer make a move, the drive was uneventful, and the three of them parked in the designated law enforcement area.

Grace led the way to Bobby's floor where she found the nurse, Yvonne Sims, at the desk. The woman looked up and smiled. "You're Bobby's sister, aren't you?"

"I am."

"I was getting ready to call you. He's awake. Still groggy but doing better if you'd like to see him."

"Absolutely."

She told Sam and Jade, then followed the nurse to Bobby's room, where she found her baby brother looking pitiful. His eyes were closed, but that didn't mean he was asleep. She walked to the edge of the bed to take his hand. "Hey, Bobby, you awake?"

His eyelids flickered open. Then shut. Then open once more. His eyes found hers and he frowned. "Grace?"

"Yeah." She pulled the chair over and sat next to him. "I love you, Bobby."

His throat worked and a tear slid down his temple. "I love you too," he croaked.

"You can't do this again. You almost didn't make it."

He swallowed and closed his eyes. "I know."

"I want to help you, but I've come to realize that's not enough. You've got to want to help yourself."

"I do."

"No, I mean, you've really got to."

"Yeah," he whispered. "I think I want to sleep, though."

"Okay. I'll be back to see you soon."

He caught her hand, his grip weak, hand cold. "Did . . . did Mom and Dad come?"

"Yeah, they did."

His eyes opened wider. "Really?"

"Yes. They're not here at the moment, but they came. I'll text and let them know you're awake."

"Do you think they still love me? Just a little bit?"

Tears clogged her throat and she coughed to get rid of the knot. "Oh, Bobby. Yes. They just hurt for you. Every time they almost lose you, it nearly kills them." *And me*, she added silently.

"I really almost died?"

"Yeah, you did," she whispered and lifted his hand to kiss his knuckles. "You did."

"Thanks for saving me, Grace." His barely-there words faded as he drifted off to sleep.

She swiped her tears and texted her parents and sister, giving them an update, then walked out of the room to find Sam waiting on her.

Sam rose. "Jade went to grab a snack from the cafeteria. You okay? Is Bobby?"

"Yeah, he's going to be okay. Once he gets a little better, we'll come up with a treatment plan for him. It's just really hard to see him that way."

Sam opened his arms and she stepped into them.

CHAPTER
TWENTY-FOUR

Friday morning, Sam took Eleni to school and reminded her that Xander would be picking her up. The reminder earned him an eye roll. "I know, Dad. Nessie told me, you told me, and Xander told me. I think I've got it."

"Sorry. I know you do. Text me when you get to Mom's."

She flashed him a grin. "Okay." Then she was out of the car and headed into the school.

Sam drove toward the prison, his schedule full for the day, but he was looking forward to some time off to watch Xander play ball that night. He'd miss Grace being there, of course, but understood her reasons for keeping her distance. He really needed to put the killer behind bars.

His fingers flexed around the wheel and he forced himself to let it go for now. He had patients to see, and if he worked up the nerve, he might even give his father another visit.

When he got to his office, he texted Grace.

What's on your calendar today?

Her response was immediate, which meant she was probably answering on her computer.

Finishing up the profile and paying attention to
some of the other cases on my desk. I'm already
at the office—and before you ask, yes, I had an
escort.

Three dots appeared, indicating she was typing another text.

Whoever this guy is, he's been kind of quiet.
Which makes me nervous.

Yeah. Just don't let your guard down.

Not a chance.

For the next seven hours, Sam met with his patients and even managed to slide in a few subtle questions about his father and who he'd been talking to in the prison.

It came down to his two cell neighbors and the guards on rotation.

Nothing earth shattering or unexpected. Those were the people in his very narrow world. Of course he talked to them.

A knock on the door pulled his head up. "Oh, hey, Mitch."

"Janice told me to knock."

"Absolutely. How are you doing?"

"Doing all right. Just wanted to check on Hal. I haven't called the hospital because I didn't figure they'd tell me anything."

"He woke up."

"Yeah? Then he's going to be okay?"

"Looks like it."

Mitch nodded. "Good. Good. So, has he said anything? Like should I request another area of the prison so there's no conflict when he comes back?"

Sam leaned back and stroked his chin. "That's not a bad idea. I'm sorry I didn't suggest it."

"I mean, just trying to think ahead. He's probably not real happy with me."

"He didn't say and I didn't bring it up."

"So, he say anything else?"

Sam tilted his head. "Yeah, he said the name Rogers. What can you tell me about him?"

Mitch blew out a low sigh. "Uh, well, he's right there in the cell next to Hal."

"He and Hal get along?"

"Yeah, seemed to. Rogers can have an attitude sometimes and a smart mouth, but when he wants something, he turns the charm on. You know how it is."

"Of course. Did you ever get the feeling he wanted something from Hal?"

"No. I don't think he thought Hal could do anything for him. Basically, they ignored each other."

Sam nodded. "Okay, thanks."

"Anything I need to be aware of? In regards to keeping the peace?"

"I don't think so. I haven't heard of anything. I was asking about Rogers in case it could help me with Hal."

"He's touchy about his sister. Keep her out of the conversation and he's not a bad dude."

"Other than the people he killed."

Mitch shot him a wry smile. "Yeah, other than that. Just talking about in here."

"I understand."

"Well, I gotta get back. Thanks for the update."

"Of course. Let me know about the transfer and if you need me to sign off on anything."

"Will do."

The man disappeared and Sam ran a hand over his face, thinking. "Rogers," he muttered. "Rogers." He pulled the man's record up. He was in for shooting his wife. He'd been a terrible behavior problem when he'd first been sentenced and had killed an inmate and a guard, which had earned him the cell in isolation. And yet, once Peter Romanos had moved in next door to him, his behavior had improved. Dramatically.

That very fact set off warning bells for Sam. He glanced at the clock. He had another hour before he had to leave, but Xander should be picking up El right about now. He sent a text to her.

> Hey, hon, just checking on you. You okay?

The three little dots appeared, then the words . . .

> I'm fine, Dad. Just waiting on Xander to get here.

> Okay. Wish you wanted to come to the game. If you do, I'll come get you.

They'd be late, but he'd get her.

> Maybe next week. Terri's coming over and we're going to play board games and binge on popcorn. Love you too. Xander's here. Gotta go.

She sent him a heart emoji and he smiled.

Eleni was not a huge fan of football, not even with a brother who was one of the starting lineup. Neither was Claire, and Brett wouldn't come without her, which was a good thing, since Sam and Brett were not exactly on speaking terms. Knowing he wouldn't run into the man at Xander's game was a plus. He set his phone aside, then grabbed it back and texted Grace.

> What are you doing tonight?

> Hanging with Julianna and Raina. They're here for the night.

> Okay, then can we catch up tomorrow?

> Absolutely.

> Great. And look into Ethan Rogers. Mark and Jerry are working on it, but Hal said his name for a reason. I have a gut feeling he might know something about the killer.

251

Will do. I hate that I couldn't be there tonight, but it's just too risky.

Next time.

Well, after this killer is caught.

Right. Talk later. Gotta run.

Tell Xander I'm cheering him on.

He tapped the last text and his choices popped up on the screen. Heart, thumbs-up, thumbs-down, et cetera. He let his thumb hover over the heart and wondered if that was a *manly* thing to do. To heart a text. He'd never done that before. Then shrugged. He did love that she was so positive about his kids and wasn't ashamed to let her know it. He tapped the heart.

■ ■ ■ ■

The killer had a message to send and he needed to send it fast. While his brain pulled ideas from nowhere, mulled over one plan, tossed it, and came up with another from the safety of his car, he watched the young girl, Eleni, cross the parking lot to climb into the vehicle. Her brother, Xander, was at the wheel. She slammed the door and her movements indicated she was buckling up.

Xander pulled from the spot and made his way out of the parking lot. The killer fell in behind them. He'd watched yesterday and found that the teen left the high school, went straight to the middle school to pick up his sister, then drove home. Chances were good that it was their routine.

Today, Xander turned left instead of right. Intrigued, the killer followed them for the next fifteen minutes until Xander pulled into a gas station. He then watched the girl get out of her brother's car and climb into the SUV parked at the gas tank. A pretty woman in her midthirties pumped and said something to the girl. The killer surmised that the woman was the mother of the two kids and was getting the daughter for the weekend.

Perfect.

Xander drove away with a wave. The woman replaced the nozzle and shut the gas tank.

The killer followed them all the way to a middle-class home in a large neighborhood.

A plan formed. A smile followed.

He'd get to Grace one way or another.

An hour later, Eleni's mother walked out of the house and climbed into her SUV.

Without Eleni.

He'd been sitting there long enough to know the kid was alone.

With an eye on the street, he stepped out of his car and walked toward the front door.

■ ■ ■ ■

Grace's phone buzzed and she snagged it, noting the number belonged to the lab. She stuck her AirPods into her ears and answered. "Billingsley."

"Carmen here."

"What's up?"

"Well, I know your intruder wasn't in the system, so I did a little something."

"What kind of something?"

"I did a search for familial DNA."

"I had a feeling you might do that. And?"

"And your guy is related to someone named Ethan Rogers."

"As in the guy who's in prison where Peter Romanos is?" Excitement built.

A pause. "I have no idea. I didn't do a background check on him. I'm just the DNA girl."

"And you're my absolute favorite DNA girl in the whole world if this guy is who I think it is." Grace let out a gasping laugh. "Oh, that's perfect. We're getting closer."

"So, this is important?"

"So very important. Thank you, Carmen." She hung up, sent the information to Mark, Jerry, and Sam, then grabbed her stuff. She'd head home, with Jade making sure she got there. Having Julianna and Raina for the night was a much-needed breather from the stress of . . . everything. There was safety in numbers, so instead of coming tomorrow as originally planned, they were on the way now. Penny's schedule had shifted, so she couldn't make it. Why the four of them actually tried to plan anything was beyond Grace. Their plans always wound up changing. She rolled her eyes and pulled her keys from her pocket.

With Jade following her, she drove home and pressed the button to lift her garage door. When nothing happened, she tried again. With a groan, she parked in the drive while Jade pulled to a stop at the curb. Grace stepped out of her car while Jade did the same. "My battery is dead, I guess. It won't lift. I'm going to run inside, open it that way, and pull in. That way the girls can park in the drive."

"That's fine. I'll hang out here. Watch the street until you're safely inside."

"Thanks."

Grace let herself in with her key, turned her alarm system off, then headed through the kitchen for the garage. She opened the door and was hit by the unusual chill of the garage. She shivered. It was as cold in here as it was outside.

She hit the button on the wall and the door still didn't lift. "Seriously?" She turned the light on, and her gaze went straight to the broken window opposite her.

"Jade!" She spun on her heel and raced back through the house to see Jade on the ground by her Bucar, curled into a ball. While Grace's mind shouted it was a trap, her feet took her toward the downed agent and her hand reached for her phone.

A man rose from his hiding spot behind the Bucar, his gun, with a suppressor attached, aimed at her. "Don't."

Her gaze swung to her neighbors' houses. No one in sight. But it wouldn't matter if they did see the guy. He looked different once again. A description would simply lead anyone to look down the wrong path. "I'll tell you whatever you want to know. Just let me get to Jade."

"Oh no. You're going to pay for all the trouble you've caused me. You're going to tell me what you said, but you're going to suffer a little too." He paused, his eyes flicking from one house to the next. "Or a lot. Probably a lot."

Heart pumping, she frantically searched for a way out. "I guess you want me to go with you?"

"I do. Toss your weapon and your phone into her sedan, then get in my car. You're going to drive."

"And if I don't?"

"Eleni dies. You don't want that, do you?"

"What do you mean?"

He held up a phone with a pink case and turned it around so she could see the back. Eleni Monroe's. "Catch." He tossed it to her and Grace snagged it midair. She looked at the screen and sucked in a swift breath. Eleni lay on her side, eyes closed, lips parted. Her hands and feet were free, but the concrete wall at her back said she wasn't going anywhere on her own.

"Oh, Sam," she whispered.

"Gun and phone, please," the man said.

She tossed them into the open car door. He was going to take her. Right there in broad daylight. "Sam is expecting me," she blurted.

"What?"

"Sam. His son is playing in the football game at the high school tonight. He's expecting me to be there. I need to text him and tell him I'm not coming. He'll be worried." There was no way to know if Sam knew that Eleni was missing. She was supposed to be at her mother's house. But texting Sam was the only way she could think of to alert him that all was not well at her house. Julianna and Raina weren't due for another couple of hours, and Jade needed help ASAP.

Oh, Lord, help me . . .

The man looked around and pointed his weapon at Jade. "Get her in her car, in the back seat. Then get your phone."

Thankfully, Jade wasn't a big woman, and Grace was able to maneuver her into the back seat in spite of her own still-healing injuries. She checked the agent's pulse. "Come on, Jade," she whispered. "Please be okay."

But the woman was unconscious, bleeding from a wound at her temple.

A hand grabbed the back of her shirt and yanked her from the car. She kept her footing but used the car to brace herself. "I need to get the phone."

"Get it."

Once she had it in her hand, she considered tossing it at him, distracting him enough to get a good punch in, but he was watchful, careful. His eyes never stilled and his hand never wavered. And he wasn't close enough.

Where the heck were her neighbors? Then again, she didn't want anyone to get hurt.

"Give me the phone."

"What? I haven't typed the message."

"You're not going to. You're going to tell me what to say. But first, get in my car before someone comes out and I have to resort to more drastic measures."

With a hard look at the man who was wreaking havoc on the lives of those she cared about, she said a swift prayer that someone would find Jade fast and obeyed. She climbed behind the wheel of his car and cranked it while he slid into the passenger seat and buckled his seat belt.

"Give me your hands."

He zip-tied them. Tight enough to make attacking him difficult. Loose enough to allow her to drive. "Tell me what to say so it sounds like you."

"I'm sorry I won't be able to come to the game as planned," she said. "Working on the case. All the best to Alexander."

"That's it?"

"Can I say more?"

"No." He tapped the screen. "There, it's sent." He tossed the phone out the window. "Now, drive."

Using both hands, she threw the transmission in reverse and slammed on the gas. Her wheels spun, then gripped the concrete with a squeal, and she backed out of the drive.

The killer pressed the weapon with the suppressor against her temple. "Keep up the funny stuff and I'll kill you right now."

Grace tightened her jaw and clamped her fingers around the wheel. "Where am I going?"

"Turn left at the light. I'll give you directions as we go."

"Is Eleni okay?"

"Yes, just gave her a little drug, but she'll be waking up soon. I want you there with her so she's not scared."

She shot him a sideways glance. He killed women and cut out their tongues, but he didn't want a little girl to be scared—in spite of the fact that he'd kidnapped her? She wanted answers, but she wasn't sure how much she should reveal to him that she knew.

"You kept your victims for a few days before you killed them."

He snorted. "They weren't victims. They got what they deserved."

"Why keep them? Were you just lonely?"

He laughed. "No. I have a job, you know. A family. Turn here and get on the interstate going north."

She followed the instructions, then stared at his man bun. "You were at the restaurant when we were there. I remember now."

"Yeah. Nearly had a heart attack, but I figured even if you might recognize me from the hospital waiting room, you didn't know my real name—or at least couldn't attach it."

Very true. If he'd turned around, they would have known exactly who he was.

"How did you decide on your victims . . . er . . ." She paused. "Well, if they're not victims, what are they?"

He was silent for a moment, then said, "They're nosy ones. The intrusive ones, the ones who should have kept their mouths shut because their words destroyed lives and families."

Well, that explained why he cut out their tongues.

She continued to drive and couldn't help wonder how far they were going, but the more she could learn on the way might give her something she could use later. "What did Carol Upton say that made you so upset?"

"She called CPS and reported my family. Mom and Dad were arguing, and they would have resolved the issue if Carol had kept her nose out of things. The cops got there and had things settled. Mom wasn't pressing charges, and they left. But then CPS showed up, and that's when Dad went nuts and got his gun. Mom screamed at him that it was all his fault and it escalated from there. Mom threw herself at him swinging, hitting. The gun went off and she went down."

"So, he didn't mean to shoot her?"

"Of course not," he snapped. "But that didn't stop the cops from arresting him and sending him to prison on trumped-up charges."

The charges weren't trumped up, but she let that go. His explanation was confirmation that she'd been right about the link. "What about the other three? Sonya, Gina, and Kristin? Did you know them?"

"No, but they made false reports to CPS as well and needed to be dealt with. And there are others. I plan to take care of them too."

"How did you find out about the false reports?"

He shrugged. "Carol and Gina were friends. They met at the restaurant occasionally."

Wait. What? How had they missed that?

"They talked and I overheard things. The other was from my aunt. Someone had reported her best friend's daughter to CPS for abuse and their investigation—such that it was—led to them taking her kids away. She said there was no way that was possible and it had to be someone with a grudge. My own *little investigation* allowed me to find out it was Kristin Davenport—a woman with a grudge against the person who got the promotion."

"The daughter of your aunt's friend."

"Exactly. I made sure she'd never do that to anyone else."

"I see." He thought of himself as some sort of hero. Getting revenge for those who couldn't avenge themselves? "What triggered this sudden killing of these people? Why now?" She kept the conversation going, but she still wanted to know about the friendship between Carol and Gina—and how that had never come up in all of the investigating.

"My father said something during one of our visits."

"Your father—"

"Never mind. I shouldn't have mentioned him. He'll be angry if he finds out I talked about him." He paused. "Then again, I don't guess it matters. He's not going to find out."

Grace ignored that chilling pronouncement. "Your father told you it was time to kill?"

"In a sense. I mean he didn't say, 'Hey, Zach, you need to go kill these people.' But yeah. He gave me the idea."

She frowned. "I'm confused."

He sighed like he found it tiresome to have to explain, but she was grateful that didn't stop him. "After my father went to prison, my sister and I went into the system—turn left at the next light—until my aunt and uncle took me in. They tried to find my sister, but the system lost her." His right hand fisted against his thigh, then relaxed. "By the time they found her, she was dead. Killed by a man who was supposed to protect her and take care of her."

"Oh no. That's awful." Would sympathizing with him work? Build a little rapport? Not that it wasn't a horrid scenario he was relating. The system *was* flawed, but there were mostly good people working in it. It was the select few who didn't do their jobs that caused the children to suffer. And that was tragic. "What was her name?"

"Jewel. She was my best friend and they killed her. Anyway, my aunt and uncle were kind and they tried to help, although their idea of helping was to take me to church and try to turn me into a religious nut like them. Some lessons stuck, I guess."

Hence the Bible verse left with the victims? "Amelia and Douglas Mason, right?"

He started and his hand lifted the weapon. "How do you know that?"

"From the license plate on the car you drove the night you tried to intimidate Sam."

He scowled. "I took Uncle Doug's Beemer and followed Sam for a while. I was going to take him to convince you—well, then I—"

"Chickened out?"

"No, came to my senses. That would be a stupid thing to do and my father—" He snapped his lips together.

"Your father?"

"Never mind, just drive!"

"I'm driving, Zachary—"

"Zach. Only my mother called me Zachary. No one else is allowed."

"Why would that make your father angry?" She dared to press.

"Because it's our thing. It's what we talk about. At first, he just told me all about the people in prison with him. The other killers. Then when I told him I'd taken care of that Chatty Cathy, he was surprised. He didn't believe me at first, but after he saw the news, he made me tell him in detail about it." He sucked in a breath and let it out slowly. "He was so proud of me."

"And that's why you want to know what I said at the scene? So you can report back to him?"

He shrugged. "Like I said, it became our thing. When my father told me about some of the other killers in the prison, I decided to pattern the killings a little after one of them. Just to keep things interesting." He chuckled. "The FBI has been running around chasing their tails trying to put everything together, and really, there's nothing to put together."

"After Peter Romanos?"

"Yeah, he was the most famous one in there. I figured why not?"

The man was talking in riddles. "What exactly did your father say that made you think you needed to kill those women?"

"That women should keep their mouths shut. That they flapped their tongues too much. If someone had shut up that Upton woman before she called CPS, then Jewel would still be alive. And it just hit me. I could save the innocents by removing the threat." His fingers flexed around the weapon and Grace said a quick prayer that he wouldn't pull the trigger. He shot her a glance. "And you're proving his point. Yak, yak, yak. Just drive."

She fell silent, noting her surroundings, trying to figure out if she could wreck the car and—no, she couldn't. She didn't know where he was keeping Eleni, but it was a good distance away. They'd been driving for thirty-five minutes. "Can you tell me more about your father?"

"No. No more questions!" He jiggled his leg. "I'm going to be late," he muttered. "This took way longer than it was supposed to. You worked later than I thought you would."

"Late for what?"

"Work, what else? Turn into the next drive. The one covered by those trees." She followed his instructions and parked. "Now, get out and walk to the barn."

"Where's Eleni?"

"I'm taking you to her. If you'll just do what I say, you'll see her in about five seconds."

Up to this point, Grace had managed to keep her fear under control, but now, it wanted to rage. She drew in a shaky breath and climbed out.

"Keep your back to me until I get out," he said.

She did so, eyeing the structure in front of her. *Oh, please, God* . . .

He jabbed her in the small of her back with his weapon, pressing on the wound already there, sending a bolt of pain through her.

"Walk." When they got to the barn door, he nodded to the wall next to it. "Put your hands there, where I can see them."

She did. "Eleni's in there?"

"I said she was."

Like she was supposed to trust his word. "What was Brenna to you?"

He laughed. "Apparently, my father likes to talk to his neighbor."

"Romanos."

"Yeah. Hal overheard my father telling what his son had done. My father was afraid Hal would talk, so he had to be taken care of. He'd already told me Hal's story. About how he'd killed all her boyfriends. She was easy to get close to. Just wanted someone to listen and understand her. Make her laugh. So, I did. Snapped a selfie and that was that."

"But how did Hal see the selfie?"

"Doesn't matter. Now shut up. I'm done talking."

He opened the door, grabbed her bicep, and shoved her inside. The musty smell of an old, abandoned barn hit her, and she glanced around to note the empty horse stalls. He opened the first stall and pointed to a huge hole in the ground with a ladder leaning against the side. "Get in."

Stunned, Grace didn't move. She wasn't sure what she'd expected, but it wasn't this.

He placed the gun against her lower back. "Move!"

She walked toward the edge.

"Go!"

She continued to the ladder and looked down. At the bottom of the deep hole, she could see Eleni on the concrete floor. She had a pillow and a blanket. The area was probably close to five feet square.

Grace's head spun. If she tried to take out Zachary and failed, Sam might never see his child again. If she went down, she had a feeling she wouldn't be coming up. "I thought you wanted to know what I said at the scene."

He paused. "I do."

"And if I tell you, will you let Eleni go?"

"Tell me."

"You have to bring her up first, then I'll tell you."

He moved the gun to center it on her forehead. "I don't have time to deal with you right now. I have to go or I'll be late. Now, down you go." He narrowed his eyes. "The easy way or the hard way."

He was out of patience with her. Grace climbed down the ladder, noting the fencing encircling the perimeter, then the concrete walls on the lower portion. As soon as she was off the last rung, he pulled the ladder up. "There's a bucket in the corner if you need it. I'll be back. Soon." The scrape of the chain-link "lid" closing them in echoed through the hole.

CHAPTER
TWENTY-FIVE

Sam pressed the palms of his hands against his temples trying to think of another route. Rogers. He pulled up the man's information once more and looked through all the visitors. He had quite a few, including a son, daughter-in-law, and three grandchildren.

Sam grunted. Bet that chapped his father's hide. Rogers's grandkids came to visit, but Peter's didn't even know he was alive. And that's the way Sam planned to keep it. He scrolled through the pictures of Ethan Rogers's family, looking for something. Anything.

The man's wife had been a pretty woman with a wide smile. In the file, there was a police report where she'd claimed domestic abuse. The pictures from the hospital turned his stomach. Eventually, she'd dropped the charges and returned home to him. Two weeks later, she was dead. That had been fifteen years ago. He'd been left with their two children, Zachary and Jewel. The kids went into the system when their father was arrested.

Sam rubbed his eyes and sighed. Then returned to his research. Jewel had seemed to fall off the radar, but Zachary had moved in with his aunt and uncle—Douglas and Amelia Mason—and eventually finished high school.

So, what had happened to the sister?

More research revealed her obituary. "Oh man, that's sad. Poor kid." He'd basically lost his whole family in a short period of time.

Sam grimaced and returned to Zach's background. He'd married right after graduation, and their first child had been born a year later. Two more children followed, and he was now employed with a local theater company when he wasn't working at his uncle's restaurant.

The base of his neck started that tingling thing it did when he had a gut feeling that needed to be investigated.

Theatre company. Costumes. Masks?

He looked up the most recent picture of Zachary Rogers and sucked in a breath. He knew that guy. Had seen him recently. Where?

At the hospital. He typed up all the information, attached the picture, and sent it to Mark and Jerry.

He picked up his phone, noticing Grace had texted him. But first, he sent a text to Brenna.

> Where are you?

Her reply came quickly.

> At the hospital. I couldn't stay away, of course.
> Waiting for my boyfriend to get here. But he's
> late. As usual.

> Stay there until the agents arrive. They've got
> some news for you.

A question mark popped up.

> Just stay there. They'll answer all your
> questions.

> Okay. Fine.

He went back to Grace's text and read it.

I'm sorry I won't be able to come to the game as planned. Working on the case. All the best to Alexander.

He texted her back.

Thought you weren't coming?

A quick glance at the time sent him scurrying. He didn't want to be late for Xander's game. Hitting a drive-thru for a bite to eat, then battling the traffic to the high school would take him right up to kickoff most likely. He groaned. He should have left earlier, but he hadn't wanted to rush Mitch in case the man had something to add that could be helpful in the investigation, and then Sam had gotten lost in his research and a very shocking discovery. When Grace's voice mail picked up after the first ring, he frowned, but filled her in on everything he'd discovered, then hurried to his car.

Just as he snapped his seat belt in place, his phone rang and he tapped the screen. "Claire? Twice in the same week. That's a record."

"El's missing, Sam."

The pure terror in her voice immediately spiked his own. "What do you mean she's missing?"

"I mean, I ran to the grocery store, and when I got home, she was gone."

The terror subsided. "Well, maybe she took a walk around the block."

"You don't think I thought of that?" she snapped. "I've driven around the block five times, I've called all of the friends I could think of that I have numbers for. No one has seen or heard from her and her phone is going straight to voice mail."

"Track it," he said.

"I tried. She's . . . offline or whatever you call it. I'm scared, Sam."

He put her on speakerphone and pulled up the app that would allow him to find Eleni's phone.

And got nothing.

■　■　■　■

Grace had no idea how much time had passed, but Eleni still slept. Thankfully, while the temperature in the hole was chilly, it wasn't freezing. Probably because the barn was heated. Grace had broken out of the zip tie, then checked Eleni's pulse and pulled the blanket tighter around the child. The longer she was out of it, the better. For her.

As for Grace, she was wound tighter than a spring and ready to release the scream at the back of her throat.

She glanced up for the thousandth time, her brain working furiously. If only she could reach the chain-link fence at the top edge of the concrete, she might be able to climb on up, but there was no way she could scale the concrete walls. And yet the only way out was up. She continued to study what was going to be their escape route. The chicken wire behind the fencing held the dirt in place. The fencing was so that he had a way to close them in at the top.

A moan from Eleni sent her to the girl's side. Grace knelt next to her and touched her hand. "Hey, Eleni?"

Eleni blinked and pressed a hand to her head. "Ugh, what happened?"

"You were drugged. Do you feel sick?"

"A little. Mostly just dizzy." She frowned. "Where are we?" And then the panic kicked in. "Grace? Where are we?" She stood and spun in a circle and stumbled.

Grace grabbed her before she fell. "Stay calm, El. Can I call you El? I think your dad does, doesn't he?"

The girl nodded, but her breathing quickened and she pressed a hand to her chest. "I can't breathe!" She dove for a wall and started walking the perimeter, pounding her fists against it.

"Eleni." Grace held her hands out. "It's okay. It is. I'm working on a way to get us out of here."

The child stopped, spun, and pressed her hands to her thighs, then bent over. "Okay. How?" she asked without looking up.

How indeed.

"Obviously, we have to go up."

"Yes."

"I can only think of one way. Did you ever play that game where you placed your feet on the doorframe and walked up it?"

Eleni straightened, her focus on Grace distracting her enough for her breathing to slow. "Yes. Sure."

"We're going to do that here."

"How? Neither one of us is tall enough for that."

"Exactly. That's why we're going to have to work together."

Eleni raised a brow. "Let me guess," she said slowly, "back to back?"

"You're one very smart girl."

"But when we get to the top, isn't that cover or lid, or whatever it is, locked?"

She shook her head. "I don't know. If it is, we may have to figure something else out, but we have to try."

"Okay." She nodded and pulled in a deep breath, then let it out slowly between pursed lips. Then again. "Okay," she finally said. "I'm ready when you are."

"How are you feeling? Any weakness at all left over from the drug?"

"Not really. The nausea's passing too."

Oh, for the resiliency of the young. Grace nodded and turned to face the wall. Eleni did the same, placing her back against Grace's. "Okay, being an ice skater, your legs are probably stronger than mine." Grace refrained from mentioning her still sore shoulders and painful ribs. It didn't matter. If they wanted out, they had to go up.

"But you work out, right?"

"I do." Probably not as much as she was going to wish she did, but . . . "Let's step up. Place one foot on the wall and balance, then wait for me to place one foot. Then we'll have to lean hard against each other to climb. Ready?"

"Yes, please. I want out of here."

"You and me both." She glanced at the blanket and an idea sparked. "Hold on a sec." She grabbed the cloth and, using her teeth, managed to get a tear started on one end.

"What are you doing?"

"We're going to use this when we get to the top." She tore it in half, thankful it was an older blanket that tore evenly. She looped one piece around her neck and had Eleni do the same. She then returned to her spot. "Okay, lean against me."

It took three tries to coordinate their first step. But finally, they made it off the floor. Grace sucked in a breath. The pull on her ribs hurt, and this was definitely going to be harder than she'd imagined, but they had no choice. "Step, step, step. Don't look down. How are you doing?"

"Fine. Can we go faster?"

Grace almost wanted to laugh but didn't want to waste the breath. They couldn't fall at this point or it was going to hurt. "Step. Step." At the halfway point, her thighs started to quiver. "Just a few more steps, then I'm going to count to two, then say 'grab.' When I say 'grab,' don't hesitate, just move and grab onto the chain-link fence, okay?"

"Got it."

"And El?"

"Yes?"

"You can't miss. Promise me you won't miss." If they fell, it wouldn't kill them, but it would definitely hurt.

"I promise." The quiet confidence eased her fears a fraction.

Please, Lord, don't let either one of us miss. "Step. Step. Stop." She shoved aside the pain and they stayed there, Grace praying her muscles wouldn't give out. Not yet. "And one, two, grab!"

She lunged, felt Eleni do the same, the warmth of her back disappearing. The fingers of her right hand clamped around the wire. Her left missed. She slammed against the concrete and stifled a cry when she jerked to a hard stop, suspended by her right hand. Her already injured shoulder screamed a protest, but she held on, braced her feet against the wall, and brought her left hand up next to her right to clasp the fencing. "El?" She gasped. "You good?"

Grace looked back over her shoulder to see the girl flat against the wall, half on the fence, half on the concrete. "Uh-huh. Yeah. I'm good. Had a little bit of a rough landing, but I'm still up here and not down there, so I'm going to say that's good."

Grace met the girl's gaze and smiled through a grimace. She was so much her father's daughter. "You're amazing, Eleni."

"I don't know about that, but thanks. What now?"

"Now, we climb. As you climb, try to move closer to me. Once we're next to each other, we're going to use the blankets to anchor ourselves and give a little protection. Ready?"

"Yeah. Let's go."

It didn't take long to clear the next six feet, and when they stopped at the top, Grace drew in a long, shuddering breath. Her shoulders throbbed and her ribs pulsed, but they'd made it. She dug her shoes into the little squares and reached up with her left hand to push against the fence section covering them.

Only to have it go nowhere.

■ ■ ■ ■

Sam didn't bother to go to Claire's house. He'd texted Xander and explained that something had come up, but he'd be in touch soon. Then he'd called his mother-in-law, who'd agreed to stay quiet about Eleni's disappearance for now. Next, he'd done a U-turn and gone right back into the prison where he requested to see his father ASAP.

He now sat at the table, waiting, while Grace's odd text kept circling in his head. Finally, he texted Jade.

Is Grace okay?

After what seemed like an eternity, the door opened and his father stepped inside. Sam met his gaze and gave him a slight nod.

"Hello, Sam," his father said. "I can't tell you how good it is to see you again."

"I don't have time for pleasantries. Someone's taken my daughter and we're pretty sure it's Zachary Rogers. He's not at home, he's not at Douglas Mason's house, he's not at work, and he's not at the theater. If you know anything, then you need to tell me now, because we both know what Zachary does to his victims." He tapped the screen of his phone and pulled up a picture of Eleni. Then spun it around so his father could see it. "That's her. That's your grandchild. The one you say you want to see so much. Well, unless we find her, it's highly likely she's going to die. And I don't know how, but somehow, it will be your fault."

His father stood and the guard stepped forward. Sam held up a hand. He wasn't afraid of the man, and if he came at him, it would almost be a relief. But he didn't. He turned his back on Sam and faced the mirror.

And Sam realized his father was shook. And thinking.

His phone buzzed. A text from Brenna.

Hal's awake and able to communicate. Mark and Jerry are here and said I may be in danger?

> It's just a precaution. Just stay put and don't go anywhere alone. Not even the bathroom.

Yeah, that's what they told me, but . . .

> Please, Brenna . . .

Okay.

His father turned, the chains clanking against the tile floor. He returned to his seat. "From what I understand, Hal was shown a picture of his sister with a man at a football game. Ethan Rogers joked that it was pure irony that Hal had killed all her boyfriends to keep her safe, and in the end, she wound up in the hands of a real killer after all. The one who cuts out tongues."

"And you know this how?"

"Because I was standing there listening to him joke about how he managed to set off Hal."

"Who showed him the picture?"

His father shrugged. "How do I know? I try to stay out of that kind of business. It's not worth losing my privileges."

"And the guy she was with, was it Zachary Rogers? Ethan's son?"

"Yes, I think so."

"Do you have any idea where he would take Eleni?"

"No, but . . ."

"But what?" Sam nearly shouted the words. He clenched a fist and forced himself to grab control. "But, what?" he asked more in a softer tone.

"But Ethan may know. You'll have to ask him." He paused. "No, don't talk to him. He won't tell you anything. Talk to Zach's wife."

"His wife. Okay. I will. Now, what else do you know?"

"What do you mean?"

"Did you kill my mother?"

His father went absolutely still. "Why would you ask that? What does that have to do with finding Eleni?"

"Nothing. I just wanted to see your reaction. Where did you bury her?"

"I didn't say I killed her."

"You didn't say you didn't either."

"Of course I didn't." The man's nostrils flared. "Your mother is probably sitting on a park bench gazing out over that lake she loved so much, surrounded by her favorite flowers and, selfishly, I might add, not even thinking about the family she walked away from. I can't believe you would accuse me of such a thing. I loved your mother. Why ask me that?"

Sam pulled a copy of his mother's letter out of his pocket and tossed it on the table, then stood. "Because you don't know how to love. If you think of anything else that might help save your granddaughter, you have my number."

He motioned to the guard, who opened the door. When he stepped out of the room, he nearly ran into Mitch. "He say anything?"

"Nothing much. Just that someone had shown Hal a picture of his sister with a killer and that set him off. You know anything about that?"

"What? No. Who could have done that?"

"Only the people who have access to the inmates."

Mitch frowned. "Which is every guard in the prison."

"Looks like I have some video footage to look at." He raked a hand over his head. "But, honestly, that's the least of my worries right now. Thanks for your help, Mitch. I've got to run."

Making his way to the exit, Sam pulled out his phone and dialed Grace once more. Again, it went straight to her voice mail. "Grace, call me." Now, he was scared. Something was wrong. He hung up and called Daria.

"Hi, Sam. What can I help you with?"

"I need a phone number."

Within seconds, he had it sent to his phone and dialed it.

"Hello?"

"Is this Julianna?"

"Yes, is this Sam?"

"It is. Could I speak to Grace? She's not answering her phone and she sent me a weird text. My daughter's missing, and I've just tuned in enough to realize Grace might have been trying to send me a message." He rattled off the words in one breath. *God, please-please-please, be with Eleni.*

"I was hoping you were going to tell me she was with you."

He frowned and a bad feeling curled in his gut. "She's not. And her phone is going straight to voice mail."

"We found Jade at Grace's house. She's been shot."

"What? Is she okay?" He picked up his pace to get to his car.

"The bullet caught her in the vest, but when she fell, she hit her head. She's probably got a concussion and is on the way to the hospital. Officers and agents just left."

"Then where's Grace?"

"That's just it. We don't know. Her car is here. We're looking for security footage to tell us what happened."

This was not happening. "Please keep me updated. I'm searching for my daughter."

A pause. "Could they possibly be together?"

"I . . . I don't know. It's possible, I suppose. I feel sure a man by the name of Zachary Rogers took her. He was after Grace, too, so . . ." He climbed in his car. "I'm headed to Rogers's house to talk to his wife and see if she knows where he is. Other agents are aware and involved."

"We'll start here with the neighbors. Keep me posted?"

"Absolutely. You do the same." He aimed his vehicle in the direction of Zachary Rogers's house and started to pray.

CHAPTER
TWENTY-SIX

"What are we going to do?" Eleni whispered, despair pouring from every word.

"Think." They'd tied the blankets around their waists, then Grace had looped the other ends through the fence and tied them off in a constrictor knot. A knot that was almost impossible to come loose. As long as the blanket fabric held, they would be all right for the next bit, and it gave her shoulders a rest. Now, she just had to figure out what was holding the top closed. "I don't see a lock," she said. "There's no wire." She forced her brain to think back to when he'd shut it. He'd simply dropped it in place and walked away. Right? No, he'd stayed there, moved something before he left. "It's just heavy," she said. "I think it has weights on it that we can't see from down here."

"So, we just need to push harder?"

"Yeah. I think if we both can push, we might be able to dislodge whatever is holding it down. And with the blanket supporting us, we might get the leverage we need with our feet to shove."

"We're really going to trust these blankets to hold us?"

She met the girl's eyes. The child was terrified, but she was focusing and listening. "Yeah. I think we're going to have to."

"Great."

"You're being a champ, El."

"Right."

"Okay, when I say go, we'll go. You ready?"

"Sure."

"Put your hands on the fencing next to mine. I'll go first to make sure the blanket holds." Keeping her feet against the wall, Grace slowly let go of the fence and placed her hands on the top portion of the wire. She bounced a little and the blanket held. With a relieved grin, she looked at Eleni. "I weigh more than you. You should be good."

Eleni nodded and mimicked Grace's movements. Feet planted against the chain-link wall and her hands next to Grace's. Together they pushed and something shifted.

"That's it," Grace said. "More."

They shoved one more time and the cage slid off. Eleni let out a choked cry and Grace laughed. "Oh, thank you, Jesus. Okay, El—"

A pair of legs appeared. Eleni shrieked and Grace jerked, caught herself, and looked up to find Zachary staring down at her, a look of shock mixed with anger on his face. "Well, I guess it's a good thing I had to come back. Did you know they know who I am? Now I have to leave the country *and it's all your fault!* Get back down there!" As he went for his weapon, she reached up with both hands, grabbed his pants legs, and pulled.

He let out a scream, toppled, and fell into the hole. The thud echoed around her. Eleni's gasping cries pulled Grace out of her own shock, and she grabbed the girl's hand. "Go."

Eleni didn't hesitate. She scrambled out, then turned to Grace and grabbed her hand to help pull her up. Grace leveraged herself out, then collapsed on her back to stare at the roof of the barn. "We did it."

"Is he dead?" Eleni asked, her voice hushed.

Grace looked down to see Zachary Rogers at the bottom of his self-made prison. His neck was twisted at an odd angle and the blood pooling under his head said he was gone. She raked a hand through her hair. "Yes, I think so. Let's go find a phone."

It took fighting the lightning pain shooting through her ribs and shoulders, but she pushed herself to her feet and grasped Eleni's hand. Together, they exited the barn.

"There's a house," Eleni said.

"Yeah, let's pray they have a landline and paid the phone bill."

"And if they don't?"

"We start walking, I guess."

The kitchen door was unlocked, and Grace stepped inside, with Eleni right behind her. The kitchen had been recently cleaned. The appliances didn't have a smudge and the linoleum floor shone with the gleam of a fresh wax. It wasn't the most updated kitchen, but it was clean.

"Do you see a phone?" Eleni asked.

"No. You?" The girl shook her head. "Let's search the house."

"Can I stay with you?"

Grace gripped her hand. "Of course you can, hon. Stick right with me." Together, they walked into the den. It was also clean. They searched the rest of the house, and finally Grace made her way back into the den and pressed a hand to her head. She had to think. "Okay, there's no phone in here. I was hoping Zachary had left his cell phone in the house, but I guess he had it on him." She drew in a ragged breath. "I guess I'm going to have to go back down the hole and get his phone." Assuming he hadn't landed on it and shattered it into a million pieces.

Eleni flinched, her eyes widening. "What? No!"

"I know it's not the ideal solution, but I drove him out here in his car and his keys are probably at the bottom with him as well. There's not much around. These are big properties, El. Lots of acreage and miles between neighbors. I have to do this."

"We can walk."

The kitchen door slammed. "Rogers! You in here?"

■ ■ ■ ■

Sam pulled to a stop in front of Zachary Rogers's home, noting the toys in the yard and the fresh coat of paint on the ranch-style house. Zachary and his family lived in a middle-income neighborhood built about thirty years ago. Most of the residents kept the yards mowed and landscaped, giving the area a cozy feel. Much like his own neighborhood. Sam walked up to the front door and rang the bell.

Within moments, he heard footsteps in the foyer, then the door opened and he recognized Mary Rogers from her driver's license photo. "Hi."

"Hey, my name is Sam Monroe. I was wondering if I could talk to you for a few minutes about your husband, Zachary."

She frowned. "All right. Is he okay?"

"Yes, as far as I know. Would you happen to know where he is right now?"

"At the restaurant working."

"Actually, he's not."

Two more Bucars pulled up, and Mark and Jerry got out. Mary's eyes widened. "What's going on?"

"We're with the FBI and have a few questions for you. Could we possibly come in and talk?" Sam asked as the agents approached.

"Um . . . yes. I guess."

"Where are your children?"

"At . . . at a friend's house. It's a playdate."

Mark came up beside Sam. "You can't be here."

Sam clenched his fists to stay calm. "My daughter's missing."

"I heard. Let us handle it."

"Let me listen, please."

The woman crossed her arms. "No, you can't come in. Tell me."

Sam glanced at Mark and Jerry, every nerve feeling raw and exposed. His child was missing. Grace was missing. And this woman's husband may know where they were. It was all he could do to keep his mouth shut and let the agents handle things now that they were on scene.

He stepped back and Mark pulled out a small notebook. "Ma'am, we believe your husband, Zachary Rogers, has kidnapped a twelve-year-old girl and possibly another agent."

She gaped. "What?"

"We have a team at the theater where he works and makes his silicone masks."

"And?"

"And our crime scene unit found the same kind of mask in a hidden compartment in a van he stole from the IKEA parking lot not too far from here. And he was caught on camera at the residence where the twelve-year-old girl disappeared from."

The woman pressed a hand to her chest and dropped to sit on the top step. "No."

"Please tell us, can you think of where he'd take her?"

She shook her head. "No. He didn't. He wouldn't."

"My father was a killer," Sam said.

Everyone turned to look at him.

"I didn't want to believe it even when I held the evidence in my own hands, but it's true. I still have a hard time believing it even after thirteen years."

"Sam . . ." Jerry frowned at him, concern written on his face.

Sam stepped forward, hand outstretched. "I'm Agent Sam . . . Romanos. I know what it's like to love a killer. I also know what it's like to have to turn one in." The woman stared at him, eyes reddening, tears pooling. "It's my daughter he has," he said. "Please, if you know where he'd take her . . . please tell them. If we're wrong, I'll get on my knees and beg your forgiveness, but please, anything you can think of would help."

Mary's mouth worked and a sob escaped her. She drew in a deep breath and swiped her eyes. "Um, I think you're wrong. It's his father who's in prison."

"And Zachary—"

"Zach."

"Zach goes to see him, right?"

She bit her lip and nodded.

"Tell us," Sam pleaded. "My little girl is waiting on me to come get her."

"Oh gah . . ." She scrubbed a hand down her face. "Um, there's some land that belongs to his uncle Doug. He likes going out there sometimes when he needs to get away from things. For a break."

"Could we have the address?"

CHAPTER
TWENTY-SEVEN

At the shout, Grace had hurried Eleni down the hall and into the nearest bedroom. She shut the door and locked it. It wouldn't keep him out for long, but she'd buy every second she could get.

"Rogers! I know you're here."

Grace frowned. She knew that voice, but from where? "Your car is in the drive, you idiot. The feds are real close to figuring out this whole stupid plan—and my part in it—so you need to go take care of Hal before he runs his mouth." He paused. "And Hal's sister while you're at it. I can't get to the man because of all the security around him in the hospital. Rogers! Answer me!" His footsteps headed in her direction. "I'm not going down for this!"

Grace turned to Eleni. "Whatever happens, you don't come back in this room. Understand?"

"But—"

"Promise me." She glanced at the window. "Go out the window and start running. Got it? I'm going to keep him busy here."

"I can't just leave you—"

"I may need you to find help."

"What if he's not alone?"

She'd thought of that. "We're going to have to take that chance." She squeezed Eleni's hands. "You can do this."

Tears welled in the girl's eyes, but she nodded. "Okay," she whispered. She ran to the window and slid it open. It squeaked on the way up, and Eleni gasped and turned while cold air rushed into the room.

The footsteps paused outside the door. Knuckles rapped on the wood. "Get out here before I break the door down."

Grace waved for the girl to go, and Eleni pushed the screen off and slipped out. Grace ran to shut the window. A foot slammed against the door and she turned, looking for any kind of weapon. But the room was empty of everything except the bed and a dresser. She pulled a drawer from the dresser and turned just as the door crashed in.

When the man stepped into the room, she swung the drawer, slamming it into his left shoulder. He cried out and she kept swinging.

He threw an arm up to block the drawer, and the impact broke it into pieces that rained to the floor. But his scream of pain told her she'd done some damage. Something else hit the floor with a thud.

His gun.

She dove for it, but he threw out his good hand and snagged the weapon from her reaching fingers.

He lifted his head to look at her, fury and pain blazing in familiar eyes. "You broke my arm," he yelled at her. "I'm going to kill you!" He raised the gun and aimed it at her.

Grace stepped back, hands raised. "Your partner kidnapped me and stuck me in a hole in the ground. I think I have good reason." She remembered where she'd seen the man. Her eyes went to the healing wound on his throat. "Mitch?"

He narrowed his eyes. "I've seen you before. Who are you?"

"Grace Billingsley. I was there when Hal took you hostage at the prison."

His eyes widened and his nostrils flared. "Why would Zach kidnap you?"

"Because he wanted to know what I said at a crime scene."

"He's so stupid."

"Actually, he was pretty smart. It was only when he started obsessing and getting desperate that he started making mistakes." She nodded to the hand still holding the gun on her. "So, are you going to lower your weapon and let me use your phone to call authorities? Or what?"

He pursed his lips, and she could almost see his mind whirling. "I can't let you go," he whispered.

Dread pooled in her gut. "Yes, Mitch, you can."

"No, because as soon as you report this, I'm going to have to explain my part in it."

"Which is?"

He glared at her. "If you must know, I showed Hal a picture of his sister with Zach."

"I'm sorry. What? You?"

"See? Now you know."

"But . . . why? You're not behind all of this. Why would you do that?"

He shrugged. "Money."

"Who paid you?"

"It . . . doesn't matter. What matters is, I did this, and you know about it, and I can't let anyone else find out."

"So, you're just going to kill me?"

He licked his lips. "I don't want to, but I don't see any other solution."

"How about we walk out of here and keep the charges to a minimum?"

"I . . . I . . . ." Sweat broke out across his brow. "I can't. I'm sorry."

■ ■ ■ ■

Sam followed behind Mark and Jerry and pulled to a stop when they got within sight of the farmhouse. From his vantage point, he could see a barn in the distance and two cars in the main drive.

Jerry and Mark and the others gathered around the lead vehicle, and Jerry pulled out binoculars.

"See anything?" Sam asked. His adrenaline had been racing for hours, fueled by fear and coffee. He'd stayed in touch with the other agents, grateful they'd kept him updated. Now, he was so close to finding Eleni. *Please, Lord, protect—*

Movement near the bush under the window caught his attention and he touched Jerry's arm. "Can I see the binoculars?"

The man handed them to him and Sam adjusted the focus.

And saw a figure hunched under the window. Eleni.

Relief nearly sent him to his knees. "They're in the house," he said. "That's El under the window. I'm going to—"

She stood and threw a rock at the window, then ducked back down.

CHAPTER
TWENTY-EIGHT

The crash of glass startled both of them but allowed Grace, who'd been waiting for an opportunity to act, to do so. She charged Mitch and slammed into him, aiming for his injured arm. He cried out, crashing to the floor. With a smooth move, she regained her balance and stomped on the hand grabbing for the weapon he'd dropped at impact.

Another scream echoed from him and he rolled. She swung her arm and swept the gun out of his reach.

"FBI! Freeze! Don't move! Don't move!"

Grace dropped back onto her rear, breathing hard.

She looked up to see Mark and Jerry, in full tactical gear, weapons aimed at the man on the floor. Jerry moved in and cuffed him, injured arm and all.

Grace stood and moved to the window just in time to see Eleni run to Sam and throw herself into his arms. *Thank you, Lord . . .*

She pressed a hand to her ribs, and all the pain from the abuse her body had taken over the last few days came crashing in. She stumbled, and Mark grabbed her arm while Jerry escorted a very vocal Mitch Zimmerman from the room.

"You okay?" he asked. "Paramedics are on the way."

"I'm all right. Rogers is out in the barn. He's dead." She walked toward the den and Mark fell into step behind her.

"Agents are already out there," he said. "They'll find him."

"I want to talk to Mitch."

"Mitch?" Sam asked from the front door.

Grace glanced back just in time to see Mark roll his eyes. "You're not supposed to be in here."

"I'm not. I'm on the porch." His eyes roamed over Grace. "You're really all right?"

"Yes. Eleni?"

"Yes. She's in the car with a female agent." His eyes reddened and he cleared his throat. "All she would say is that she's fine and you saved her."

"She just saved me by throwing that rock in the window. It was the distraction I needed to go after Mitch." She went to Sam and slipped her arms around his waist. "Don't hug me back. Everything hurts too much."

He rested his hands on her head and that was okay. Then he kissed her forehead. "Mitch was behind this? Prison guard Mitch?"

Grace nodded and stepped back, hand pressed against her side. It was hurting more than it had before her tackle. "But there's more going on than he shared. He's the one who showed the picture to Hal of Brenna and Zach, but someone paid him to do that."

Sam blinked. "Who?"

"He never said, but someone knew Hal would lose it when he saw that picture. Who would know that?"

"Anyone he talked to," Sam said. "All he talks about is his sister."

Grace nodded. "Well, Mitch knew what was going to happen when he showed that picture to Hal. Find out who paid him and that will explain a lot."

"It wasn't Zach Rogers," Mark said. "We looked at his financials as soon as we connected him."

She shrugged. "All I know is that Zachary was doing the killings and reporting them back to his father."

"So, I was wrong," he murmured. "My father was never involved?"

"I'm not sure. I can't answer that."

"Once Mitch gets his medical attention on that arm," Sam said, "I'm going to have a lot of questions for him."

She shook her head. "I think Hal is the one that's going to be able to answer most of the questions. When Mitch came inside, he was hollering for Rogers, saying that he needed to take the man out before he talks."

Sam clutched her hand and his gaze bounced between her and Mark. "Then let's go talk to him?"

Mark shook his head. "Jerry and I tried to get him to talk earlier. He had nothing to say."

"But that was when Mitch was still free," Grace said. "He may be more willing to talk now."

Sam looked at Mark. "You okay with me talking to him?"

Mark sighed and rubbed his eyes. "Sure. He was asking for you when Jerry and I were there trying to get information out of him. We did tell him that we knew it was Ethan and Zachary that were behind the killings and we were in the process of chasing them down."

"What'd he say to that?"

"That we didn't know the half of it. Then shut up and asked to talk to you."

"Okay, then," Sam said. "But first, I need to make sure my daughter is okay. She's my priority right now."

"I'm fine, Dad," she said from behind Sam.

Sam whirled. "El, I was coming. I just needed a few more minutes."

"I wanted to make sure you were okay."

Grace's heart hurt for the agony on Sam's face. "I'm fine. Come on. We'll get you checked out at the hospital—"

"Hospital?" She frowned. "No way. I'm fine."

"But—"

"Dad, how many times are you going to make me say it? He

didn't hurt me. I heard the doorbell ring and thought it was my friend. I opened it and got a face full of whatever it was he sprayed." She held up a hand. "I know, I know. I should have checked to be sure it was her. Anyway, the next thing I knew, I woke up and Grace was there." Tears filled her eyes and she sniffed. "And I'm very glad she was there. Otherwise, I would not be as fine as I am at the moment."

Sam nodded and pulled his daughter into a tight hug. "Okay." He kissed the top of her head and turned to the others. "Then let's get out of here."

■　■　■　■

With Eleni safely ensconced in her grandmother's arms and being waited on hand and foot by Xander, who'd forgiven Sam for ghosting the football game, Sam rode the elevator to the ICU floor with Grace, Mark, and Jerry at his side. Forensics would be a while going over the farm and the theater where Zach had made all his masks. And now it was up to Sam to get answers from Hal while Mitch was being questioned.

The others stood just outside the room. When he stepped inside, Brenna was seated by her brother. He was cuffed to the rails and she held the hand nearest to her. She looked up, tired and weary, shell-shocked. "I was dating a serial killer?"

Sam shoved his hands into his pockets and pursed his lips. "Brenna—"

"Boy, I can pick them, can't I?"

"It wasn't your fault. You were played."

"Nevertheless, I allowed it to happen." Anger flared her nostrils and quickened her breathing. "*I* did this."

"You're going to blame yourself no matter what I say, aren't you?"

"No." The whisper came from the man on the bed. "No, Brenna. Not your fault."

Sam moved closer and met the man's eyes. "Hal, Mitch has been arrested. We know someone paid him to show you the picture. He also held a federal agent at gunpoint. So, he's going away for a long time."

"Really?"

"Yes."

"Then I can tell?"

"Yes, Hal, you can tell. You're safe. Brenna's safe. Everyone is safe."

"I lied before . . ." The raspy voice was almost too low for Sam to hear. "When I had to blink to answer. You asked if I knew who the killer was. I said no, but I did."

"I know. But tell us the truth now."

Hal rested for a moment, then said, "I overheard them talking . . ."

"Can I record this, Hal?"

"Yeah. Don't think I'll have the strength to tell it twice."

Sam pulled out his phone and hit the recording app. "Please note that I have Hal Brown's permission to record this conversation. Hal, can you please say you agree if you agree?"

Hal agreed.

"Okay, Hal, go on."

"I overheard them."

"Who?"

"Ethan and Peter. Ethan was bragging about his son righting the wrongs that had been done. Killing people. Cutting out their tongues. They saw me listening." He swallowed and winced. "Ethan said if I talked, they'd go after Brenna. I promised to stay quiet, but I . . . guess they didn't believe me because Mitch showed me that picture of Zach and Brenna. It . . . it . . . I'm sorry, Sam. I snapped."

"Yeah. Can't say I blame you." He sighed. "So, my—I mean, Peter, knew?"

"Yeah."

Sam nodded. "I see," he said, his voice low. After a brief pause, he asked, "Was Peter in any way behind the killings? Like coaching Zach what to do?"

"No, but Peter and Ethan talked about them after Zach left," he rasped. "I know they did. They tried to talk low, but I always managed to deliver the books after the boy left and I'd stand outside the cell and listen." He tried to chuckle but cut it off. "That's how they caught me. Mitch saw me listening and told them." He drew in a deep breath and closed his eyes.

Sam let him rest a moment while his eyes burned and a rage built from the center of his chest to spread outward. Would he never be free of his father's evil? Swallowing his thoughts, he nodded. "Okay, thank you, Hal. But why show you that picture when they knew it would set you off?"

"They told me if I said anything, that he would kill her."

"*Her* being Brenna? And *he* being Zach Rogers?"

"Yes. Peter said he'd been bored a long time and finally had some worthwhile entertainment, and I wasn't to spoil it or he'd have someone not only cut out my tongue but Brenna's too. I believed him. And it just . . . I don't know. Like I said, I saw red and I snapped." The man's eyes flickered and shut. "I didn't mean to explode, Sam, I really didn't."

"I'm guessing Mitch didn't count on that." They'd known Hal was protective of his sister, they just hadn't factored in the lengths he would go to make sure she was safe. Including taking a prison guard hostage. And Mitch had taken the opportunity to try to take out the man who could end his career.

Sam raked a hand over his head. "Who paid Mitch, do you know?"

"Peter did, I think. S-said he was bored and it was worth the money to finally have some fun again." He paused. "He used the word 'bored' a lot."

Sam's gut churned. "Thanks, Hal. Get better."

"S-s-sorry. I should have told sooner, but was . . . scared." He finally gave up the fight to stay awake and closed his eyes.

"Let him sleep, Brenna."

"Yeah." She leaned over and kissed her brother on the forehead.

Sam turned off the recording and sent the file to Mark and Jerry with instructions to check the financials of his aunt. He had no doubt they'd find she was following orders from her brother to pay for his . . . *entertainment*. Because if Hal told what he'd overheard, Zach would be caught and unable to visit the prison to talk about his killings. Thus ending whatever morbid pleasure his father took from hearing about them. So, he'd once again used his money for evil. As a result, innocent women had died.

But it was over now. Finished. And Sam was going to make sure his father couldn't hurt anyone ever again.

He got up and walked out of the room.

CHAPTER
TWENTY-NINE

TWO WEEKS LATER

The skating rink was busy but not packed. Eleni and her nine friends were showing off their skills. Some were better than others, but it looked like they were all having fun.

And that's all Sam cared about at the moment. Even his mother-in-law and her doctor friend, Connor, were out on the ice. Xander and one of his football buddies were also out there.

And Grace's three best friends. Penny and Holt Satterfield skated hand in hand while Julianna and Clay did the same. Raina held on to the side, laughing, while the girls tried to convince her she could let go. Eleni skated up to her and held out a hand. Raina shook her head. Eleni insisted. Finally, Raina put her hand in his daughter's and came off the side.

"Everyone seems to be recovering," Grace said, handing Sam a hot chocolate.

"Yeah." He curved his hands around the warmth. "I'm just standing here trying to wrap my mind around the fact that we're here. That you're not dead." He couldn't help the emotion behind his words. His father had set up such an elaborate plan, bided his time, then used Ethan and Zach to implement it as soon as he had all the pieces in place. It was mind boggling, and he was trying not to let it consume his every waking moment. "I'm grateful."

"Good." She slid an arm around his waist and leaned a head on his shoulder.

"How's Bobby?"

"He's doing okay, I think. Like, I'm surprised, actually." He knew she'd stopped by her parents' house on her way to the rink.

"And your parents?"

"Working through everything. When I told them that Bobby wondered if they loved him, it nearly killed my mother. So, they're working a little harder on the relationship there."

"And with you?"

"Yeah." She smiled up at him. "And me."

"I'm glad."

She shifted. "What's wrong?"

He raised a brow. "What do you mean?"

"You have that look on your face. What?"

"I really am an open book, aren't I?"

"No, I'm just getting to know your looks."

He sighed. "I just learned that my father was transferred back to the supermax prison in Colorado where he will spend his days in isolation away from anyone and everyone. And it's a place where he will *not* have access to a phone or my new number. I made sure of that."

"Are you okay?"

He pulled in a deep breath and kissed her. A light peck that promised more later. "Yeah," he said. "I'm okay. Grateful you're with me and willing to put up with my baggage."

She gave his arm a light punch. "Hey, that goes both ways."

"I know.

His phone rang and he held his breath when he recognized the number.

"Sam?"

"I have to take this, okay?"

"Sure. Of course. Want me to leave so you can have some privacy?"

He shook his head and gripped her hand. "Stay." He pressed the phone to his ear. "This is Sam Monroe."

■ ■ ■ ■

After his initial greeting, he went quiet, listening, face tightening, eyes turning red. He blinked and looked at the floor. "Thank you," he said, his voice hoarse. "Thank you for letting me know." He hung up and his hold on her hand spasmed, then he drew in a ragged breath and lifted his head.

"Sam? Who was that?"

"That was my buddy who works in the police department with the K-9 unit. I asked him to search a certain area in one of the local parks."

"Okay." She had a feeling where he was going with this, but wanted to let him tell it in his own way, at his own pace.

"My father never admitted he killed her, but he said something at our last confrontation—sorry, can't call it a visit—and it clicked. He described a place that she loved. A park with a lake and a bench. The place is surrounded by wildflowers in the spring, and she used to take me and Harmony there when we were little. The cadaver dog found a body and they've already dug it up. He waited until they had a positive ID to call me."

"It's your mom?"

He nodded and swiped a tear from his cheek. "Yeah."

She wrapped her arms around him and held him. "I'm sorry."

"I am, too, but I'm not surprised. I've always wondered if she was dead, I was just too afraid to find out for sure. But now I know. Now, I can have closure."

"Yeah."

"I'll call Harmony later, but for now, I want to enjoy the rest of the day with my family. And you." He kissed the top of her head. "Thank you for today," he said. "Your friends are wonderful and amazing. Just like you."

"Thank you for asking them to come."

He cleared his throat. "So, think we could have dinner tonight? The kids will be with Claire and Brett doing their celebration, Vanessa will be with Connor, your friends have to leave by five, so it can be just us if you're open to the idea."

"Dinner, huh?"

"Yeah."

"Why don't we call it something else. Just for the heck of it."

He laughed in spite of the news he'd just received. "That's not a bad idea."

She kissed his cheek. "You're a good man, Sam Monroe."

Emotion flickered in his eyes. "Thank you," he said. "I need to hear that every so often."

"I'll tell you every day."

"For the rest of our lives?"

"If that's where this is heading."

"I have a good feeling about that."

She smiled. "I do too."

THE THRILLS
DON'T STOP HERE!

Turn the page for a sneak peek at the next book in the Extreme Measures series.

COMING SOON

SUNDAY MORNING
MID-JANUARY

Flight paramedic Raina Price looked out of the window of the chopper and pointed. "There! Two of them as reported."

Penny Satterfield piloted the aircraft with an expert touch, aiming them toward the two stranded hikers on the side of Bull Mountain. Raina grabbed the binoculars and held them to her eyes. "One is on her back. I see blood on her head. The other one is moving and appears unhurt. She's waving at us and looking pretty frantic."

"There's no place to sit this bird down," Penny said, her low voice coming over the headset.

No, there wasn't. Not even for Penny, who could land pretty much anywhere. "Looks like it's a day to go rappelling," Raina said.

"Looks like," Holly McKittrick, the nurse practitioner, echoed.

Raina didn't particularly enjoy hurling herself out of the chopper—not like some who actually hoped for it. But she was skilled at it, and if it saved someone's life, then . . . okay.

She worked quickly, efficiently, strapping herself into the gear. She'd go down, assess the situation, and radio her findings.

After fastening the medical bag to her belt, she clipped the rope to the other hook and nodded to Holly. "Ready. You?"

"Ready."

Holly would lower the basket and, if necessary, follow it down. Other emergency personnel lined the edge of the cliff, but no one had been able to get down to them.

"A little closer, Penny."

"Getting there."

Raina slid the door open, shuddering at the blast of cold air followed by a face full of snowflakes. She looked back at Holly, who had the stretcher ready to winch down. "Okay, here we go."

"Let me know if I need to come down too."

"I will. Stay tuned." She stepped out of the chopper and began her descent.

With precision, Penny moved her right to the ledge that jutted from the cliff. Less than a minute later, Raina was next to the girls while Penny continued to hover close, but not so close the wind from the blade interfered with the work.

"Help her," the nearest teen pleaded, pointing. "She hit her head."

The gash had stopped bleeding, but she'd taken a hard hit. "What about you," Raina asked. "Are you hurt?"

"No. I climbed down." She pointed to the rope behind her—the one still tied to her waist. "Sadie tripped and fell, then rolled over the side of the mountain." A sob ripped from her. "I thought she was dead."

"She's not, hon." Not yet anyway. *Please God, don't let this child die.* "Sadie, huh?"

"Yeah. I'm Carly."

"Hang in there, Carly, we're going to get you both out of here, okay?"

But the head wound was concerning. A gust of wind cut through Raina's winter clothing and she grimaced, shoving aside the cold and focusing on the patient.

"When I saw how bad she was hurt," Carly said, shuddering, "I was too scared to move her. I . . . I didn't know what to do, but I have my dad's SAT phone, so I called for help."

"You did exactly the right thing." She lifted Sadie's lids to check her eyes. Concussion. "All right, Carly, you're doing great. Where are your parents? Have you called them yet?"

"Yes. They're completely freaked out. I called them after I called you guys."

Raina could understand freaked out. If this was her child—
But it wasn't.

She cleared her throat. While she talked and gathered information, Raina triaged the unconscious girl, speaking into the headset
to those on the other end. Blood pressure, pulse, breathing status.
"And uneven pupils indicative of a concussion. The gash on the
side of her head is going to need stitches." She moved down. "Broken right tibia." Raina ran her hands over the girl's body as gently
as she could, searching for more injuries. A low moan escaped
Sadie when Raina's hands grazed her ribs. She unzipped the light
windbreaker and lifted the girl's shirt. The bluish area under the
skin alarmed her. "We've got some internal bleeding, maybe some
broken ribs." She listened to the girl's lungs once more. "Breath
sounds are still good, so no lung punctured." Yet. She got the
cervical collar on, then worked to stabilize the broken arm.

More chopper blades beat the air. Farther away, but close
enough to capture her attention. She took a moment to shoot a
glance in the direction of the noise. "Great," she muttered under
her breath. A news chopper. *Ignore it and focus.* It was all she
could do.

That, and keep her head down.

"Hey!"

Raina's head jerked up at the shout that came from above. So
much for keeping her head down, but at least her back was to the
news chopper. A man leaned over the side of the cliff. "I'm Larry
Owens with the fire department. If I throw this line down, can
you send up the uninjured girl?"

"Sure can! And I need someone to come down here and help
me get Sadie in the chopper basket." Holly could do it. Would do
it if necessary, but she absolutely hated to rappel down.

"As soon as she's up, I'll come down."

"Perfect."

"No." Carly clutched Raina's arm. "I want to go with Sadie."

"You're both going to the hospital. They'll let you see her when
you get there, but we need to focus on Sadie right now, all right?"

Carly bit her lip, then nodded. "Yeah. Okay."

In less than two minutes, she had Carly in the harness and Larry was pulling her toward the top.

"Send down the basket," Raina told Penny.

"On the way."

And so was the firefighter named Larry. Working together, they got Sadie into the basket.

"She's ready," Raina said, "take her up." Raina watched her lift gently off the ground and head for the belly of the chopper. She turned to Larry. "Thank you."

"Anytime. See you around." He signaled his readiness to return to the top and his team moved into action.

"Ready," Raina said into her mic. She noted the location of the news crew still hovering in the sky and positioned herself accordingly, never more thankful for the helmet and other gear covering most of her face. The line pulled her up off the ledge, and she started her ascent, following the path the basket had taken just a few moments earlier.

The line lurched and Raina gasped, fingers clutching the rope. "Penny? What was that?"

"No idea."

The line jerked again and Raina dropped another twenty feet before it stopped. "Penny! Holly!"

"Something's wrong with the winch," Penny said, her voice low and controlled. "Hang tight." A pause. "No pun intended."

Raina almost laughed but couldn't quite get the sound through her tight throat. "Don't let me fall."

"You're not falling. Just hold on a sec."

After what felt like a lifetime but was only about sixty seconds later, Penny's voice came through the headset. "Bringing you up."

Raina started moving upward once more. She held on tight and decided not to look down, while steeling herself for another abrupt drop. Thankfully, that didn't happen, and soon, Raina was back in the chopper, kneeling next to Sadie.

Holly looked up from the still-unconscious girl. "You good?"

"I will be when my heart rate gets back to normal. Then again, I'm here, so we'll count that as a win."

Holly nodded. "Definitely. All right, Penny, take us to base."

■ ■ ■ ■

Vincent Corelli sat on the couch that belonged to his best friend's fiancé, Julianna Jameson. The big-screen television mounted on the wall across from him held a fraction of his attention. Mostly, he was interested in the dark-haired woman chatting with Holly McKittrick, Penny Satterfield, and Grace Billingsley.

Raina Price. Beautiful, but . . . haunted, distant, seemingly unreachable. Yet for some reason those facts didn't stop him from being drawn to her. Her sage green eyes with the hint of yellow had captivated him from the moment he'd met her about a year ago when he'd been invited to watch a football game at this very house. Julianna, who was getting ready to marry Vince's best friend, Clay Fox, in three weeks. Vince smiled. He was happy for his friends. Clay and Julianna had been through so much. They deserved their happily ever after.

But he couldn't help wonder if he'd ever find his own. Not that he was looking.

Much.

Again, his gaze settled on Raina.

Okay, he might be looking *now*.

"Hey, Raina, what did they say was wrong with the winch on the chopper?" Penny asked. "Have you heard? I haven't checked."

"Mm, yeah. That it needed to be replaced, but thanks to all the safety measures, I was never in any danger of it coming disconnected."

Penny snorted. "Well, I suppose that's good to know."

"It is."

Vince noted Raina's absent agreement and rapt attention on the television. It was halftime and the station was doing a special report on Olympic hopefuls.

A young boy identified as Michael Harrison, age thirteen as of yesterday, according to the banner in the bottom left-hand corner of the screen, stood on a snow-covered mountain in Colorado's Arapahoe Basin, snowboard in hand. Raina moved closer to the television, no doubt trying to hear over the chatter. But it was the fact that her face was two shades whiter than normal that made him frown. She snagged the remote from the mantel and turned on the captions.

"How does it feel to be the youngest person ever to qualify for the Olympic Snowboard Team? Not only in halfpipe, but also slopestyle?" the reporter asked. She held the mic out to the boy while the words continued to pop up on the screen as they spoke.

"It feels amazing. And, of course, disappointing that I'm too young to actually go. But I'll get there one day."

"In four years?"

Michael laughed. "Exactly, but at least I've been invited to the trials and get to hang out with everyone who's going to the Olympics."

"And watch the competition?"

"Not the competition," Michael said, "my future teammates."

"What an amazing young man you are." The reporter turned and the camera panned to a wider angle. A woman came into view. "Mrs. Harrison, has this always been a dream of Michael's?"

"Always is pretty accurate. The dream started when he was about four years old and watched the snowboarders that year on the Olympics. He pointed at the television and said, 'I want to do that.' My husband went out the next day and bought him a snowboard and signed him up for lessons. He took to it right away, and it finally got to the point that we had to make some decisions about what to do. Four years ago, we moved from the Burbank area of California to Colorado, and snowboarding has been our life ever since." She gave her son a warm smile. "I wouldn't trade a minute of it."

The reporter nodded to the button Mrs. Harrison was wearing. "I see you're pro-adoption. Is there a story there?"

"Of course." The woman shot a look filled with intense love at her son. "I'm not able to have biological children, so my husband and I went through the adoption process. We took Michael home the day he was born, and he was legally ours shortly thereafter. We're so grateful to Michael's birth mother for giving us the chance to be this kid's parents." A sheen of tears glimmered in her eyes, and the camera zoomed in to catch the expression.

"Aw, Mom, stop." He rolled his eyes but grinned at her, and she ruffled his hair before he could duck.

The reporter stepped back. "All right, Michael, it's time. Show us what you've got."

Michael strapped his feet into the board and took off. The camera followed him as he glided to the bottom of the hill, then returned to the reporter.

"This is Camille Johnson with *NewsBreak*, providing you with the latest and breaking news. Thank you for joining us. I know we're all excited to see if young Michael Harrison can bring home the gold in the next Olympics. He'll be almost seventeen years old when that rolls around, and I know we'll be there to cheer him on."

The station cut to another site where another Olympic hopeful was in the middle of an ice skating rink, but Raina had lost interest even though she still held a frozen expression. Then she blinked, cleared her throat, and excused herself to slip into the kitchen.

Vince waited a good sixty seconds, then followed her, only to find her with her back to the door, her arms braced against the kitchen counter, head down, gulping deep breaths. Her phone lay face up in front of her, a number programmed. He couldn't tell if she'd dialed it or not. "Raina?"

She squeaked and jumped back, the blazing fear in her eyes cutting him to the core. He stood still and waited for her to realize he posed no danger.

Finally, she shuddered, then sighed.

"You okay?" he asked, knowing the question was a dumb one but asking anyway.

"Yes. Fine. Sorry. You just startled me."

"You were pretty deep in thought there."

"Hm."

"Anything I can help with?"

"No . . . I . . ." She looked like she might say something else, then, "No. Thank you."

He nodded. "Because I'd be more than happy to help you out. If you needed it."

She shook her head, then tilted it up to stare at the ceiling. "I'm okay. That kid on the news just reminded me of someone I used to know." She lowered her gaze to meet his. Her green eyes had shuttered and gave nothing away. "Seeing him brought back a lot of bad memories."

"The kid did?"

"Yeah."

He waited, but she bit her lip and looked away. "Okay," he said after several seconds of silence. "I'll leave you alone then." He turned to go, hurt she wouldn't confide and frustrated because he'd done nothing but try to reach her, to show his interest. To let her know she could trust him. That he cared. At times, he thought she felt the same, but he honestly didn't know. Maybe she just wasn't into him. And while the thought made him sad, it was what it was. He'd move on. And yet he found himself unable to leave, his eyes caught on hers as he looked back over his shoulder.

ACKNOWLEDGMENTS

So many thanks go to Dru Wells for helping me brainstorm the occupations of Sam and Grace, the timelines of their careers, and more. I can't even list all the ways she helps keep the story on track and legit. Any inconsistencies or mistakes all belong to me.

And as always, a big thank-you to Wayne Smith. Your guidance and inclusion of the little details make me sound so smart! LOL. I appreciate your willingness to offer correction and input into the stories. Get ready, I've got another one coming! HA!

Thank you to my agent, Tamela Hancock Murray of the Steve Laube Agency, who always works tirelessly on my behalf. And thank you to the amazing Revell team. You guys rock every story from edits to cover design to marketing. I can't express my thanks enough.

A special thank-you to Barb Barnes, who catches all my mistakes and keeps me from looking like a doofus. And keeps my timeline straight! Because—inside scoop—I'm terrible at timelines!

Thank you to the readers for buying the books. You're the reason I can write the next one.

Thank you to my family, of course, for all their patience and encouragement to get the story done. I love you all to infinity and beyond. And back.

Thank you to Jesus, who allows me to do what I do. I always pray that his fingerprints are on every page.

Lynette Eason is the *USA Today* bestselling author of *Life Flight* and *Crossfire* and the Danger Never Sleeps, Blue Justice, Women of Justice, Deadly Reunions, Hidden Identity, and Elite Guardians series. She is the winner of three ACFW Carol Awards, the Selah Award, and the Inspirational Reader's Choice Award, among others. She is a graduate of the University of South Carolina and has a master's degree in education from Converse College. Eason lives in South Carolina with her husband and two children. Learn more at www.lynetteeason.com.

Still can't get enough of the Extreme Measures series?
Check out *Life Flight* and *Crossfire*!

"A heart-stopping, breath-stealing masterpiece of romantic suspense!"

—**COLLEEN COBLE,** *USA Today* bestselling author on *Life Flight*

Find **HIGH-OCTANE THRILLS** in the **DANGER NEVER SLEEPS** Series

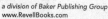

Also from Lynette Eason:
The WOMEN OF JUSTICE Series

"I enjoyed every minute."
—DEE HENDERSON

WOMEN OF JUSTICE

TOO CLOSE TO HOME

LYNETTE EASON

"A fast-paced thriller."
—BOOKLIST

WOMEN OF JUSTICE

A KILLER AMONG US

LYNETTE EASON

"The suspense is high."
—SUSPENSE MAGAZINE

WOMEN OF JUSTICE

DON'T LOOK BACK

LYNETTE EASON

Revell
a division of Baker Publishing Group
www.RevellBooks.com

Available wherever books and ebooks are sold.

THREE WOMEN. THREE MEN.
THREE UNSUSPECTING TARGETS.

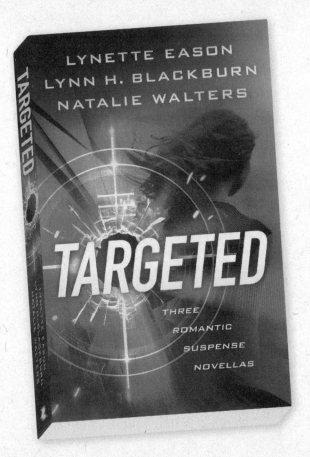

In this novella collection, an FBI computer hacker, the vice president's son, and a CIA officer each find themselves in the clutches of merciless criminals. These thrilling stories offer excitement, intrigue, and romance—and hit the bull's-eye every time.